YOU LOOK DIFFERENT IN REAL LIFE

ALSO BY JENNIFER CASTLE

The Beginning of After

YOU LOOK DIFFERENT IN REAL LIFE

JENNIFER CASTLE

HARPER TEEN
An Imprint of HarperCollins*Publishers*

HarperTeen is an imprint of HarperCollins Publishers.

You Look Different in Real Life
Copyright © 2013 by Jennifer Castle
For information address HarperCollins Children's Books,
a division of HarperCollins Publishers, 10 East 53rd Street,
New York, NY 10022.
www.epicreads.com

Library of Congress Cataloging-in-Publication Data
Castle, Jennifer.
You look different in real life / Jennifer Castle. — First edition.
        pages   cm
Summary: "Five teens starring in a documentary film series
about their ordinary lives must grapple with questions of change
and identity under the scrutiny of the camera."—Provided by
publisher.
ISBN 978-0-06-198581-2
[1. Documentary films—Production and direction—Fiction.
2. Interpersonal relations—Fiction.   3. Celebrities—Fiction.
4. Identity—Fiction. 5. Family life—New York (State)—Fiction.
6. New York (State)—Fiction.]   I. Title.
PZ7.C268732You   2013   2012051743
[Fic]—dc23   CIP
                                                      AC

Typography by Laura DiSiena
13 14 15 16 17   CG/RRDH   10 9 8 7 6 5 4 3 2 1

First Edition

For Bill,
because we see the world
through the same lens

S ometimes, I hit pause at a random moment when I'm on film and stare at my eyes, and try to figure out why they chose me.

With the others, it's obvious. Rory says those accidentally hilarious things, and Felix keeps bursting into song. Keira reads an advanced-level social studies textbook aloud. Then there's Nate, with that whole Johnny Appleseed vibe. Maybe I was picked because my favorite answer to their questions was "Grrrr," or because I wore pajamas to school three days in a row, or simply because they needed a girl with brown hair. It could have been all of these things, or none of them. So I search those eyes, those eyes I once saw the world through, and remind myself they're the same ones I see it through now. But in all the searching, I've never found the spark that says, *Watch this one.*

I'm guessing Ian Reid didn't find it either, and this is why he dumped me.

"You're awesome, Justine," he said as we sat in his vintage Jeep, not going inside to the party we were supposed to be going inside to. "But I feel like we're better off as friends."

Translated, I'm pretty sure that means: *The thought of kissing you—or touching you at all, really—makes me want to hurl, and when you look at me with love you resemble a chipmunk.*

My heart doubled over from the punch, hacked a bit, then fell to the floor of its little heart studio apartment.

But on the outside, I just nodded and spun out words like *okay* and *fine* and *cool*. That was before Christmas and now it's March, and there isn't a single hour when I'm not thinking about the fact that for seven weeks I had someone, and then I didn't, and how that works exactly.

This hour, I'm pondering it while sitting on a low stone wall outside the town library. It's snowing again, falling in bite-size chunks so fluffy they look fake. I've got an overdue copy of *The Graduate* on DVD tucked inside my parka and I'll go in and return it, eventually. Well, yes, the stone is cold down there. Very, in fact. But this is so peaceful, with my mother at the supermarket and thus out of nagging range, and I love the way Main Street looks before the plows come through. The air feels eerie-hushed, and above me, everything is colorless, a striking shade of utter blank.

In the distance to the west, I can see our town's mountains. They're not normal mountains with peaks. They're ridge mountains, low and wide and gracefully deformed. You know they're beautiful but have no idea why. On top of one is a stone tower visible from miles away with windows that look like eyes, and if you stare at it long enough, it always seems to be staring back.

I imagine that Ian is here, perched on the wall beside me, with his arm around my waist, his chin on my shoulder, and this time I don't care how we look or that some idiot might yell, "Get a room!" No, wait. We lie down on the lawn and make snow angels. I know that's the stuff of trite Hollywood movies but maybe that's where I went wrong. Maybe that's what he wanted.

When we got together, people called us *JustIan*. The sun looked different in the sky, like it recognized me.

And with that thought, the hurt comes again. It's a familiar hurt, and literal too. It starts at my belly button and pushes into me, as if someone's trying to dig a tunnel straight through to my back but dammit, there are all these organs in the way.

"Justine?"

3

The voice pops against the stillness of the air. Sharp and high. Familiar, but not really.

I turn toward the voice. There's a man and a woman standing five feet in front of me, wearing ankle-length puffy down coats and matching fleece hats right out of the clearance pages of an outerwear catalog. He's in black; she's in silver. They're each holding a cup from the chain coffee place across the street.

Then I realize who these people are, and the cramp goes supernova inside me.

"Is that you, Justine?" the woman asks again.

I don't see how I can deny it.

"Yeah, it's me." I force myself to say her name. "Leslie?"

In that moment as her eyes widen, her brows lift—her face expands in every direction—I think about how I've seen *her* over the last five years, in pictures, but she hasn't seen *me*, and that makes me feel a tiny bit powerful.

"Oh my God!" she says, quickly passing her cup to the guy, her husband, Lance, and stepping forward. Her hands fly toward my cheeks, and I let them land, feeling the jolt of warmth transferred from her cup; then they jump to my shoulders to bring me in for a hug. My stomach still hurts, and for an instant, ridiculously, I think maybe she'll notice.

"You're so grown up," she says, squeezing tight. Her breath used to smell like cigarettes; now it stinks of a Cinnamon Dolce latte.

4

"That's what happens," I say, and throw a look at Lance, who just winks. Lance is the kind of guy who can get away with a wink regardless of unfortunate outerwear.

When Leslie releases me, I ask the question.

"What are you guys doing here?"

"What do you think?" asks Lance.

Uh-uh. I need them to say it. I look at Leslie.

Taking the cue, she says, "We've got the go-ahead for *Five at Sixteen*."

"*Five at Sixteen*," I echo.

In December, after my birthday, I was expecting the phone call, but it didn't come. Then the holidays paraded by, and nothing. Winter dragged on. At the end of every day without hearing Lance or Leslie's voice, breathing got 0.5 percent easier for me.

"I didn't think it was going to happen," I say after a slow-motion moment. It's all I can do not to ask, *Who's going to give you any more money after last time and that other movie you made that just plain sucked?*

"Neither did we. But it was meant to be, Justine, and it's happening. We're in town for a few days to talk to people at your school and line up somewhere to live for a few months."

"We were going to call you and your parents tomorrow," adds Lance.

"Running into you like this—it's just so perfect!" continues Leslie. "I saw your face from across the street and instantly knew it was you. Like I said, meant to be! I have a feeling this film is going to be kick-ass."

For the record, Leslie is way too old to say things like "kick-ass."

"You *will* be part of it, won't you?" adds Lance. At least he's actually asking.

"Have you talked to the others?" I nonanswer.

"Just Nate so far, because he called us last week," says Leslie. "They're all on board over there. You were next on my list, because if we don't have you . . . Well. That's a lot not to have."

They're wrong and don't know it. "When would you start?"

"We'll begin preproduction next month," she says. "But we need paperwork signed in the next week or so, to keep things rolling."

I know my line here should be, *Of course I'll sign your paperwork! Why would I not?* In some alternate reality, I might add, *I can't wait for you to slice open my life for the world to examine and poke at with sharp instruments!*

I don't say that.

We're all silent for a few long seconds.

Finally, Lance says, "We should let you go, Justine. We're due at the Realtor's office up the street. We'll talk later, yes?"

I just nod. Leslie touches her cheek to mine and squeezes my shoulder, and I wonder if that's some new version of good-bye they're beta testing in Los Angeles. Lance pats me on the back, in the same way he's always patted me on the back. Then they are gone, gliding away from me like graceful, overdressed angels of doom.

My mother steps through the kitchen door with two steaming cups of cocoa and a bowl of popcorn, as if we were in a scene from a feminine-hygiene-product commercial. In this commercial, I sit at the table and she puts my drink and snack in front of me, then eases into my sister Olivia's usual chair across from mine.

"You think I should do it," I say to her. It comes out sounding like an accusation, which it sort of is.

"I do. But the decision is yours." As she leans down to blow on her cocoa, I notice the streaks of gray hair now woven through her blond highlights. When she came to pick me up at the library and I told her about seeing Lance and Leslie, her eyes, which have looked so tired lately, suddenly sparkled to life.

I don't know what to say next, so I blurt out the first moronic thing that comes to mind.

"I always thought I'd be thin in time for this one."

Instead of coming up with a *You're not fat!* or *You look great*, my mom stares into her cocoa, then offers an encouraging smile. "You could still lose a few pounds before they start shooting."

She thinks she's being helpful. That's my mother, in

a nutshell. I just shrug and make a mental note to seethe about it later.

After a few moments I say, "Leslie said that if they don't have me, that's a lot not to have."

"Oh, I agree with that. So do the people who loved the first two films. I know that's hard for you to hear."

A line from one of the reviews my mother keeps in a scrapbook ticker-tapes across my mind: *The real break-out star of* Five at Six *is the sharp-tongued yet funny and sweet Justine, whose early rebellion gives you a sign of things to come.*

Things to come. Gah.

"The intrusion will be a problem," I say. Grasping. "I'm supposed to be getting my school act together, remember?"

"It'll just be for a month or two."

"Why is it so important to you?" I'm curious to hear what she'll actually admit.

Mom thinks for a moment, her expression warm but a little pained, and I'm glad for the pained part.

"I guess I still believe in it. The original idea of it. From the very beginning, it seemed like such an honor."

That sounds sincere but I know there's more. After the last time, her custom birthday cake business got a nice bump from the exposure. Now she's branched out into cupcakes and what she calls "food art," which mostly means bananas on sticks with candy faces, and she could use the free advertising. Then there's the thing she won't mention:

It made us all kind of famous for a while.

"You'll feel better after the whole idea settles in," says Mom now. I can see she's hiding a flash of excitement behind the concern. "I have to get started on a T. rex with red frosting."

I go upstairs to my room and open my laptop, unable to shake that dark-shadow feeling.

The original idea of it.

My hands, which seem to be much more motivated than the rest of me, open a Web browser and type the address I know so well but refuse to bookmark.

Here it comes, loading into place: the website for the *Five At* movies. I used to go on here a lot, watching video clips of the films or interviews with Lance and Leslie. Every time I went back, I'd expect to see something new. Like it might tell me secrets I didn't already know about myself. When I realized it never would, I stopped. But now I'm here again, and it's like the site has been waiting for me all this time, that home page with the familiar logos of the first two films. Dangling them. *You know you want to.*

Five at Six. The word *six* is carefully designed to look like some kid's doodle, colored faux-sloppy with

9

red crayon. In the *Five at Eleven* logo, the word eleven is written in chunky block letters with alternating polka dots and stripes.

Then there's the tagline:

The award-winning documentary film series that's captured hearts and minds everywhere.

As corny and cringeworthy as ever. But I click on the *Five at Six* logo, which brings up a page of information about that movie, and start to read.

Five six-year-olds, all assigned to the same table in their kindergarten classroom in a college town in New York's Hudson Valley . . .

For the record, that's bullshit. I remember us getting moved to that table together right before the cameras came in. After they'd interviewed a hundred kids in a converted janitor's closet, then twenty-five, then twelve, before finally finding five in one class who they liked best. Five of us, with the right shapes to fit together and make some bigger picture.

Who are they? What do they care about? What are their hopes and plans, and what are their families' hopes and plans for them? What can five kids and their families, their school and community, tell us about our times? Filmmakers Lance and Leslie Rodgers create a brilliant portrait of these children and their world, and ultimately our world . . . and begin what will become a most amazing journey for all of us.

The "most amazing journey" thing always makes me want to laugh, or barf, or *larf.* Maybe Lance and Leslie think it's amazing. First, their humble credit-card-funded documentary was the toast of the film festival circuit and hit theaters in several big cities. After it ended up on cable TV and won a bunch of little statues, they announced their idea—and the big funding to go with it—to do a follow-up documentary every five years until we were twenty-one.

They never asked us to commit for three more films. They just assumed we would. So far, they've assumed right.

On the page titled "The Kids," there's a picture of each of us at six years old, paired with one from when we were eleven. At six, I have shoulder-length, straight light brown hair with a barrette to keep it off my face. I'm looking at something above the camera with an arched eyebrow, a slightly slanted expression of *Are you freaking kidding me?*

The photo next to it shows me with a short pixie cut, my hair brown-black then, my mouth open in the process of saying something, because in the second movie I was always saying something. Of the five of us, I'm the one who'd visibly changed the most. People thought that at eleven I'd dyed my hair and wow, that is so rad and how did her parents feel? Truth is, it just got darker naturally. But I didn't correct them.

I try to imagine what the new picture will be. My hair is once again shoulder-length. Sometimes I use a single barrette to keep it off my face. So it's possible that I could just look like a larger version of my kindergarten self.

Shudder.

I've had five years, since they shot *Five at Eleven*, to get ready for this. After what happened that time around, I was sure the amazing journey had screeched to a halt, sparks flying, brakes burning.

This is not a soap opera, folks. This is my life.

And it is absolutely, positively as unamazing as you can get.

TWO

The next morning, my sister, Olivia, drops me off at school on her way to class. She's a freshman at the college now but has discovered that zipping through her old haunts is a quickie feel-good fix. Like, she may still be living at home and failing two classes and been through three boyfriends already, but at least she's not in high school anymore.

"I'm stopping by Dad's house tonight. I really can't break the news yet?" she asks as I get out of the car. It's my father's handed-down Saab station wagon, which has turned out to be a surprisingly awesome set of wheels, even if it does have a forever-stink of moldy bagels and spilled coffee. She calls it Sob or, alternately, S.O.B., depending on whether or not it starts on a cold morning.

"I know it's torture for you, but no, you really can't."

We've decided not to tell Dad about Lance and Leslie until we can all be together to talk about it. Olivia makes a pouty face and starts to drive away, then screeches to a stop. I hear the *whirr* of the passenger side window lowering and see Olivia's oversize black sunglasses peeking out.

"Hey, Justine?" she yells.

"Yeah?"

"You can just say no if you want to!"

Despite the big round shades covering her eyes, Olivia is able to deliver a glance loaded with meaning, and then she speeds off.

You can just say no. Is that true?

My cell phone chimes with another text message—I've gotten about a dozen so far this morning and that's an alarming statistical spike—and I head inside to check them. Once I step into the main entrance lobby, I look up at the rushing current of students moving past me. Most of them are doing something unusual in my direction: smiling, or flicking their eyes sideways, or actually saying hi.

I know a lot of people. Some of them I hang out with and consider friends. Fortunately, it's been five years since *Five at Eleven* and most kids have forgotten that my face was ever on a movie poster. There's no reason for anybody to dislike me—at least I hope that's the case—but I'm nothing special. I just sort of *exist* at this school.

All that's about to change, because when I glance down at the first message, I see it's from a girl in my homeroom and it says, *SO excited about the movie!*

Oh, crap. Word is out. And I know, instantly, how that word got a jet-powered blastoff on its speedy journey through the cell phones and social networks of our student body.

I'm going to kill him.

"Why, Felix? *Why?*"

"Oh, come on. You know you love it."

"Yeah, I'm pretty sure I don't."

We're in line for lunch in the cafeteria, where at least all the staring is concentrated in one place at one time. By now, there isn't a single being at this school—not the kids nobody talks to, not even the French teacher who won't let you address her in English—who doesn't know. All morning, people have been asking me questions I can't answer.

When do they start filming? Is everyone else doing it too?

My standard response is to shrug, while in my mind, I'm curled up at the back of a closet with the door closed, pleading *go away go away go away.*

Felix, though, grins at them, all teeth and confidence. His face is so bright and open, his enthusiasm so uncomplicated, that for a second, I see the world he sees. It's not a bad world. I'm sure it would be a lovely place to visit.

"Haven't you been waiting for this?" he says to me as he grabs a bowl of pudding. "I mean, I've got plans! If I can get two new videos online by the time they come . . ." His eyes light up. "Actually, they could shoot me *shooting* the videos!"

Felix is a first-generation American, says the *Five at Six* website. *The son of immigrants from the Dominican Republic, he's already navigating a tricky multicultural, bilingual landscape. Will his parents' American dream for him happen?*

When I worry about how well I know this stuff, I think of Felix. If I have it memorized, you can bet your ass he has it framed on the wall. (Well, that's not quite fair. I've been in Felix's room. He does have it framed on the wall.) Judging from his daily photo blog and the video clips he posts of himself performing original songs on his electronic keyboard, Felix would like nothing better than cameras following him 24/7.

We reach the cash register and when we're both done paying, I start to follow him toward our usual table. "Oh," he says, looking over his shoulder at me. "I'm having a screening party on Saturday. To watch *Six and Eleven*. You have to be there."

I frown hard at him. "Do you have any idea how narcissistic that is?"

Felix's smile drops, but only a little. "I thought it would help people get used to the idea of the cameras being around."

He's not watching where he's going and when he turns forward again, he almost walks right into another kid.

Oh. Not another kid.

Nate Hunter.

How do I sum up Nate Hunter? Let's just say that if I merely exist around here, Nate blazes, through hallways and classrooms and the swimming pool. He blinds and dazzles, if you're into that sort of thing.

Nathaniel is about as "homegrown" as you can get; he lives with his mother, who is young and single, and his grandparents, the owners of a long-established local farm.

Felix and Nate stare at each other, frozen by some invisible force field between them. If I could snap a picture, it would be a study of opposites: Nate is blond and green-eyed, pale and lanky, his hair short and even vertical in places, while Felix is dark and small and shaggy-headed. This kind of moment with Nate happens sometimes, when Felix is distracted and not on his guard. Usually, I grab Felix and snap him out of it, but right now we've both got these damn trays in our hands. It's extra awkward today, given the news about the film. All I can do is stand there and watch, and wince.

Felix tries to like everyone and be the universal buddy, but I know if there's one person he would want to make disappear from the planet, it's the guy who was once like a brother to him.

Nate looks away from Felix, then quickly around the room as if searching for someone, anyone, else. His gaze lands on me for a split second, then jumps off as quickly as possible. That's all I rate.

I remember what Leslie said, that Nate actually *called* them to see if there would be a third film. Well, of course he did. He's got the best story out of the five of us. His will be the most dramatic "Then" and "Now" footage, and all I can feel is angry. For what he did to my best friend, and what he did to himself.

Nate continues to search the cafeteria beyond Felix, then, apparently finding what he was looking for, moves away.

"Come on," I say, walking in front of Felix. I snag our table and he follows, still a bit dazed. We eat in silence for about a minute, both trying very hard not to look over to Nate's table, which is filled with other swim team guys and their assorted female counterparts.

"Hey, Justine," says a voice, and I glance up to see Ian standing there with his tray, my face reflected in his thick-framed so-uncool-they're-cool glasses. He tosses his head to flick back a lock of curly black hair. "Do you have room?"

There's just Felix and me at the table, so *duh* we have room. But I just nod and slide down the bench to make space for him.

Felix shoots me a look, one eyebrow raised, and in return I pop my eyes at him so he gets the hint. "Oops," he says to me, too dramatically, "I forgot napkins. Be right back." He gets up and walks toward the napkins, but stops on his way to chat with two guys at another table.

Ian sits and shakes up his bottle of juice, which is something that always drove me crazy (*I like the froth*, he'd say), then slides his straw wrapper down to an accordion. Those hands. I remind myself that those hands used to stroke my hair, rub my shoulders, hold my face right before he kissed me. I do this because clearly, I'm a masochist.

"How do you feel about this movie thing?" Ian asks, and the fact that he's the first person to care, the first person to consider that maybe the news is strange and difficult, pierces me a little.

"I'm not sure," I reply, the closest thing to the truth I've got at the moment.

Ian smiles, takes a bite of his hamburger, then considers while he chews. "I can totally understand how it would be weird. But I've got to tell you, I thought the first two movies were awesome."

We'd never talked about the films. I kept waiting for him to ask about them, but he never did. I took that to mean he wasn't interested and I sort of loved that.

"I haven't seen them in a while," he continues. "But I remember how funny they are." He glances at me, then down at his burger. "How funny *you* are."

"Oh yeah? Funny good or funny bad?" I try to make it sound like I'm teasing, not fishing.

"All good," Ian says.

Would you care to elaborate? I want to ask. Because it was my understanding that for him, being funny did not equal being totally hot and datable.

Instead I shrug and mumble, "I never know who's seen them and who hasn't."

"My parents bought the DVDs. It made them so proud that it was our town and our school. For a while they begged me to be friends with Nate so he'd have more kids to stick up for him."

We laugh. It's hard to remember a time when Nate Hunter needed charity buddies.

Then we're silent, and I'm trying to think of what else to say during this sweet, surprise treasure of a few minutes together.

"Well," Ian finally says. "I think it'll be cool to have the cameras around again."

Something about his manner feels off. Then comes the thought I shouldn't have but do anyway, because we already know I'm a masochist: Is this news about the film the only reason he came over to sit with me? I don't know what to do with that. Let's just toss that under the table with those hard, runty french fries that always end up on the floor.

Instead, I'd like to make him laugh somehow. If I can say one thing that will make him bust out, it'll rocket me onto a high so lovely I can make it through the rest of the day. *See? I really can be that kind of girl.*

"Smile!" he'd always say to me during those seven weeks he was my boyfriend. We'd be out somewhere, doing something categorized as Fun. We'd be in a group of people and someone just said something hilarious. We'd be kissing, his hands so warm and mine so cold. Then he'd stop and look at me, and brush my hair away from my eyes and examine my face like he'd never seen it before, and say it. *Smile.*

I couldn't. Not just like that, on cue, as if taking direction. But that wasn't the worst part. The worst part was, I thought I *was* smiling.

He's gulping down his juice in a very unsexy way I'll ignore, and I'm about to chirp something at him when the notion hits: Whatever we are, or might possibly, miraculously, be again, would be part of the new movie. There would be no escaping it.

A girl from my biology class is suddenly next to me. "Hey, Justine," she says. "I heard about the documentary. Do you know if they're going to need interns or assistants or anything?"

"I really don't," I reply, trying to sound disappointed for her, "but I'll let you know what I find out." I look over to Nate's table again. Nobody's coming up to him like they are with me. Although with Nate, maybe you have to request an audience in writing. I don't know how popularity works.

Felix returns with a handful of napkins and follows my gaze. After a thoughtful moment, he asks, "Do you think Keira will do it, after last time?"

Oh. Yeah. That is the bonus winner-take-all question.

Then I realize why Felix has asked this. Normally, Keira would be at the Nate Etcetera table. But she's not there.

"Has anyone seen her this morning?" I ask.

"She wasn't in homeroom," says Ian.

So Keira has skipped school, probably knowing what was in store. Smart girl, they always say about Keira, and today she does not disappoint.

Felix is waiting for me after school in a window booth on the second floor of Muddy Joe's, the bakery/coffeehouse/laptop mecca in town. It's the realm of college students too cool to hang out on campus and they're all LBNF: Loud But Not Funny. The space looks great but has terrible acoustics. You can't even hear yourself drink.

"Hey," I say as I sit down across from Felix, who has his computer open on the table. "Thanks for the assist at lunch."

"Just spreading the joy because, guess what? My visitors more than doubled since news broke about the film."

He slides the laptop over so I can see the screen. It's a graph of traffic statistics for Felix's blog, where he posts a lot of sci-fi fan art and stills from *The Big Lebowski*, with what he thinks is brilliant commentary but is really stuff like, "The Dude is the bomb, yo!" And then there are videos of him performing original songs on his electronic keyboard while sitting on the floor of his bedroom. His music is either brilliant or awful, I'm still not sure. I tell him it's the former.

"I'm happy you're so happy," I say.

"I hope my stats will climb even more between now and the start of production. Lance said they'll be here in a month."

"Maybe that's enough time for me to figure out a hobby."

Felix tilts his head and regards me with a sad familiarity. "You watch a lot of movies. Even the old ones nobody's heard of. Being a film buff—that's a hobby, isn't it?"

"I think that involves way too much lying around in sweatpants to count."

"If you start a hobby now, won't it be obvious you're

just doing it for the cameras?"

I shrug. Yeah, maybe. Probably. That could be my "story." Justine at sixteen, trying to find something to keep her from dying of boredom.

I glance out the window, which overlooks the sidewalk in front of Muddy Joe's. One of the employees is on her break. She's leaning against a tree with her apron thrown over one shoulder, smoking a cigarette. It's this striking, almost bittersweet picture because she looks totally at peace with the world, but it's wicked cold and I know she only gets a few minutes before having to go back to the kitchen to decorate five hundred red velvet cupcakes or something.

"Be right back," I suddenly say to Felix. I grab my jacket and head downstairs. Outside, the snappy air hits me hard, but I try to look unfazed.

The girl tips up her chin in greeting. "Justine, right?"

"Hey." I have no idea what her name is although she's waited on me countless times, and they even wear name tags.

"What's up?"

"Would you . . . can I . . . bum a cigarette?"

She smiles at me in this condescending, *Oh, you little high schooler* way. After a long few seconds where I get the sense I'm being appraised, she produces the pack and holds it out to me. I hook my finger around a cigarette and

24

slide it out. She's ready with a lighter and a hand cupped around it, and I lean forward to get the thing started.

I don't smoke. Olivia does, sometimes, and she taught me how to do it one night when we were home alone during a thunderstorm and the power was out. I didn't feel one way or another about it, which I took to be a sign that it wasn't worth the trouble.

I take a drag on the cigarette, avoiding Felix's *What the hell?* face in the window above. I blow the smoke out slowly, remembering Olivia's coaching. Fight back a cough. It feels a little great. Even shivering and with the bakery girl watching, I get a sensation like, *I could do this.* It would give me something. All the people who wanted me to be some kind of symbol of youth in revolt would expect nothing less.

I'm on my third drag when I turn my head casually and see this sudden weirdness: the petite figure of Rory Gold walking down the street, her too-big, aggressively puffy down coat zipped all the way to her chin. She stops dead when she sees me. I'm wearing a long-sleeved T-shirt that says "STOP WARS" in the *Star Wars* logo, and the familiar blank look on Rory's face stabs me a little right on the *O*.

Rory Gold and I have not spoken in almost five years. To my credit, or at least I like to think, for the last year I've been meaning to change that.

There are best friends Justine, whose parents are enjoying professional success, and Rory, whose family is struggling with recent job layoffs. The two families have been close since the girls were babies. Will their friendship be affected by their changing economic situations?

I wonder how the press release might read for this new film. I wonder how Lance and Leslie will figure out what happened, what I did to my friend, and how that story will get told.

I'm so surprised that I blurt out, "Hi," before I can remember all the reasons not to.

Rory says, "Hi," softly. Her eyes shift to the cigarette in my hand, which I didn't have time to hide.

We're caught like this for many more seconds. I notice Rory's just got her dark blond hair cut again, super short like it's been since we were eleven, and the style flatters the bold features she's grown into.

My tobacco benefactor is done with her smoke and walks past us, smirking, to get back indoors.

Then Rory speaks, addressing the cigarette. "Smoking causes one in five American deaths. It kills more people in the U.S. than AIDS, drugs, homicides, fires, and auto accidents combined."

"I don't really smoke," I sputter. "I was just . . ." She's locked on to it like RoboGirl with a targeting system. It still unnerves me when she does this stuff, so I add, "Did

26

you talk to Lance and Leslie? Are you doing the film this time around?"

Now she looks at me, actually at my eyes—no longer than a blink—then at the hedge next to me.

"Yes. My parents feel strongly that I should continue."

"Mine too." I throw the half-smoked cigarette on the ground now and rub it out with my foot the way I've seen Olivia do. Rory watches me. These long pauses feel way too familiar, even though it's been years.

"Well, maybe I'll see you, then," I offer, "when they start shooting."

Now Rory's eyes meet mine once more. They dart away, as if trying to escape, then back. It's strange to see her face straight on like that.

She asks, "Are you going to do to me what you did last time?" Her voice isn't accusing at all. It's mostly flat, as always, with the slightest twist of curiosity, like she's asking me what I'm having for dinner. Eyes away, and back again. I can tell this is work for her. I heard that a therapist at school has been helping her with social skills. "I would just like to know," she adds, "so I can make a plan for how to deal with that."

I used to hate Rory's directness. It irritated the hell out of me. But right now I can't think of anything more refreshing.

"No, I'm not. I mean—"

She cuts me off. "I'm going to be assertive here and say, please don't. It hurts too much."

Then she turns and continues on. If Rory thinks about these things, if she's at all typical in certain kinds of ways, I'm sure she's muttering *bitch* on her way down the street.

THREE

B eing the daughter of a local pediatrician has its insider moments, for sure. My father often gives me sealed, unmarked envelopes to pass on to the school nurse—medical forms and get-out-of-gym notes, stuff like that. I could be privy to a lot of juicy gossip, if I were a different kind of person and could steam open an envelope.

A few mornings after the Day Everyone Heard, I walk into the nurse's office with two small letters. When Mrs. Underwood sees me, she looks relieved.

"Oh good," she says. "I've been waiting for these. Let

me check to make sure they're complete. Can you hang out for a minute?"

"Sure," I say, expecting this. Dad has a bad habit of leaving important things blank, and then I have to bring the whatever-it-is back to him.

As soon as Mrs. Underwood is distracted with the envelopes, I scope out the office. There are two doors against the rear wall, each leading to a small room with a cot. The door to one is ajar and the light is on. Just inside I can see a pair of long legs in jeans stretched out on the bed, crossed at the ankles. Black leather Mary Janes with embroidered flowers and chunky heels. Shoes that look familiar because I'll admit, I've admired them before.

Then I remember something Felix said to me about Keira the other day.

She went to the nurse with a headache again. That's the third trip in a week.

I wasn't prepared to care about how often Keira Jones goes to the nurse or leaves early or looks depressed or hangs her head or breathes. But the fact that she's acting like anything besides the confident, bright, and gorgeous light she's known to be is pretty damn interesting.

I take a couple of steps to my right and now I can really see. There's Keira, sitting up, one hand holding an ice pack to her forehead and the other grasping a book. Her dark curly hair's long and loose, her glasses are sliding down her nose a bit.

I could say hi. Just an everyday hi, not too loud, and normal–friendly. But then I think of her glancing up and not saying it back, and that's not someplace I want to go.

"Looks good!" says Mrs. Underwood. "Thank your dad for me."

I just nod and get the hell out of there.

Sometimes I think of an invisible cord connecting Nate and Keira and Felix and Rory and me. It's made of something thin and deceptively powerful, like the stuff Spider–Man squirts out of his wrists. Then I wonder who spun it. Was it Lance and Leslie? Was it everyone who's ever watched the *Five At* documentaries? Or maybe it was me. All I know is that it's always there. It stretches and winds but will never break.

I'm home after school and my sister has sent me an email with this persuasive note:

Dude, you have to read this post about the Five At *films.*

Olivia has pasted a link below it, but I don't click yet. Just like I've avoided the series' website, I've avoided the stuff an online search might dredge up. Sometimes when I'm bored, I'll type out "Five At films" or my name, but never actually hit the search button. Like when you're terrified to call someone, so you dial the first nine digits over and over but always hang up before pressing the tenth.

Today, though, I dial that tenth digit. I click the link.

It's an entry from a blog by someone who calls himself DocuGeek, dated about a month ago.

When I was in college, a girlfriend dragged me to what sounded like a snoozer of a doc called Five at Six, *about a group of kids in the same kindergarten class in an upstate New York college town. Precious, right? Mundane and probably someone's vanity project, I was sure.*

I was wrong. Five at Six *was the opposite of a snoozer: It was a wake-up call. It was funny and fascinating, probably one of the best films I'd seen in a long time, thanks mostly to the gifts of Lance and Leslie Rodgers, whose choice of subjects and tragicomic sensibilities are brilliant. It remains one of my favorite documentaries ever.*

Five at Eleven *is right up there too, for different reasons.*

It's been five years. These kids are sixteen now, so we're due for another installment. Is it coming? I emailed Lance Rodgers but got only a vague reply of "We're working on getting things in place."

So for the time being I have to just wonder about Justine, Keira, Nate, Rory, and Felix. They must be sophomores in high school. Who are they now? I could do some online detective work, but what's the fun in that?

(Although I will admit I happened upon Felix's personal blog; I've included one of his videos below.) Instead, I'm going to make some predictions.

I read on.

According to DocuGeek, the most likely scenario is that Rory's been diagnosed with some kind of autism spectrum thing (okay, that is eerie) and Nate has been bullied out of school (so way off) and Felix, based on the personality shown in his videos, is the most popular kid in the class (he wishes). He's got a couple of theories about Keira: She probably rebelled and is a total pothead (not that we know of), or she and her father moved cross-country to start fresh after all the heartbreak (which nobody would blame them for, but this is a miss too).

What's really striking, and I'm not being egotistical here, is that this guy, who's probably blogging from his man-cave surrounded by gaming consoles and sex dolls, is mostly wondering about me.

Justine was the one who always snagged my attention. Much of the drama in Five at Six *revolves around what happens after she's rushed to the hospital with terrible stomach pain. She was fascinating to watch at age six and again at eleven. So now, at sixteen, I see Justine having started a badass girl band or become the star of the drama club. She could be into painting, or designing clothing, or writing an underground newspaper. She's the class president or has dropped out of school.*

I don't read any more, although I notice the bottom of the post says "24 Comments," which means DocuGeek's readers have weighed in as well. I slap the laptop shut and put my head on my desk.

I am none of these things people have wanted for me.

I am none of these things because I am nothing in particular, period.

What comes to mind suddenly is my last sit-down interview in *Five at Eleven*, where Leslie asks me a question I don't have a smartypants answer for.

"What do you think the next five years will be like, Justine?"

"They'll be super awesome." At eleven I'm fast and loose with the double adjectives.

"Rephrase part of the question in your answer, please." She still needs to remind me.

"The next five years will be super awesome."

"Why? What's going to happen?"

"I'll be in junior high and then high school and be a teenager and get a boyfriend and wear makeup. And I'll be a great guitar player by then too."

"That does sound awesome," says Leslie, and you can hear the smile in her voice. Not because she wants that for me too, but because I just gave her a great sound bite.

"Yeah, I can't wait to be sixteen," I say. And of course that's what they use for the last line of the movie. I would bet the classic anime shelf of my DVD collection that they'll use that in the trailer for this next one, too.

I couldn't wait to be sixteen. Now I am. I don't have a boyfriend, and actually hate wearing makeup except for ChapStick and a little eyeliner. I stopped playing guitar three years ago. I feel so sorry for eleven-year-old me.

Don't rush, Justine! You may have peaked in fifth grade!

It still blows my mind, sometimes, that so many strangers watched me go through what I did when I was six. Those tests they did in the hospital, the alien probes that snooped around in every possible orifice. My parents let Lance and Leslie film some of it (not the gross parts, but certainly the tense parts), because my father the pediatrician wanted other parents to learn from his process of figuring out what the hell might be wrong with his kid.

The doctors found nothing. The pain kept coming. Eventually, they suggested it was caused by stress and I should see a therapist. One of them dared to wonder if it was related to the experience of *being the subject of a documentary*, but of course that didn't appear in the film.

The cramps went away for a while, so the therapist idea did too. I don't tell anyone, but they come back from time to time; we seem to have a drop-in-whenever arrangement. I've developed tricks for dealing with them. The tricks seem to work. I am fine.

Except right now.

Get inside the pain. Okay, what does this pain feel like?

The way it felt to see Lance and Leslie by the library. The way it felt to wonder why Ian came to sit with me at lunch. The way it felt for everyone to look and whisper and question.

Olivia's words from this morning are in my head now.

You can just say no if you want to.

I know she has an ulterior motive. My sister came off terribly in the second movie: a fourteen-year-old airhead who represented everything I didn't want to be—obsessed with clothes, boys, and hair, like she ordered her entire personality from the back pages of a teen magazine. Plus, she hated how it all affected our family. When our parents split up, so perfectly timed after the film experience was done, she accused them of keeping things together just long enough for the cameras to go away.

Olivia was right, of course, but they didn't have the guts to admit it.

Could she be right here? Can I just say no? That seems impossible. Or maybe it's one of those things that only seems impossible because you've never questioned it.

Dad still has a place at our table, even though he hasn't lived in our house for almost four years. When he sits at it, every Thursday night without fail, he reminds me of a little boy who's been plopped onto the driver's seat of a fire truck. He's not really in control, but he likes to pretend to be, and by the look of pure pleasure on his face this must be the highlight of his week.

After *Five at Eleven* came out and the publicity died down, my parents took Olivia and me to our favorite mini-golf place, and in between the pirate ship at hole nine and the giant caterpillar at hole ten, told us they were splitting up. "We decided that we're better off not married," said my dad. My mom just nodded, and then later when we were driving home with ice cream cones, decided to add, without looking at us, "You can love someone, but not be *in love* with them."

So now they "love each other" but are not married, which equals the Thursday night dinners. When Mom doesn't have another Three-Week Boyfriend and Dad isn't dating one of those moms who think pediatricians are automatically hot, he stays over—and it's not on the couch—and he makes breakfast the next morning like there's nothing messed up about it. I chose to stop being confused by this years ago.

On these nights, it's easy to pretend our family is the way it used to be and my parents cared enough to fight for their marriage. It's easy to keep eating and talking despite the side dish of bittersweet that always seems to sit at the edge of the table, untouched.

Olivia tries to take the salad bowl from Dad, but he holds it teasingly just beyond her reach.

"Grow up," she snaps, and grabs it from him.

Once we all have our food, Mom clears her throat and announces, "Jeff, we have some news." I gave her permission to be the one to do this.

Dad looks at her, then me, his eyes lit up mischievously.

"Lance and Leslie Rodgers are in town. It looks like the third movie is a go."

"I heard a rumor about that from one of my patients," he says simply. I won't ask who it was, because then I'll picture that person in a white paper gown, and sometimes that picture is not pretty. Now he turns to me. "That'll be exciting, yes?"

My parents' clueless grins. Olivia's silent scowl. My window of opportunity is open, and I can fit through.

"Actually, no," I say. "I don't want to do it."

Now Olivia explodes into laughter and offers her hand for a high five. I gently oblige.

"What?" asks Dad.

Mom overlaps with, "Why not?"

"I've thought about it, and I have my reasons."

"Is everyone else doing it?" asks Dad.

"Are you going to tell me that if everyone else does it, I should too? Isn't that the opposite of the standard jumping-off-the-Empire-State-Building speech?"

"Consider what it means," says Mom, who looks at Dad

for approval. He nods back. "Not just to Lance and Leslie but to the other kids, and the fans, and—"

"And to you?" asks Olivia. I'm so glad it's her and not me who says this.

"To *us*?" asks Dad. "Why, what would it mean to us?"

"Oh, please," says Olivia. "Like you don't want all the attention and publicity."

Mom and Dad exchange a sharp glance and Mom lets out a sigh.

"We've talked about this before," says Mom. "Don't for a second think we have our own interests at heart."

"We made a commitment ten years ago and I think we should stick to it," adds Dad. "Unless you have a really good reason not to. Justine, do you have a really good reason not to?"

I look at my parents' faces, serious and united now.

Olivia reaches out and touches my wrist. "Don't let them pressure you."

"Justine?" Mom nudges. "Why would you say no?"

These are my parents, and they're always telling me I can be honest with them about anything. They tell me this so much it's annoying and makes me want to do the opposite. But right now, maybe I should give it a try.

"I just . . . I'm not . . . I'm not what I was hoping I would be by now."

My mother melts a little. "Oh, sweetie." Which means she doesn't get it.

"Mom," I say evenly and, I hope, firmly. "You can't even get me to be in family pictures. Why do you think I'd want a camera crew on my tail?"

It's so much more than the way I look, but I've thought about this and decided my best strategy is to focus on what they already know about me.

Dad leans back in his chair and nods; maybe I hit the mark with him. "Remember when I didn't want to go to my twenty-fifth high school reunion because of my bald spot?"

"No way," says Olivia. "If you tell that story again, I'll puke."

"It applies!" Dad's raising his voice now.

I look at my family squaring off against one another and my resolve falters. If I hold firm, the pressure would make life a living hell that would be worse than the much briefer living hell of just doing the film. Either way, I will hate them for it.

Olivia leans in and whispers, "Don't cave."

I stare at my plate. "I won't."

"This makes me sad," says my father.

"Yes, because it's all about you!" shouts my sister, as she pushes away from the table and huffs upstairs.

A stunned, hear-a-pin-drop silence follows. Mom is making shapes with her potatoes, and Dad squeezes the bridge of his nose with his thumb and forefinger like he does when he's thinking or sad.

I'm not sure what to say now, so I just turn to Mom and ask, "Will you call Leslie and tell her for me?"

Mom pauses, staring into my eyes, then, mercifully, nods.

Dad says, "Jussie, you wanna walk me out?"

Usually I invite him to stay and watch a movie with me, but tonight I just get up and find his coat.

FOUR

S aturday afternoon, Felix calls. I know his "screening party" is tonight and he still wants me to come. I let it go to voice mail.

Then he texts me. *Cmon u know u want to be there! Plzzzzzz!*

I haven't told anyone about my decision. It's easier if the whole thing begins as a rumor, so I'll just ask Olivia to start a blabfest; she excels in that area.

The truth is, the only thing I've been able to think about today is all those people from school watching me on the screen in Felix's basement. Making comments about my hair, my clothes, what I'm saying. And I can't stand the idea of not being there to feel insulted by it.

This is why, at 8:30 p.m., I am pulling my dad's car into the driveway of Felix's house. There are a dozen cars, and for a second, I'm happy for him. Felix is always trying to be Mr. Social, always grasping for anything that resembles popularity. He's got other friends besides me, a tight-knit gang of techie-music nerds, but nobody takes him seriously. Unless he has something special to offer, like this screening with the digital projector he bought with his own savings.

I knock loudly on the front door and Felix's mother, Ana, answers. "Hola, Justine!" she says, as she hugs me. I haven't seen her since the last time I stopped in to the Hunter Farms store, which she runs, and it's weird seeing the lower half of her body because she's always, you know, behind a counter. Over her shoulder in the living room, the TV is blaring a news program in Spanish. Felix's dad, who is also named Felix and manages all the Hunter Farms employees, swivels in his La-Z-Boy to wave at me. I wave to him. He swivels back to the TV.

Ana asks me the standard questions about my family and school, and I nod, saying "Yes" and "Good" while inching toward the door to the basement. Finally, she lets me go and I'm making my way down the stairs.

I hear the sound of Keira's six-year-old voice.

"My daddy doesn't let me watch TV," she's saying. It

comes out proud, but she pauses after she says it and her mouth twitches downward.

Good, we're just a few minutes in. I hang back and check out the room. There are at least thirty kids sprawled on two faux-leather couches and countless floor pillows, munching popcorn. I spot Ian's friend Dashiell, which makes my heart spazz.

When Ian and I were in that brand-new sunshine-and-rainbows phase, I'd thrill at the sight of his friends, because I knew he was nearby. There he is. Ian, on the floor in front of Dashiell. I can't see his head but I know it's him by the clothes.

And now I'm instantly sorry I came. Or not. It's very confusing.

The movie is showing on a giant white sheet tacked to the wall. It doesn't hang completely straight, and Keira's light cocoa skin has strange wrinkles in it, her curly hair has extra swirls.

Felix is sitting behind everyone, next to the projector. Jotting things down in a little notebook.

"Has your daddy told you why he doesn't want you to watch TV?" asks Leslie's voice. Sometimes I have to remind myself that most people who watch this have no idea what Leslie looks like. They can't see her small, intense eyes and her nail-biting, her hands running nervously through her hair, as she listens to what you're saying with a camera pointed at you.

Keira stares off for a moment. She thinks, then shrugs one shoulder.

The next shot is Keira and her parents sitting on the floor of their living room, playing some math board game. Keira's mom is lying on her side, her head propped up by an arm, and she's rolling the dice for Keira. I forgot how beautiful Mrs. Jones was and feel a terrible pang of grief for this family scene that can't exist anymore.

Suddenly, there's a hand on my elbow and I jump.

It's Felix, smiling. Not smugly, like he could be, but as if he's genuinely happy to see me. "I'm so glad you made it," he says. "Here, take my chair." And I don't protest, because I'd rather not shift my eyes off the screen. I've watched this movie many times in the privacy of my bedroom—too many to count, and nobody knows that—but seeing it big like this is a different story. Keira is nearly the size of her real kindergarten self projected on the sheet, and it's pretty weird, like having your memories yanked out of you and tossed onto the nearest wall.

"We don't watch TV because there's no interaction there," Keira's father is saying in his booming English-professor voice. He's a tall, stunning African-American man. Everything he says sounds automatically correct. "How can we use our imagination or problem-solving skills if we're just passive consumers of a medium? Instead, my family plays. We play games, we play with toys, we read books to one another, we do activities outside. It's old-fashioned and we like it."

Then we see Nate. He's sitting in a miniature plastic chair covered with cartoon characters, eating dry cereal out of a bowl, two feet from a giant TV blaring cartoons.

Everyone in Felix's basement cracks up, just like they're supposed to.

The camera pans over to Nate's mother, sitting at a nearby table in her dental hygienist's scrubs, talking on the phone. For a full ten seconds all we hear is her saying, "I know . . . Oh my God . . . yeah, as if . . . ," to whoever's on the other end, and Nate crunching his cereal so loud I wonder if that wasn't juiced up in the editing room.

I glance over to Felix, but his face is too shadowed for me to read his expression.

One of the kids on a couch yells, "Go, Nate!" and I know what's coming next. That will be Rory and me, dressed in princess costumes, dancing around my kitchen while *The Nutcracker* blasts through the stereo.

This is an excellent time for me to go to the bathroom.

For a few minutes, I just listen to the audio I know so well. And then, laughter from Felix's basement audience. Ian, surely part of that laughter. I cover my ears.

I've been in there a while—too long, apparently—when Felix knocks on the door.

"Justine? Are you okay?"

"I'm fine."

"Can I come in?"

"Uh, no? Gross."

"I know you're not doing anything in there." He's right, of course. I'm sitting on the toilet, but it's closed and I'm dressed.

I sigh and unlock the door. Felix enters, shuts the door behind him, and leans on the sink. It's a salmon-colored thing, with chipped gold-toned fixtures, lost in the seventies. The rest of the Cortez house has been beautifully remodeled, but Felix refuses to let them alter the retro-cool vibe in the basement.

"You're missing the best parts," he says.

"Felix, I've seen this movie. So have you. I wonder who's seen it more?"

He shrugs. "It's different when it's not just you in the room."

"It's different when you know it's all going to happen again."

For a second, I forget that I'm not going to be part of it. Then I remember and realize I'm going to have to tell him.

"It's nice to talk to someone who gets it," he says softly. Then he looks me square in the eye. "Let's go out this week. I'll buy you dinner."

And now we've got this again.

"We've been through that stuff before, Felix."

"But I like you *so much*!"

I can't even feel flattered.

"I like you too," I tell him. "You're one of my favorite people in history. But, uh, how fake would that look, that you and I start dating right before shooting starts? Lance would probably force us to dump each other just so nobody would accuse him of setting it up."

"So if they weren't coming, you would say yes?"

Okay, I walked right into that, and now I have to tell him the thing he doesn't want to hear.

"No, Felix. I wouldn't. I don't think of you that way and I don't think you think of me that way either."

"I've always thought of you that way, Justine. Forget that total douche Ian. You and me, we have a connection."

"Yeah, courtesy of Lance and Leslie ten years ago."

The thing I won't tell him is that, fabricated or not, I love our connection. Talking to Felix is sometimes like talking to myself.

In the years after *Five at Six*, we were always in different classes and when I did see Felix, at school or around town, we were both too shy or weirded out to say anything to each other. Then *Five at Eleven* was released. There was all the attention and the controversy, and then suddenly there was no more of either, and one day in the cafeteria I found an apple cider donut in my backpack.

It was tucked into a Ziploc bag with a bow, alongside a sugar-dusted note that said, simply:

You look sad. Please don't be.

I held the donut in my hand and thought about what I did to Rory, and Keira's face in that scene in the film, and my dad moving out, and then put those thoughts away in a place so deep inside me, they could bang and bang and I wouldn't hear a thing.

I ate the donut, licked the note clean. After school I asked my mom to drive me to the Hunter Farms store and found Felix in the back room, arranging strawberries in green paper containers.

"Hi," I said to him.

He turned and smiled, and just like that, I wasn't alone anymore.

Now, Felix is staring at the wall—also salmon, with iridescent gold flecks in it. "I would feel this way without the films, I swear."

So would I, I'm about to tell him. But I stop myself. Felix grows suddenly quiet and I don't know if it's because he knows I'm going to say that, or because he's listening to the movie in the other room. It's Nate's voice, answering questions on-screen.

"Listen, I could use some advice," Felix says after a few moments, taking a deep breath. "Nate emailed me after our little standoff in the caf."

"What? *Contact?*" I ask, exaggerated, but Felix remains serious.

"He wants us to agree not to talk about certain things on camera, when shooting starts. You know Leslie will ask why we're not friends anymore. I mean, in *Five at Eleven* there's that whole scene with us down at the pond, catching salamanders, like we're freaking Tom Sawyer and Huck Finn."

I try not to think about that scene, because it reminds me of Rory.

"But we were never real buddies," he continues. "My parents work for his grandparents, so I'm basically hired help. Sometimes I think when we were little, they all bribed me to spend time with him. His mom was always giving me his old toys."

Now, of course, I'm dying to hear more because this is the most Felix has ever talked about Nate, but he's come to me for help and this feels good and I don't want to blow it.

"So what do you want my advice on?"

"Well, you're always great at avoiding the question when Leslie asks something you don't want to answer."

"Am I?"

"You make some funny smart-ass comment and it's like gold, and then nobody cares that you didn't answer. They only care that you gave them something good on camera. I need some tips in case I get into a corner. Because I'm not like you. I find myself wanting to please them so bad, I'll tell them anything."

"You make it sound like torture."

Then we look at each other and laugh. We both know that it *is* a little like torture. Or, a lot.

"I guess that's the difference between you and me," I say, and think hard about how to put this into words. "You like to please them. I like to piss them off."

Felix snorts, then smiles and takes my hand. "The real difference, Justine, is that pissing them off *is* your way of trying to please them."

This statement rolls over me like something big and fast with a hundred wheels. I can't recover from it right away, and I can't deal with what it means, and I don't want Felix to know either.

Finally, I compose myself and offer this: "Try to think of every question they ask you as the setup to a joke."

"Oh, that's good," says Felix, taking his notebook out of his back pocket.

As he writes, it echoes in my head. *Pissing them off is your way of trying to please them.* Something rises in me.

"I have something to tell you," I say. Felix lifts one eyebrow into his hungry, gossip-munching look. I take a breath deep enough to push all the words out. "I'm not going to do the movie."

His face is empty for a few seconds. Then he bursts into laughter. I'd be totally insulted by this reaction if I didn't expect it.

"Ha! Good one."

"I'm serious, Felix."

"Let me see."

He leans in to examine *my* face now. I keep my mouth

in a flat line and nod slightly. He leans out.

"Hmm. Well, maybe you are. For the moment. But there's no way you'll stick to that."

An F-sound dances on my lips and I know it would feel so good to say the word, to throw it at him. Candy good. But post-Ian, I've been fighting my potty mouth tendencies.

Instead I just say, "I can prove you wrong."

He smiles. "Keira said no too."

"How do *you* know?"

"I have my sources. But I guess Leslie talked her into it."

"Of course she did," I say. Leslie's left me two messages that I haven't returned.

A sudden roar of laughter from the other room draws Felix's attention from me, and without a word he bursts back through the bathroom door to check it out. I follow him.

There's me on the sheet-screen. I'm standing on a makeshift stage in our elementary school cafeteria, wearing red top-to-bottom long johns. Our teacher is off to the right, giving me line cues as I perform the lead role in our kindergarten version of *The Emperor's New Clothes*.

A few of the kids in Felix's basement turn around to see me hovering nearby, their faces alight with pure entertainment. One of them flashes me a thumbs-up, and I just smile politely. It always feels strange and a little wrong to take credit. What was I doing, besides getting up, going to school, doing my thing, living through the day? I wasn't trying to amuse. At least, I don't think so.

I move a bit so I can see Ian's face. He's grinning, totally enjoying what he's seeing.

Felix turns to me with both eyebrows raised. "You need this," he says, almost tenderly. "You just don't know it."

"You don't know what I don't know!" Yeah, that sounds moronic but whatever. I rocket toward the stairs and up, up, up to the outside world.

In no time I'm driving back to Dad's, thinking about the totally screwed-up-edness of people watching me and for some reason enjoying themselves. The rhythm of the tires against the uneven road slowly curls itself into a pattern of almost-words.

The pattern sounds like, *Felix is right, Felix is right, Felix is right.*

The next afternoon, there's a message in my email inbox from an address I don't recognize. No subject line either.

Justine,

Please change your mind about the movie. I think I understand why you're saying no. You may not be able to see it now, but good things will come out of it. I'm sure about that.

We are part of a whole, and without you, nothing will work. If you're doubting that this came from one of us, then I'll just say:

Five stickers under the table. Yours was the polar bear. See you soon, I hope.

The first thing I do, of course, is feel tremendously creeped out.

Then I think, *This is a trick from Lance or Leslie.*

But they wouldn't do this. They would potentially ask one of the others to do it, but my gut feeling says that's not the case here.

There was a day in kindergarten, after shooting ended, when our teacher had to duck out for an hour and left an aide in charge. The aide was new and young, and many of the kids saw their chance to mess around. Rory, Felix, Nate, Keira, and I all decided to do sticker art on the floor. (It was my idea. I wonder if they remember that too.) A few of the stickers ended up on the rough underbelly of our table. Yes, mine was the polar bear.

I look at the email address again. I didn't notice this before, but the first part is "lancehasbananabreath." I laugh. Who else would remember that? And who else would care whether or not I say yes or no? Felix. This is from Felix. And although he gave himself away, he managed to get me where I'm most vulnerable.

Part of a whole.

Well, dammit.

I go down to the kitchen to stress-chug a whole can of diet soda before I call Leslie and tell her I've changed my mind.

FIVE

M y morose princess!" says Amelia as I slide into her chair. "The usual trim today?"

Amelia is the hippest hairstylist in town in the un-hippest salon in town, a cruddy little place wedged between a comic book shop and an insurance office. She will tell you that because she has a couple of piercings and a borderline offensive tattoo on her neck, nobody else would hire her. But I know that as soon as the secret's out—that she doesn't suck the way everyone else does and actually knows what to do with hair—she'll soon be able to buy the shop for herself.

"I need something," I say, shaking my head hard, my

hair falling loose and a little wild so it says *Style Me!* like one of those big disembodied Barbie heads. It's been two weeks since I agreed to do the film, and it's taken me this long to get up the courage for this.

"Anything in particular?"

"Just different. Maybe a little surprising."

Amelia bites back a smile and runs her fingers through my hair. Her eyes grow intense, and okay, I'm a little scared now, but it's already too late.

"Are you sure?" she asks.

"Yes, I'm sure." I'm so glad to feel this way about anything.

Lance and Leslie will be here any minute.

They're coming to shoot their first sit-down interview with me, and my mother is making scones. She does this when she's nervous about impressing someone. They are Mango-Anxiety scones.

Olivia, who has chosen not to sign the paperwork because she doesn't want to appear in the film *for one freaking second*, as she so clearly put it, has agreed to stay away all day.

I'm still cleaning up my room, aka taking most of my dirty clothes, shoving them into my closet, and trying to get the door closed, when I hear the doorbell and freeze. The sound of Mom's footsteps from the kitchen to the foyer, the grinding noise the front doorknob always makes when you turn it. Then a chorus of high, loud voices.

I've thought about this and have decided I'll wait until Mom calls me down, like I was so engrossed in something I completely forgot we were expecting visitors. But now that I'm standing by for my cue, it all feels sort of Scarlett O'Hara.

Mom yells, "Justine! Lance and Leslie are here!"

I check myself in the mirror. Outfit looks uninspired but functional: blue jeans and a black V-neck sweater, with my special-occasion silver-toned sneakers. It's rare for me to wear something completely plain like this, unadorned by a graphic or funny comment. I feel naked and overdressed at the same time.

Mentally, I trim twenty pounds off my body. If I'd lost the twenty pounds I'd wanted to lose but somehow couldn't—because, let's be honest, I just didn't try hard enough—would my face be less round, my chin pointier? Would this part of my hips be gone? Would I look like how people imagined I would look? Or rather . . . how *I* imagined I would look?

The fact that I go right to thinking about *people* aka *audiences* makes me mad, and the fact that I don't know how to change that makes me even madder. But what can I do? They've got what they've got and maybe that should be my punishment. For not having the willpower, for being so lazy. I deserve for them to see me on-screen and whisper to whoever's sitting next to them, *Whoa. She chunked out.*

I've taken a preemptive Zantac for my stomach, which I know won't actually help but it's nice knowing it's in there.

Then I make my way down the stairs. Not too fast, not too slow. Leslie, Lance, and my mom are waiting at the bottom in our foyer.

When Leslie sees me, she blurts out, "Justine. Oh my God!"

"Hey," I say.

Now Lance looks up but his face is stone. His eyes travel slowly from my head down to my toes before he cracks one side of his mouth amusedly upward.

"I almost didn't recognize you," says Leslie, trying to hide the shock in her voice. I wish I could take a picture of the contrast between her expression and her husband's.

"That's been happening," I say.

She steps toward me, tentatively like she's not sure it's really me, and reaches out to touch my hair.

"What's a color nobody's ever seen you wear?" Amelia asked me at the salon.

"Pink." It popped out of my mouth like a bubble, catching a rainbow with the light.

So now my hair is chin-length, sliced into choppy chunks with the help of a razor blade. The pink that streaks through it is dark, dramatic, a shade you might see in a once-a-year sunset.

60

It's so not me that it's suddenly, totally me.

I can tell Leslie's fighting a battle: Wanting to Seem Excited vs. Being Inwardly Horrified. My mom had the same satisfying reaction. Finally Leslie just says, "Well, then," and pulls me into a hug.

Leslie has her long blond hair in a neat ponytail, with a rhinestone-studded headband looking pretty but unnecessary. When she draws back and turns to say something to my mother, I notice a frown line between her eyes, which was obscured by the hat that day outside the library, and it's much deeper than the one I remember. In the pictures I've seen of her at the premiere of their last film, the frown line is not even there, and I wonder how much makeup it takes to spackle up a crevice like that.

Lance steps forward and gives me a quick hug, grinning like he just won a grand prize. Ethically, he's not allowed to encourage us to look or dress a certain way. But I'm guessing he likes it when things work out for him in that area. The ratty superhero T-shirt I wore every day in *Five at Six* and that gray fedora I was partial to at eleven. Now this, with the pink streaks.

With his head uncovered, I can see Lance has less hair than he used to but it suits him, and he also looks deeply tanned. I flash on a conversation I had with Rory when we were eleven.

"Don't you think Lance is kind of a hottie?" I asked her as we were sitting on the floor of her room, doing a particularly brutal puzzle that was nothing but a photo of sand.

"Lance is nearly three times our age and would get arrested for even looking at us the wrong way," Rory had said, pressing her fingertip hard into the corner of the puzzle box, over and over. "But I've heard my mother say he's handsome."

I follow everyone into the living room and when Lance and Leslie nab the couch, leaving a cushion-length space between them, I'm left with the overstuffed chair-and-a-half that makes me feel like someone just blasted me with a shrink ray. My mom comes in with a steaming plate and there's a burst of scone-related rhapsody.

The light catches on the chunky ring on Leslie's finger as she reaches for her scone. She and Lance got married in Hawaii right after they finished shooting *Five at Eleven* but before the film actually came out. They must have had a short honeymoon period.

Now we've all got coffee and my mother drags in a dining room chair, settling in next to me.

"You guys got here just in time for the thaw," Mom says. "Two weeks ago, there was snow everywhere."

"Well, that's the way it works now that we live in Los Angeles," says Lance. "We're big-time filmmakers, we can order the weather around."

Leslie rolls her eyes but my mother and Lance laugh.

Then they're all looking at me like I'm supposed to add something snappy.

"I'm sorry your last movie tanked," I blurt out. Probably a little more snap in there than they wanted, but oh well.

It's silent, and then my mother shakes her head. "That was rude, Justine."

"No, Diana, it's cool," says Lance. "That's not anything we haven't heard from the most important people in Hollywood." He pauses, takes a sip of coffee. "Yup, our film tanked. That's actually putting it nicely."

"Apparently we need to stick to documentaries," says Leslie. "Although I have to say, I really loved the whole process of writing a script, casting it, doing retakes. My original dream was to direct fiction films, you know." She sighs. "I hope someday we get a second chance."

We're all quiet again. Lance looks at Leslie with a mix of annoyance and affection, then chirps, "In the meantime, we've got another story to tell! That of you, Justine, and your friends. I can't tell you how grateful we are that you decided to participate."

The word *friends* takes me by surprise, a little slap that stings. I don't know what hurts more. The thought of Rory shuffling past me in the hallways at school, me being afraid to even say hello to Keira that day in the nurse's office, or Nate's gaze bouncing off me in the cafeteria as if I could just be ignored out of existence.

"So, how are you *doing?*" asks Leslie, leaning forward to the edge of the couch. "Both of you. Since the divorce."

Mom and I look at each other and she jerks her chin toward me in a *You go ahead* gesture. I have no idea what to say to this.

"You know it happened a while ago, right? I was, like, twelve."

"A tender age for you," says Leslie, giving a nod that I recognize as her Prod Nod. The one that says, *I may or may not be interested in what you're saying, but I really want you to keep saying it.*

"I guess it was. But my parents breaking up was kind of mellow. Dad lives right in town and I'm there half the time."

"We had an amicable split," adds my mother, proudly. "In fact, Jeff still comes over for dinner every week. We're still a family."

Argh. I'd heard that so many times in the year after the divorce. That, along with its hideous inbred cousins: "We both love you no matter what" and "Divorce does not define us."

Leslie looks at me and I just smile blandly, backing my mother up. Then she glances at Lance, and he gives the tiniest eyebrow raise, which I think, if my eyebrow-to-English skills are as sharp as they ever were, means *There goes that idea.*

"Have you been shooting home video during the last

few years?" asks Lance. We all know he's talking about the camera they gave each family when they finished shooting *Eleven*. The expectations were obvious.

"Oh, yes," says my mom with a smile. "As much as she'd let us. I have some stuff saved and labeled for you. We can look at it whenever."

"Fantastic," says Leslie. She turns to me and adds, "Justine, if there's anything you took yourself, even with your phone, we'd love to see it."

"Okay," I say, and leave it at that. I have more than "anything." I have quite a bit. But I haven't yet decided to share.

We're all quiet for a few seconds and then Lance says, "Well, then. I think we're ready to get this girl on camera."

"I love it," says Leslie, looking around, even though there's really nothing special about my room. The walls are teal green, because I liked that color for six minutes three years ago, and the only thing breaking up the obnoxiousness of it is my bookcase full of DVD's, my bulletin board, and a big denim chair.

I don't respond to Leslie because I'm too busy sizing up the unnervingly tall person in the corner. His name is Kenny, and he's the sound guy. Lance and Leslie called him in from the car after we were finished with our getting-reacquainted session. Now he adjusts the boom microphone on a stand and I'm reminded of how much the mic looks like something you'd use to dust window blinds: a furry gray thing attached to a long metal pole. When we were six, we'd take turns petting it and giving it names.

Lance walks over to the chair and asks me, "Is this where you want to sit?" I nod. "Can we move it away from the window? There's some glare." Then he does it before I answer, to a spot underneath my bulletin board.

Fortunately, I've already prepped that, knowing it would be in a shot. I removed some of the weirder stuff, the celebrity tabloid headlines I like to cut out and post out of context, the collages where I take two magazine ads and blend them together into one extremely screwed-up one. Front and center are a few pictures of Felix and me, and one of my cat, Blue. Then I've carefully posted a few of the photos I've taken with my cell phone and printed out. A shot of a trail leading off into woods. One of Olivia in a yoga pose, talking on the phone to a boyfriend. They are fuzzy and low-res, and the colors are off, and I think that's what makes you look twice.

"You should learn how to do photo editing," my mom said one day, peering at them. But I liked when they came out this way, random yet perfect.

"Are you all right?" asks Leslie now, and I snap out of it.

"Yeah. Well, you know. Jitters."

"You? Of all people?" She smiles warmly, but her comment has just made things worse. It has just made the ceiling lower, the floor higher, the walls closer.

"Can we get started? I'll be fine once we start."

"Is it cool if I put a mic on you?" asks Kenny, stepping close. I nod. We're all quiet, serious, as he attaches the tiny microphone to the collar of my sweater—a *lavalier* microphone, I know they call it—and it's a strangely intimate gesture, as if he's pinning me with newly gifted jewelry. Kenny then hands me the wireless transmitter, so I can clip it on the waistband of my jeans. I run the cord under my sweater and plug it in. Amazing how quickly this stuff comes back to me.

The transmitter will send my voice into Kenny's mixer, a big electronic box with enough knobs, jacks, and cables to stump a bomb squad. He wears it in a case slung across his chest and it looks heavy, unwieldy, but he'll never complain. He'll just listen with his headphones and make sure every sound that goes through the mixer on its way to Lance's camera is sound they'd want in the film.

"Can you sit down and then talk for me?" Kenny asks.

What? Oh. He wants to test the mic. I sink into the chair. "My name is Justine Connolly. Are you ready to rock?"

Lance and Leslie laugh, and Kenny grins while he fiddles with the mixer, but the tension-break is over in a nanosecond and now, if anything, the Dread is worse.

Blue, who's been curled on the floor by the heating vent, jumps into my lap. He is black and because I'm wearing black, I actually wonder if the cat will make me look fatter.

"Is it okay if Lance and I sit on the bed?" asks Leslie. "It's a good angle."

"Sure," I say, swallowing what feels like ash in my throat, it's so dry. I don't remember being like this before.

"Try to forget that we're filming and that this is a documentary," says Leslie, picking up on how nervous I am. "We've known you since you were six years old, Justine, and we really want to know how you're doing."

In one of my interviews for *Five at Six*, I'm lying on the grass with my head resting on my hands. They shot it while standing on a ladder above me. I wiggle my legs a lot and stare up at the sky, squinting into the sun and scratching my behind way too much.

In *Five at Eleven* there's a scene where I'm standing in front of a full-length mirror with a guitar strapped on, playing chords and talking at the same time.

Who the hell was that kid? Didn't she know how it would all look?

Of course, it looked fine. It looked fantastic, actually. But now it seems impossible that I could re-create that fantasticness.

Whether I can or not, here is Leslie nodding at me, then at Lance, and then I know he's recording and I'm looking down to pet the cat, imaging how the shot must look on the camera's little LCD display.

"Justine," says Leslie. Her voice catches and sounds froggy. She clears it and tries again. "Tell me about a typical day for you."

"A typical day for me would be . . ." I pause, glad I remembered to start it off like that, so it will sound better when edited. "I get up. I go to school. After school I come home, or go to my dad's, or walk around Main Street, or hang out at Muddy Joe's with Felix." What else do I do? "I go online or watch movies in my room. Homework, of course." Wow. In other words, a typical day for me is a staggeringly boring pile of crap.

Leslie pauses, glancing at her notebook. I can't read her face. "Are you doing any afterschool activities?"

"Not at the moment."

"I thought you played guitar." She's tried to frame that softly, curious and floating, but it still hits hard.

An image jump-cuts into my head. I'm thirteen, seated on a small stage in a church basement without windows, sweating and suffocating from heat and all-over panic. I'm holding a guitar. There are dozens of faces fixed on me, including my parents and sister in a back row. I'm playing "Scarborough Fair" and although I've been practicing this song for weeks and I know the chords by heart, my fingers aren't doing what they're supposed to. My voice is soft and scratchy, and the ages-old air inside the church seems to be swallowing it up. I'd been taking guitar lessons for two years, and there were seven-year-olds at the music school who played circles around me.

"Practice makes better," my dad said to me afterward. "Keep it up and by next year, you'll sound amazing."

But it wasn't that I sounded awful. It was that I didn't like it. My guitar gave me no joy. The thing with strings didn't call to me from its closed case in the corner while I played video games or trudged through homework. So after that total fail of a recital, I'd stopped taking lessons and never played again.

"Justine?" says Leslie.

I've been spacing out, staring blankly at the wall behind Leslie's head. On camera.

"Any hobbies you want to tell us about?" asks Leslie. Her brow is crinkled with a careful, pleasant interest.

But I've got nada. I give a Nada Shrug. Leslie glances at her notebook.

"So what about guys? Do you have a boyfriend?"

Now I snort. Involuntary reflex.

"Negative." The only truth I will give them. There's no way they can know about Ian.

"Okay," she says. "Should we try something else?"

I nod.

"I hear you're not friends with Rory anymore. What happened there?"

I look at her accusingly. *Try something else* was supposed to mean a softie question about school or what music I like to listen to.

"We grew apart."

"Full sentence?"

"Rory and I grew apart, I guess." *Pull this one together, wise-ass.* "Don't look so shocked. Are you still friends with the people you played with when you were little?"

"That's different. You and Rory . . . you seemed special. I remember when her mother called me a few years ago to tell me about the diagnosis. I thought, well, at least she's got Justine. You two had been friends since you were babies."

Now I'm angry. I don't remember Leslie making judgments like this, but I guess after ten years she's invested.

"Our *moms* had been friends since we were babies."

"Did something happen in particular? Did she do something?"

I don't answer. I let the silence hang there. An image of Rory comes back to me, from five years ago.

I'm glad you want to go to this movie with me, Justine. I like having popcorn but I can't eat a whole one and now we can share.

We were eleven and it was a month before Lance and Leslie were coming to start shooting the second film.

"Make an effort with Rory," my mother had urged. "You don't want to seem cruel, especially in the film. Her mom is still one of my best friends."

It had been close to a year since we'd hung out, with

me preferring to spend my time with a couple of other friends. *Normal friends,* I remember thinking. When we went to that movie, some boring historical drama, she kept looking over at me and touching my arm, like she wanted to make sure I was still there. That it was real, having her friend back.

During the two months that Lance and Leslie were in town with their cameras, Rory and I did all the things we used to. Which wasn't much, but I know to her it seemed like an embarrassment of riches. We hung out at her house and did puzzles. We went for walks in the woods. I didn't sit with her in the cafeteria, because I couldn't risk losing my friends, but I'd meet her after school and we'd get snacks at the Stewart's convenience store. Lance and Leslie filmed us doing all this.

Another image fades in, as I stare at that lens again.

Rory waiting for me outside our middle school, in her hands a fresh five-dollar bill earmarked for salt and vinegar potato chips and an iced tea at the convenience store. And then her face after I told her I couldn't go anymore, that I had something else after school every single day from now on. Her face, not getting it, as she asked me when I *was* free. On the weekends, maybe? As soon as school ends for the year?

I didn't have to see her face when she called to invite me to that summer's Renaissance Faire. This is when I finally told her we weren't friends anymore and to stop calling and stop talking to me, period.

"You must have been relieved to find out," Leslie is saying.

"What?" I shake my head, coming back from Mars.

"About Rory being on the autism spectrum."

"Oh."

I'd done some searching online. Things made sense. But it had been too late and in the end, it wouldn't have mattered. Rory was Rory. I was me. I didn't want to hang around her anymore and by then, I had Felix.

Leslie taps Lance on the leg, who pulls away from the camera and says, "What? What do you want me to do?"

"We need to stop. Or at least, take a break."

"You *think?*" he snarls.

"Don't be an asshole about it."

"I'm sorry, Les. I'm just getting a little frustrated and tired."

"Tired of what?" I ask. *Tired of me?* I know what they must be thinking. *This can't be the same girl.* The eleven-year-old who expertly mimicked famous movie lines and liked to answer Leslie's questions as a made-up hippie character named Starlight Lovepeace.

Leslie rubs one of her eyes wearily. "This is the third interview we've done where we're not feeling . . . we're not getting the kind of material we'd like. It was the same with Nate and Keira."

Something about the way she says this enrages me.

"Maybe you should just write us a script," I say, "and we'll follow it."

Leslie looks quickly at me, then at Lance, and Lance takes the camera off pause.

"That's not what I meant, Justine." Leslie smoothly steps out of the way and into the corner of my room.

"What kind of material do you want? What are you not getting?"

"We wish you guys would open up more. It's like we keep hitting these dead ends with everyone. There's so much you don't want to talk about."

"Uh, yeah. Because we're *teenagers.*" And as soon as I say this, I know I've given them another great sound bite. Dammit.

"I guess we were just expecting to have . . . more to shoot," says Leslie. "With you."

"Our producers at Independent Eye really wanted you to be positioned as the focus," adds Lance.

"The focus? What, like, the *star?*"

Leslie shrugs. "You've always been the most popular one."

I know this is true. I know Felix would be jealous to hear this. Nate too, probably.

"I'm sorry. I'm sorry I don't have a story this time around." It comes out sounding pissy and I like that.

Lance turns off the camera now and replaces the lens cap, so I know it's not coming back on. The room expands to normal size. I can breathe. But there's this overwhelming feeling of having let someone down. Who? Them? Myself? I feel a tickle in my nose like I might cry, but *no no no, none of that, young lady.* That is so not an option right now.

Leslie has been examining me, carefully, with concern. I get the feeling this might be who she really is, when she's not playing producer.

"Justine," she says evenly. "Everyone has a story. It's simply a question of finding it."

I want to help them. I want to help myself. I'm not sure if those are the same things in this situation, but I'm feeling a little desperate.

"The community theater is doing a musical in June," I say softly. "I could . . . you know . . . audition. That would be something."

Lance and Leslie share a sad, knowing kind of look.

"We don't feel comfortable with that," says Leslie. "We've never created a situation to shoot. We've always tried to focus on naturally occurring scenes."

"It changes the kind of filmmaker you are," adds Lance, "if you set things up."

If you set things up. Should I say it? Yeah, what the hell. I'm not feeling desperate anymore. Just mad.

"So what was that with Keira, last time?"

Leslie looks down at her notebook, and Lance winces like he's been poked in the ribs.

"That," Lance says slowly, "was a conversation that Marcus Jones would have had with his daughter regardless of whether or not we were there."

I remember reading that same line as a quote from Lance in a magazine story.

But you didn't have to put it in the film, people said. *You could have cut away at any one of several moments.* And they were right. I think.

Suddenly, Blue, who's been curled in my lap this whole time, for some mysterious important cat reason launches off my legs and onto floor. In his mad dash out of the room, he ricochets off my floor lamp, knocking it off-balance, and down it goes with a big clang.

And that's a wrap for the day.

Mr. Jones sits by himself on the stone bench in the garden, his back to the camera. His eleven-year-old daughter, Keira, walks into frame. She looks confused and surprised to find him here, and for a moment, glances back over her shoulder as if to ask an unseen someone, Is this where you want me to go?

"Hi, Daddy," she says tentatively. Her hair is gathered in a tight bun off her face and she's wearing a ballet leotard underneath her hoodie and jeans.

"Hello, Sprite," says Mr. Jones, because a well-regarded English professor at the college would only have a literary, classical-sounding pet name for his little girl.

"What did you want to talk to me about?" asks Keira.

"Have a seat." And Keira does, but you can tell she'd rather not, because when someone tells you to have a seat before they talk to you, something is about to suck.

Mr. Jones takes a deep breath and you can hear it rattle into the microphone he's wearing.

"You know how Mommy had to go to Massachusetts for a few nights?"

"To visit her friend," says Keira.

"Right. Well." Another rattle, amplified. "You need to know that she's not coming back."

Keira is facing away from us, but we see her head cock sideways, the body language equivalent of a question mark.

"What do you mean?"

"She's going to live somewhere else."

"I don't understand. How can she live somewhere else when we're here?"

Mr. Jones looks at his daughter for the first time, and she looks back. Now they're both in profile.

"That's a good question, Sprite. I wish I knew the answer. She told me she needs to be away for a while."

When you hear this, you think of the earlier scenes in the film. The scene where Keira's mother starts crying at dinner and locks herself in the bathroom. The interview where she seems only half there, lighting up a clove cigarette in the middle of the conversation, to the shock and horror of her husband.

"But she'll come back, right?" asks Keira.

Even you know there's no way to answer that. You think for sure Mr. Jones will say something like, "I hope so," like most people would. But he does not. Because Mr. Jones has said that he's a proponent of constant honesty with his child, he says, "No, Keira. I don't believe she will."

Keira is silent for a moment as this truth, this reality that suddenly seems inevitable even to us, sinks in.

Then she turns to the camera. She swivels her entire body to the other side of the bench and slides away from her father. In her effort to hide her expression from him, she is showing it to us.

Her face.

Take eleven years times a million, and that's how much pain is on her face. That's how much confusion, despair, and betrayal is on her face.

The camera does not cut away.

Instead, it zooms in close.

Keira starts to sob.

The camera does not move.

For twenty long seconds, she weeps, and we watch. When the camera does cut away, it's to a shot of Keira and her mother walking along the old Rail Trail that runs through town. Mrs. Jones—Allison—is a willowy blonde with skin several shades lighter than Keira's, and she's always seemed a little in awe of her daughter. In this brief scene, she ambles along behind Keira. Keira realizes she's gotten ahead of her mom and stops, waits for her to catch up. Reaches out her hand. Mrs. Jones takes it and for a few steps they're connected like that, until she releases Keira's grasp and bends down to pick up a rock.

She tosses the rock into the woods and the camera catches it bouncing once, then twice, then skidding to a stop in the dirt.

To put a child's worst moment on film, to turn her unspeakable heartache into entertainment for the masses, is absolute exploitation, said one critic. *Don't believe for a second that it's anything else.*

Later, in interviews, Lance and Leslie said that Mr. Jones wanted them to film this scene, so somewhere out there, his ex-wife would know what she did. So other parents in similar situations, who had to have equally horrible conversations with their children, would feel less alone.

But it was the way they did it, argued one writer. *That unflinching cut. Most of the audience glances away from this girl's face. Out of instinct and decency. Why didn't the filmmakers have the same instinct and decency?*

Lance and Leslie never really answered that question, and that's probably because there was no good way to do it, and they also knew they were wrong. I could see it in

Leslie's face during one interview that I sometimes watch online.

Meanwhile, Keira disappeared from school for a while. Mr. Jones took a leave of absence to teach in Paris for two years. When they came back, Keira had changed, and not just because she had clothes everyone swooned over and this way of tying a scarf that defied physics. There was something confident and powerful about her, about the straightness of her neck and the glow of her skin. It seemed organic and not processed, and people flocked to it.

When it came to Mrs. Jones, the parent grapevine offered up only a few tidbits. She was gone, for sure. Divorced, definitely. There were rumblings about mental health problems for which she refused to get treatment. Where she was, and whether or not Keira ever saw her— that was anyone's guess. They guessed a lot, and then eventually, as the news got old and something else took its place, they stopped guessing.

SIX

Leslie once told me that a film isn't made by shooting stuff but, rather, by editing it. The shooting is the inspiration and the ideas and the paint palette. The editing is the artist actually picking up the brush to accomplish the *doing*, the making something out of nothing.

I think about this as the alarm clock snaps on with a radio commercial at 6:30 a.m. This is a big day. My first— and maybe only—Follow Day, where the crew will be tailing me morning to night, hopefully getting a wide and colorful palette full of Justine. Everyone else will get at least one as well, but for some reason they've chosen to start with me.

The alarm is unnecessary, because I woke up at 3:00 a.m. and couldn't get back to sleep, thinking about the Follow Day. Outlining it in my head. Punching it up with jokes here and there. For instance:

Justine comes down for breakfast and opens the fridge. Upon seeing all the foil-wrapped blobs of ULOs (Unidentified LeftOvers), she says, "This isn't a refrigerator. It's a halfway house for good food gone bad!"

Funny. Like she used to be. Back when she didn't have to try.

After I get out of bed and take a shower, I put on my pajamas again, which feels just wrong but this is what's been asked of me. I open my door to call down to Lance, Leslie, and Kenny, who are waiting in the kitchen with my mom.

"Fancy meeting you here," I say as they appear in the upstairs hallway. Yes, that's a gem I came up with at 4:23 a.m.

"Another day of cinema vérité," says Lance, yawning.

"We'll make it a good one," says Leslie, but without any of her usual enthusiasm.

Kenny just nods at me. He's a quiet type; maybe, as a sound guy, he's used to letting other people make all the noise.

As we prearranged, I let them into my room so they

could get some shots of me picking out clothes. Surely to be intercut later with scenes of the others in their morning routines, chosen carefully for contrast and comedy.

Of course I've already planned the outfit: black jeans, red low-top sneakers, and a navy blue T-shirt with a picture of a rock, a piece of paper, and a pair of scissors as gunslingers in a three-way standoff. But I pretend to look for these items, thumbing through exactly three other tops in my closet before tugging the chosen one off its hanger.

Once I'm dressed, we put on my lavalier mic. I blow-dry my hair and keep my eyes on the pink streaks in the mirror, and not on the camera. I put on my eyeliner, then, as usual, rub most of it off.

Downstairs, my mother already has breakfast and juice out on the table, leaving me with no excuse to open the fridge. Middle-of-the-night brilliance fades into early morning brain-deadness and I can't think of a single damn witty thing to say here.

Mom is baking her Panda Bear cupcakes for a last-minute order. She uses Thin Mints cut in half for ears, and Leslie finds this fascinating. She and Lance spend so much time trying to get some good shots of the little black-and-white faces that we get behind schedule and I'm going to be late for school.

"It's okay," says Mom, "I'll write you a note." She needs this attention and frankly, I'm happy to share it. I pretend to be anxious to get going, and she pretends she doesn't know I'm pretending. So far, we are playing ourselves just right.

I pull open the heavy door to the school lobby and hold it for a moment, so Lance, who's got the camera rolling, then Kenny, then Leslie, can follow close behind me.

At the office, the front desk aide hands me my late pass and is much friendlier about this than she normally is about everything. On my way out, I catch sight of the bright green notice on a bulletin board. It's the one that went home with every student two weeks ago, notifying them and their families of Lance and Leslie's imminent presence at the school, along with a release letter that every parent had to sign if they were okay with their kid ending up in the film. I'm sure a few parents weren't and didn't, like the last two times. It was fun to see people's faces blurred out in the finished product. I wonder who it will be this year.

But we are on the move and I have to stay focused and aware, with the camera watching like this. I've missed homeroom, so our first stop is Journalism class, which starts in a few minutes. I can see Lance exclaiming over a latte: *Journalism! The irony!* Also, the class features not just me but Nate too, so that's a whole lot of bang for their shooting buck.

Here's some information for the record. Length of time

since this class began: twelve weeks. Number of times Nate has lowered himself to talk to me during said class: zero.

Inside the classroom, our teacher, Mrs. Zandhoffer, is pushing four desks together so they make a little island of metal and Formica. There are several other islands like it throughout the room. She looks up and nods at Lance and Leslie, and I can tell they've already met. The crew quickly moves to a corner to get situated.

Mrs. Z notices me scanning the desks and indicates one near her, saying, "Justine, you sit over here. I'm putting everyone in groups for a new project."

The bell rings and within seconds, the doorway has filled up with students. Everyone freezes when they notice the reconfigured desks and the camera and the boom mic, causing a bottleneck in the hallway. Within minutes, Mrs. Z has everyone assigned to their desk islands. Sharing mine are Lily and Michael, who are cool. There's an empty seat.

I notice that at the same time I notice Nate hasn't arrived yet.

On cue, he bursts in and does the same freeze everyone else did. But when he sees Lance and Leslie, he smiles. Waves with one hand, brushes his cowlick—a little chunk of blond hair that's always sticking out to one side—with the other. Nate somehow makes this cheesy move seem natural, like something you've been hoping to see all day.

Mrs. Z points at our table. Nate just nods and falls into the empty desk, then scans the three of us. His gaze catches on mine for a second, and one corner of his mouth twitches up like he knows he should smile at me, but just can't make himself do it.

Lily steals a look at the crew, then pulls out some lip gloss and begins to apply it. Heavily.

"Act normal," I say to her. "Remember, they're just *observing.*"

I realize I've just spit out one of the things Lance and Leslie kept telling us when we were six, and then again at eleven. *We like to pretend we're in kindergarten too,* Lance would say with a wink, and our whole class would giggle. I look around to see who's buying that line now. Most of the students in the class are busy getting settled, but a few keep glancing toward the camera. One kid, known jackass Marco Marretti, waits until Mrs. Z's back is turned and waves both middle fingers at the camera, then laughs at this stroke of pure, subversive brilliance.

"Today we start our unit on feature journalism," announces Mrs. Z when all is finally quiet.

I thought we weren't supposed to do this unit until June.

Lance has the camera pointed at us now. Kenny, behind him, holds the boom mic above his head with both hands, sticking it as far into the room as he can.

Mrs. Z continues. "Each group is going to produce a newspaper supplement focused on whichever subject area you pull from this bowl." She holds up a Tupperware dish and shakes it; something shuffles around inside. She walks over to the group nearest her and holds the bowl out to one of the kids, who reaches in, pulls out a piece of paper, and unfolds it. "Arts and Entertainment," he announces, and his islandmates cheer.

Mrs. Z makes her way around the room as the assignments are drawn. Health and Fitness. Money and Finance. Science and Technology. Finally, she comes to us, and offers the bowl to Nate. Of course, always Nate. Nate makes a show of feeling around for the last slip of paper, making everyone (but me) crack up, then produces the paper and opens it with a flourish. "Travel and Recreation. Boo-yah!"

Mrs. Z smiles and says, "This edition will focus on *local* travel. No darting off to Atlantic City on your parents' credit card and blaming it on your assignment." Then she turns to the rest of the class. "I'm going to give each group a couple of examples from real newspapers. Your goal for this period is to figure out story assignments or at least a list of what you might want to cover."

Out of the corner of my eye, I see Lance's camera and it's still trained on Nate and me. It takes everything I have not to turn and stare it down.

"Okay," Nate says as Mrs. Z plops a couple of newspapers in front of us. "Why don't we do two stories on travel and two on recreation?"

"That makes sense," says Lily. "What about a Top Ten

list of places to visit in the area?"

"It should have more focus than that," says Michael. "Like, historic sights, or sights for nature freaks or shop-aholics."

"We could do the whole section as a collection of Top Ten lists . . ." adds Nate.

Mrs. Z brushes past us. "Cute idea, but that doesn't sound like it would require much actual reporting." And then she's gone.

"What do you think, Justine?" asks Lily, like she's just remembered I'm here.

What do I think? What *do* I think? I glance at Nate, who has this *Cameras? What cameras?* look on his face that makes me want to wrap my hands around his neck, right at the spot where that gigantic Adam's apple sits.

"I think I need to be right back."

I get up and walk over to Mrs. Z, who has just sat down at her desk with a big sigh. Her hair, a neat black bob with bangs, barely moves as she looks up at me and frowns.

"Yes, Justine?"

I hook my finger at Lance to come join us. He turns off the camera, places it gingerly on a bookcase and does as I've asked. Leslie follows. Kenny lowers the boom mic and leans against the wall.

"What's up?" asks Lance, leaning in for a huddle.

"You guys arranged for Nate and me to be in the same group."

88

Lance and Mrs. Z exchange a guilty glance.

"Is that a problem?" asks Mrs. Z. I can tell she was reluctant to do it.

"It makes it easier for us to shoot you both," Lance says matter-of-factly.

I look at Leslie, expecting a comment, but she's just staring at one of my pink stripes.

"Well, it feels fake to me and we'll be self-conscious," I say, "and that will affect how we do on the actual assignment."

For a second I think they get it. Mrs. Z is nodding slightly.

"I don't feel self-conscious," says a voice behind me. Nate steps up and slides into our huddle.

I turn to him and he's looking at me. Really looking at me, not just brushing a glance across the space I occupy. His expression is soft and friendly, and for a second I flash on the Nate he was five years ago in *Five at Eleven*. His hair was longish then, his green eyes larger, even though I know that's impossible because eyeballs never grow.

Is it Nate's fault, really? He didn't set this up. So why do I want to close that open look on his face? Zip it, lock it, pull it shut with a drawstring?

"It feels fake to *me*," I finally say, looking back at Nate for a second. "Fake," I say again, to him. For him. The word seems to hit its mark, landing deep behind the carefully composed lines of his face. He looks at the floor.

We're silent for a moment, then finally Mrs. Zandhoffer takes over. "Okay, Justine. Your performance on this project is what matters most to me. We'll switch you with someone else."

For the rest of the class, in my new location on the Arts and Entertainment island, I have no trouble ignoring the camera. I get assigned a story on an exhibit at the college art museum.

The bell rings, and within seconds I'm out the door toward history class. I can't face Lance and Leslie. I don't want to answer their questions about why I can't just play along. But four steps down the hallway, I feel someone touch my shoulder. I turn around, expecting Leslie and her Diplomatically Concerned face.

But it's Nate.

"Do you have a problem with me?" he asks hesitantly, like he already knows the answer.

"No," I lie. *Just go away go away.*

"You called me fake."

"I said the situation—"

"Be careful what names you throw around." Nate cuts me off, then adds, with an exaggerated glance at my hair. "Especially that one."

Then he's off, and I watch him go.

It's all I can do not to yell it after him. That stupid, hateful nickname from years ago, the one you used to see scrawled on his locker. For a second, I feel the thrill of imagining what he would do if I resurrected it, right here in the crowded hallway.

But I hesitate too long, and then he's gone. I look back in the direction of Journalism class. Lance is standing not five feet behind me, the camera lens rotating. My microphone's been on the whole time.

Nate opens one of the hutches and reaches in to pet a large white rabbit. It's fluffy—ridiculously fluffy. It looks like it could float up any second now to its home against a teal-blue sky. It's the kind of animal little girls feel giddy about.

But Nate's not a little girl. He's an eleven-year-old boy, and the way he looks at this animal with a mix of awe and devotion, well frankly, it makes you a little uncomfortable.

He gently lifts the rabbit out of the hutch and toward his chest. "This is Nimbus," he says tenderly, like a proud parent. "She won a blue ribbon at the county fair last summer."

The rabbit has a very rabbity way of looking both bored and terrified. Nate coos to her with baby talk, and the camera stays there just long enough so you feel the beginning of a cringe.

The cutaway shot is to a wall in Nate's room, covered in colorful awards, then another back to Nate's hands as he combs the rabbit with a steel comb. "Nimbus was my first English Angora. My grandpa got her for me when I turned eight. The trick with these guys is that you have to groom them enough so they don't get wool block, which is like hairballs, but not so much that they don't show well."

This next moment always cracks people up: the combination of Nate's calm and practiced hands, working quickly on Nimbus's fur, paired with Nimbus's expression of surprised pleasure.

Nate continues: "Usually she stays in the house but on nice days, I like to have her out in the hutch with the others. Plus people who stop at the farm store can buy some hay for fifty cents and come down and feed them. It's good for business."

Now we see a shot of the farm store driveway. Two boys Nate's age are standing at the edge of it, peering across the lawn at Nate and the rabbit hutches behind the farm store. The light looks different; some time has passed.

"Hey, it's Bunny Boy!" yells one.

"And his girlfriend!" calls the other.

Nate turns his head the other way and wraps his arms protectively around Nimbus, covering her ears as if he doesn't want her to hear the taunts.

"Or is it a boy rabbit?" we hear one of the kids shout, the camera still on Nate. "Because if it's a boy rabbit, that would make you a total fag!"

A cut now to Felix standing outside the farm store, a

few feet from the other boys. He's apparently heard the commotion and come out the back door.

"Go away!" Felix yells at them, but only after some hesitation.

One boy turns to him and makes a dismissive gesture with his hand. "Felix, YOU go away," he says. "Go back to picking fruit or whatever it is you people are good at."

"He has to protect his boyfriend!" says the other. "That's so sweet!"

We can see Felix take that double hit, absorbing it, letting it explode inside him but trying not to let the aftershock show.

"Yeah," he finally says. "We're boyfriends because we hang out together. I guess that makes you guys boyfriends too. Should we all have a gay party?"

One boy lunges at Felix but the other catches him, his eyes on something else: a mom, who comes out of the store now and ushers them away. Felix watches them disappear, then turns to look at Nate.

We don't see Nate's immediate expression because when the scene cuts back to him, a few minutes have passed. He's standing up straight again and Nimbus is moving on the table, and Nate's been asked a question.

"No, the names don't bother me," he says flatly, like one of those computerized voices. "Those guys are jerks. Felix didn't need to stick up for me."

He looks at the comb in his hand.

"They can call me Bunny Boy all they want. They don't understand the rabbit thing. My grandmother says it's just ignorance."

The camera zooms in on the comb, the way Nate is fidgeting with it, his fingers running over the teeth in search of some kind of reassurance tucked between them, where it's hardest to get.

It's a shot that will get repeated later in the film. The nervous, searching fingers plucking at the metal of the comb. It's the day Nate comes home late from school to find the hutch empty, Nimbus nowhere to be seen.

They found Nimbus in the orchard the next morning, alive and well and just as fluffy as ever. She'd been rabbit-napped but otherwise unharmed, unless you count the licorice someone had fed her, which resulted in a memorable scene involving red-streaked rabbit poop and Nate yelling, "She's bleeding internally! Call the vet!"

Everyone assumed it was Aidan and Tony, the two boys who taunted Nate on camera. What you saw on film was only a tiny bit of what we saw in school. They persecuted Nate relentlessly, and everyone but them got bored and annoyed by it. Even the teachers stopped paying attention, until the thing with Nimbus. Nate's grandfather visited Aidan's parents in person. That's another great scene. So great—an old weathered farmer, a pillar of our community, ripping those people a new one—that sometimes I wonder if Lance and Leslie put him up to it.

But Aidan and Tony denied the bullying, and nobody could prove otherwise. Mr. Hunter asked Lance and Leslie if they'd shot anything that would prove how badly Nate was being persecuted, but they claimed they had nothing. It was the people who didn't believe that who helped make Lance and Leslie's life hell when the film came out. The thing with Keira was bad enough, but if they had footage that could make sure these kids got disciplined, why wouldn't they share it?

It's always been easiest for me to believe they were telling the truth.

SEVEN

If I could edit together a montage of Follow Day at school, from *my* point of view and not the camera's, it would look like this:

The faces of people who don't normally sit with me at lunch, sitting with me at lunch.

The thin blue lines of my class notebooks, filling up with much more writing than usual.

The lacrosse goal in gym class as I smack a ball into it, because I'm secretly terrific at lacrosse.

The reactions of other students as they notice the crew, then pretend they don't notice, but act differently anyway.

It's fascinating to watch how some don't seem to care and some care way too much.

Oh, and the whole sequence would be set to electronic music that's pretentiously dramatic and slow, because that's how it all feels.

I can't stop thinking about what the lens is seeing as I move through my routine. I open up a little screen in my mind where I can imagine how the shot is framed as I sit uncharacteristically quiet in class or eat tomato soup in the cafeteria. (And why did I get soup anyway? Nobody looks good eating soup.)

So it's not only the camera watching me, but *me* watching me, and by last period Spanish, I am damn seriously sick of myself.

This is where I get a stomach cramp, and in a sense, I feel like I've been waiting for it all day. It grows more intense; it's going to be a Mega. I send all the painful energy into my toes and curl them inside my sneakers where nobody can see—another trick I've developed over the years. But soon, this can't contain the *ow*. I clench a fist, then two, and bite my lip.

Leslie's noticed; her frown line is creased deeper and darker. Before I can think about it, I'm raising my hand for a bathroom pass.

Pass granted, I don't look at the crew as I leave the room and step into the blissful solitude of the hallway, where I can really breathe now. They won't follow me right away.

They'll assume I'll be back in a few minutes. But I could use more than a few, and suddenly I don't care if I have to steal them. I can always make up an excuse later.

I head directly for the stairs to the east wing, at the end of which is the gym and the locker rooms. The girls' locker room will be deserted this period, and since it's got a bathroom, my pass might keep me covered if anyone questions what I'm doing there. I've done it before.

Once inside the locker room, in the quiet half-dark that feels like a secret, I sit on a bench and breathe through the cramp as it loosens its hold, then goes away completely. Some time passes. My cell phone chimes with text messages from Leslie, wondering where the hell I am. The final bell rings and there's the rumble of mass exodus, people getting out of school as fast as humanly possible. When all sounds calm again, it feels safe to leave. I know I should let the crew know where I am, but I just can't yet.

I'm in the hallway for all of four seconds when I hear my name echo against the walls.

"Justine!"

I freeze. There's a silhouette moving out of the shadows.

"Justine," the figure says again, more softly. It's starting to look like Ian. I find myself actually happy to see him after my long, long night and day.

"Isn't this like a scene from a zombie movie?" I say, putting the grin in my voice. Maybe this is what he was talking about when he said I felt more like a buddy to him, but I can't help it.

Now he's almost reached me and I notice he's wearing gardening gloves. He stretches out his hands, curling them into giant claws, and changes his walk to an Undead march.

"Rawrrrr . . ." he growls.

Yeah, he's adorable. And he smells like damp earth.

"What's up?" I say fake-casually. "I mean, before you kill me or eat me or whatever, we should exchange pleasantries."

He releases his claws and looks suddenly embarrassed. "I'm trying to get to all the classroom wastebaskets before the custodians do. Long story that involves recyclable plastic containers and a science fair project."

So, not earth. Just plain old garbage, but garbage never smelled so good. I get a sharp body pang from missing him.

"Well, I would say that's weird, but remember, I know you."

Ian laughs. *Score!* "Where are you headed?" he asks.

"Just outside to wait for my mom." If I'm lucky, he won't notice that I don't have my bag, or anything else that would make me look ready to be picked up from school.

"I'm headed that way too," he says, pointing his head sideways as if to say, lazily, *after you.*

My phone chimes again. I ignore it.

"How's the filming going?" Ian asks brightly as we walk.

"It's going. That's all I know for sure right now."

"I haven't gotten a chance to tell you, but I think your hair looks great," he says.

Something inside me takes off in flight. "Thanks," I say, and then swallow hard.

"I hear you made a secret appearance at Felix's party that night," says Ian.

"Yeah, well . . . I didn't plan it to be secret, I just . . . it was a lot harder to be there than I expected."

Ian nods thoughtfully. When we reach the door, he holds it open for me. It's a gesture so simple, so normal, but thrilling. The first time he did that, on our first date, I knew we were really going out.

Outside, the air feels warmer than expected. Ian takes off his gloves and stuffs them in his back pockets. He squints into the late afternoon sun, hanging over the ridge in the distance, and takes a deep breath.

"I have to tell you, I kind of miss hanging out," he says. "I miss our friendship."

Another body pang. *Oh, you mean the friendship that you declared we should have after you BROKE MY HEART FOR NO APPARENT REASON? I'm sorry if it's not everything you imagined it to be.*

But here's all I can mutter before my throat clenches up: "Me too."

"It feels like you've been avoiding me lately. Are things just overly weird?"

Yes, I've been avoiding him, which means fighting every impulse I've got. It's worth it though. If I'm not around him, the camera isn't around him, and there are no humiliating questions about who he is and what happened.

"Things are weird, yes," I say, trying to pull out the strands of truth, the ones that won't make me feel like a total fake liar girl. "I just have a lot going on right now."

"Well, if you feel like you need some fun, let me know. The trails up on the mountain are clear and we could go for a hike."

When we were JustIan, I put up with the hikes. I put up with the blisters in my Converse high-tops ("You're not supposed to wear shoes like that," he'd said) and the constant, panicky breathless-but-not-in-a-good-way feeling of trying to keep up with him.

"It might be something cool for, you know, the camera crew to film."

He must notice my expression. Actually, if he didn't, he'd be a moron because I'm looking at him like someone just slapped me with a wet rag.

"I mean, it's so beautiful this time of year," Ian quickly adds, and by his face I can tell he wishes he could just back up, up, up from that thing he just said.

Is this what he wants? Does he want to be *in the movie?*

My stomach tightens again.

"Justine?" a voice calls from around a corner. Leslie.

"Gotta go," I squeak, not caring what Ian thinks, all flight response. I'm prey and the crew is my predator. I dart back toward the door and fling it open, letting it bang shut behind me as I rush inside.

The hallway is darker now but I move farther down, into the shadows. At the end of the hall there's one classroom door open, a trapezoid of light projected onto the floor. I walk toward it because I'm a fugitive from my own absurd life and have nowhere else to go.

Closer to the classroom now, I hear happy voices—I can tell from the musical upturn at the end of each comment. Someone laughs. I reach the doorway and peer into the room.

There's one girl cleaning the whiteboard at the front of the room. Another is moving desks around.

The first girl is Rory. I'd know by her clothes even if I couldn't see her face: Rory always wears button-down blouses and track pants with white stripes down the side. The second is a girl named Aimee who I've often seen talking to Rory.

My afternoon is about to get even more bizarre.

"Justine?" asks Rory, seeing me.

I step all the way into the room. "Hi," I say.

Silence. Ugh ugh ugh.

"What are you guys doing?" I ask casually, like it's

normal for me to just appear at this moment.

"Setting up for a History Club meeting," says Aimee.

Rory's eyes are on me, then off me.

"What are *you* doing?" asks Aimee.

"I was just . . . looking for someone." Got it! I can say Ian. Ian was probably just here checking the wastebasket and voilà, plausibility.

Rory puts down the paper towel and Windex she's been using to clean the whiteboard, then steps a little closer, all without making eye contact.

"Me?" she asks.

"You?" I echo, stupidly.

"Were you looking for *me*?" Now here comes the eye contact. One, two, three. I meet her there, in this small space where we are staring at each other, and all the things we ever shared, all the adventures and secrets and daily ins-and-outs of friendship, are jammed in tight.

There are footsteps in the hallway.

"Justine!" calls Leslie, because she can see me, and I am stuck.

I turn and hold up my hand in a wave. "Sorry," I mutter.

Leslie looks pissed. I can't see Lance's face because he's focused on the camera, which is pointed at me and most definitely on.

"Justine, you can't . . ." Now they've reached the doorway, and Leslie glances into the classroom. "Rory!"

Rory doesn't react. She's been staring at the top of the doorframe above my head, but now she glances at me again.

"Were you?" she repeats. "Looking for me?"

A strange question for anyone but Rory to ask in this situation, but she makes it sound like it's so obvious, it would be strange if she *didn't* ask it. It feels like if I tell her, "No, I was looking for Ian," or even if I tell the truth and say, "Actually I wasn't looking for anyone; I was just trying to avoid these guys," it would be profoundly disappointing. So I just nod.

"Yeah, I was. I was looking for you."

"My mom said you might," says Rory, nodding back. "She said I should be careful."

I take a step into the room, then glance back to see Leslie, Lance, and Kenny gathered in the doorway. Kenny steps inside the door and to the side, holding out the boom mic so it's above our heads but out of the camera's frame.

This is not how I wanted it to happen, with Rory. But I want to say the words. If I could just say them, it wouldn't matter what happened next. They would be out and I could move forward with my life. The fact that the camera is here and they're recording this suddenly doesn't matter. It feels like a perfectly reasonable part of my punishment.

"Your mom must have been pretty upset, when we stopped being friends." Then I correct myself. "When *I* stopped being friends with *you*." I correct myself a second time. "When I stopped, then started, then stopped again."

I think of how much her mother must have hated me while she was warning her daughter that I might pull the same crap again. I wonder if she counted all the carpools and outings and meals and sleepovers where I was part of her family. I know what I did ruined the friendship between her family and mine, but that's something Mom and I never talked about.

Rory looks at Lance and Leslie. "Is that why you came down here with them? So you could say all that to me on camera?"

"These guys? No. They . . . just followed me. It's my Follow Day."

Rory blinks slowly. Aimee is frozen in place on the other side of the room. It suddenly seems possible that we could all stand here silent forever. The world could end and they'd find us petrified like this, covered in ash. I still haven't said the words. Why can't I just say them? The camera watches me, knowing. Judging. I want to push farther into the room and grab Rory by the shoulders and just tell her. *I'm sorry. I'm sorry.* Instead, I feel myself retreating.

Before I know it, I'm in the hallway again and walking as fast as I can without actually running, because we're not supposed to run in school and my body's conditioned to obey this rule. Multiple footsteps are behind me, and together we all drum a rhythm on the floor. There's light over by the stairway, through the window of the door to outside, and I stop there. Let them catch up to me. Let them catch me.

"Justine," says Leslie, panting, her face filled with concern. "Are you okay?"

It seems genuine and this makes me feel so ashamed. "I'm fine." We're silent.

"You didn't plan to run into Rory like that?"

"No. That was an accident."

Lance and Leslie exchange a glance, one of those quick, wordless conversations they often have.

"A fantastic accident," says Lance. He's still shooting, but he's also grinning like he just got a surprise treat in his cereal box. "I can't believe we got that."

"It's the best thing we've shot since we started," says Leslie, and for a second I feel really flattered. Like maybe I've got my groove back.

"I'm sorry you didn't get more. I wanted to say more."

"Oh, Justine," says Leslie, putting her hand on my arm. "That's real life. We almost never get to finish a conversation the way we want to."

"Next time you see Rory, maybe you can pick up where you left off," says Lance.

"But I'm confused," says Leslie. "What were you talking about in there?"

I sink down onto the second-to-bottom step. Leslie does the same, and it surprises me, how different this one little gesture feels. She's not standing near the camera, observing. She's participating. Lance shifts a bit with the camera, and Kenny with him. But Leslie is right here, so I look at her face, which seems interested in what I might say.

And I talk.

I tell her about the new friends when I was eleven, and about my mother's request, and being with Rory during the time they were shooting, and then about the ditching. I describe what it's been like to see Rory alone every day at school, and how heavy five years' worth of guilt can be. I even tell them about feeling jealous that Rory found some place where she belongs.

When I'm done, they're all quiet and I close my eyes to the feeling of relief. It's all out. It's messy and gross and they probably wouldn't come near it except to poke at it with a long stick, but I don't care. I feel better instantly. The footage they got today, the thought that Ian might be hoping for screen time—all things to toss and turn about later.

This is where somebody might say something along the lines of, "It's okay, Justine. We all do things we regret."

Instead, Lance asks: "Les, what do you think?"

"I'm thinking we can use the narration as voiceover later. Right? She was looking at me and not off camera, so we'd have to."

"I was thinking the same thing," says Lance.

I used to tune out this kind of chatter between them. It

always seemed boring. *Just put the camera back on me, will you?* But now I understand what they're doing. They're thinking about both sides of the process at once. While they're shooting they have to mentally edit too. I don't know how I know this. But I can see it in my head as if I've tapped into some psychic wire between Lance and Leslie.

"We have to include that in the first rough cut," says Leslie.

"You're already doing a rough cut?" I ask.

"The people at Independent Eye want to see footage every few weeks," Lance says.

"The suits," Leslie adds, smiling.

"Our *producers*," says Lance, shooting her a serious look, and Leslie's smile goes away. "They need to see if we're on the right track."

So this is their punishment for the *Five at Eleven* fallout. No more artistic carte blanche. They're being monitored now, which is maybe a small price to pay to continue the series. Or a huge one.

"Thank you, Justine," says Leslie. "Thank you for giving so much of yourself today." They needed this.

I didn't plan on the giving, but on the other hand, they didn't force me to hand anything over.

So how, and why, do I keep doing exactly that?

Rory uses a metal skeleton key to open the tall wood-and-glass cabinet. It's an antique piece, lovely in that cold, untouchable way. Not something you'd expect to find in an eleven-year-old girl's bedroom.

"This is my Tudor Monarchs collection," she says a bit anxiously, running a hand through her dark blond hair. It's cut short and elfin, just like her best friend Justine's. "It's about three years' worth of stuff, ever since I was eight and the school librarian gave me a biography of Henry VIII. It was five hundred pages long and I read it in like a day."

There's a cut to a drawing by Rory of King Henry. It's pretty terrible, almost a caricature, but Rory's had it matted and framed. Surrounding it are six smaller, equally unrecognizable portraits of his famous wives. Now Rory unscrolls a paper banner on which she's created a computer-generated flowchart of Tudor-era family and political relationships. "I have another one of the timeline, but I'm still fiddling with it."

What follows is a series of shots where Rory's showing off the various treasures of her collection—books and figurines, a "Bloody Mary" Christmas ornament, replica jewelry—pulling them out of the glass cabinet one by one, then replacing them carefully when done. The montage ends with Rory emerging from the closet wearing a floor-length Queen Elizabeth I costume, complete with ruffled collar and curly red wig.

She spins for the camera and laughs. "I'm going to be volunteering at the Ren Faire this summer!"

In the next shot, she's sitting on her bed in the gown, fingering the curves of the collar. "Why do I like this stuff so much?" she asks, in response to a question. "Because it's full of characters who are more interesting than the ones in any fiction book I've read, except these were real people. The more I learn about them, the more I learn about people in general."

There's a cut to Rory walking up the front steps to a house, still dressed in her costume. We know from earlier scenes that this is my house. "It's the Spring Carnival at school," she says toward the camera. "Justine and I are going together."

She knocks. After a few moments, I open the door. Look her up and down with an expression of pure wonder, but not the good kind.

"What. Are. You. Wearing?" I ask.

"I'm Queen Elizabeth I, the Virgin Queen, sometimes known as Good Queen Bess."

"You look ridiculous."

Rory pauses. "Do I?"

"Was this the thing you spent six months' worth of allowance on?

"Yes," says Rory. "You're supposed to dress up at a carnival."

I glance at the camera, then turn back to smile at her, a little forced. "It's not . . . that kind of carnival. This isn't the Renaissance."

Rory nods slowly, frowning, as if filing a mental note. "Sorry," she says. "Do you want me to change?"

The question seems too large for the moment. A guilty look travels across my face.

"Come on," I say, almost tenderly now. "You can borrow something of mine."

Rory turns to pick up the hem of her gown and when she does, the camera catches the disappointment on her face. But she follows me into the house and the door closes behind us.

It was the last scene in *Five at Eleven* with Rory and me together.

I never saw her in that costume again, and I have no idea if her collection has grown to two more cabinets or five more or twenty. But this *is* a small town with a thick grapevine, and I know that at some point, Rory discovered an online community of people all over the world who, like her, have a thing for that particular pocket of history. Every year they have some big convention and at the last one, Rory was asked to be on one of the panels. On the heels of that, she started the school History Club, and it even has a few members.

Rory has a passion. She gets recognition for it. It connects her with people.

I have never felt so jealous in my life.

EIGHT

on't! Mess! Don't! Mess! Don't mess with the best! 'Cuz the best don't mess!

If you think that cheer sounds stupid, imagine it shouted against hundreds of feet stomping on ancient wooden bleachers, pounding an echo across the grungy tile and glass surrounding the college pool. I look down at the water from my perch near the top of the bleachers, the way it's jiggling slightly, like Jell-O. I bet the world is blissfully muffled down there, and that's the draw. Maybe that's worth wearing a Speedo in front of all these people.

I'm sitting with Felix, and this is some kind of important

swim meet for our high school boys' team—our school doesn't have its own pool, so the team swims here. We're supposed to care about who wins and who goes splashing away in shame and defeat. This is my first time at an event like this. And really, I'm not here by choice.

I look for Lance and Kenny and there they are, standing in the aisle alongside the bleachers. Lance is panning the crowd as it whips up this inane cheering. Felix is actually participating while I actually am not. The only reason I'm even mouthing the words, sort of, is because we've got Leslie positioned in the aisle next to us, shooting the smaller camera they sometimes use for extra footage in big crowd scenes.

Here comes the team out of the locker room wearing sweatshirts and track pants. There's Nate, rolling his neck and his arms around. He raises his hand to the crowd and smiles, and they go crazy.

Several rows below us and off to the side, I see Rory. She's sitting by herself with headphones on, reading a book, which makes me suddenly burst out laughing. If I could do that, I would. But Rory doesn't care that it looks ridiculous. She's not even doing it because she wants to make a statement or create a terrific shot. It's just what she wants at the moment. I'd like more than anything to climb down, sit next to her, and crack open a book of my own.

"Ah, her Royal Highness has finally graced us with her

presence," says Felix, nudging me and pointing with his chin toward the door. Keira has just entered with two of her friends. The front row is full but people make room for them, and their heads disappear into the crowd.

So we all got the same call from Leslie the night before. It's always Leslie, when they want us to do something special.

"We'd like all four of you to attend Nate's swim meet," she'd said to me on the phone. It had been a week since my Follow Day. In that time, they'd done Nate, Keira, and Rory.

"Isn't that against your usual, you know, method?" I'd asked.

"Yes, we wouldn't normally be asking this. We'd try to find an organic situation where you're all together. But things are different than they were five years ago. Your high school is much bigger than middle school and your interests are, well, varied. We need to have all five of you in the same place at the same time, at least once."

"But I don't go to these things. Neither do most normal people."

"Can't you just pretend . . . I mean, suppose . . . Felix asked you to go? Just as something to do on a Friday night."

So I had *supposed*, and now I'm here. Watching Nate Hunter take off his sweats. Okay, I will objectively admit that he is a beautiful boy. But I admire him the way I'd admire a male model in a magazine underwear ad, glossy and glistening yet one-dimensional and ultimately, not real. He's got lines on his body that seem carved by some high-precision tool. I let myself look for only a moment.

True to form, Lance and Kenny are quickly poolside, just close enough to get good shots without disturbing the Swimming Messiah.

Leslie pans the crowd with her camera, then suddenly travels to the other side of the bleachers, where Keira is sitting. With the cameras distracted and Felix engrossed in the meet, I decide to step outside so I can regain my hearing for a minute.

The hallway of the college gym is decorated with trophy cases and banners, and I start reading about a student named Maeve O'Bannon who, back in 1978, apparently did superhuman things with a volleyball. On the other side of the doors to the pool, I hear a starting horn and splashes and more cheers, and then the opening and thudding closed of the heavy metal door. I look up.

It's Keira. She's wearing a khaki shirt dress with a big buckle and high brown leather boots, and anyone else would look overdressed for a swim meet, but with her you get the sense this is maybe something she just wears around the house.

"Oh," she says, bored and distracted. Like this is her version of *Hi*.

"I'm hiding out," I say.

"I'm taking a very long trip to the restroom," she says without any twist of sarcasm, and starts walking toward it. She has to pass me on the way, though, and I offer her a smile as she goes by. She smiles back, but only half as much.

I don't know why it's so important for me to talk to Keira. I'd liked the way Leslie had whined, "None of you guys have anything to do with one another anymore," on the phone last night. Taken some pleasure in it.

But for me, Keira is different. Maybe I'm just like everyone else, caught by her mysterious tractor beam of charisma.

"How has it been, so far?" I call after her as she's reaching for the restroom door. Now she stops and really looks at me, almost amused.

"It's great. Terrific. Just lovely." She smiles for a second. A fake smile. An almost mean smile. "And how about you? You always seem to have so much *fun* with this."

When Keira says the word *fun* her brow crinkles and she bites down hard on the *f*.

"Do I?" I ask.

"Don't you?" says Keira, and now she snorts. It's a haughty little sound. She swings open the restroom door and moves through it, letting it slam.

Keira Jones hates me. She hates me, and I have no idea why.

I liked it a lot better when I thought she didn't care about me.

I would leave this place. Right now. Except my stuff is back at the bleachers and something drives me forward into the restroom. Keira's just standing at the sink, staring blankly into the mirror, as I step inside and let the door slam just like she did.

"What did I ever do to you?" I ask, and there's something about addressing the back of her head that lets me be brave. "You haven't lowered yourself to look at me, let alone talk to me, since we were eleven years old. What exactly is your problem?"

Keira does glance at me now, but in the mirror. It's disconcerting. At least I have her attention.

"*My* problem?" she asks, genuinely surprised. "Aren't you the one who pulled a total diva in Journalism?"

When I don't answer, she turns to face me head-on.

"Do you have any idea how that made Nate feel? That you wouldn't do a simple group project with him on camera?"

Her face is softer now, and she reaches up to her hair with both hands, twists it behind her head into a temporary bun. This seems like a pretty weird thing to do in the middle of what I see as a face-off, but then again, it is Keira.

How would *Nate* feel?

"Why do you care so much about how he feels?" I ask.

"Are you guys going out? Or maybe just doing it?" As soon as it comes out of my mouth, I cringe. I may think hateful things like that all the time, but I know better than to say them.

Keira's expression hardens into a look of contempt, a strange mixture of anger, pity, and disgust. Then she releases her hair and walks past me out of the restroom.

I stare at the door after it closes behind her, the straight, clean lines of it, wishing everything in the universe could be so neat. There's cheering coming from inside the pool area and I really, really just want to hang out here by myself, but eventually I'll be missed. When I think of people calling me a diva, it hurts, and my absence from the pool will just reinforce that.

I go back and sit down just in time to catch another starting horn and there's Nate, diving off the block and into the water, disappearing for a second before popping up, and wow, he's fast. I look over at Felix, who is watching him too.

There's one of the cameras. On me.

"Go Nate!" I find myself yelling.

Before I can think of why I bothered, the race is over and Nate has won.

Three days later, it's Felix's Follow Day and he's invited/ cajoled/begged me to hang out with him after school. We take the bus to his house, the crew riding along in the way-back row of seats, then we all walk a few blocks to the used music and video store on Main Street.

It's weird to be in town with the camera in tow. At school, people have gotten used to it. But here, it's still exciting. Some people, film students and older locals mostly, look at us knowingly. Others have no idea what's going on and take a moment to watch. I put on mental blinders and pay no attention.

We're at the record store for five minutes, Felix and I browsing through the 99-cent DVD bin, when I glance up to see Ian moving toward the opposite corner of the store. He's examining, with great interest, the *New Mint in Box Never Opened!* wall of comic book action figures. This strikes me as off, because I know he doesn't like action figures and, in fact, considers them a stupid waste of money.

After a few moments, he turns and sees me looking at him. And seems surprised.

"Justine!"

"Hey."

"What are you guys doing here?" he says, coming over. Felix shoots me a sideways glance and moves to another aisle, but the crew stays with me.

"I'm doing my weekly check for movie bargains." Then I point with my thumb at the crew. "Plus there's *this*."

He looks at the crew and acts surprised again.

But it's suddenly so obvious.

He is totally not surprised. He has totally followed us in here.

It feels like my stomach drops about a hundred feet. Equilibrium vanishes so quickly, I could tip over.

Ian raises his hand in a wave. "Hi, folks," he says.

Leslie, Lance, and Kenny all murmur hello. Leslie surveys Ian with an alert curiosity. Yes, this is someone you haven't shot me speaking to yet. A guy. Move along because there's nothing to see here.

"Find anything good?" Ian asks, leaning in to look over my shoulder. I can smell his hair and despite everything else I'm feeling, there's that unpushawayable *Oh God can I please just put my face in it and breathe for a few minutes?*

I pull out the DVD I was just handling. It's *Love Actually*, which was one of my favorite Christmas movies until I realized that both main female characters end up miserable and two of the male characters fall in love with their maids.

I hold it up to him because I don't seem to be able to speak. My mind is busy with some other questions, not the least of which is, *Do I do this now?*

I look at his face in profile and think about the first time he kissed me. Felix and I had run into him and his buddy Milo at a pizza place one afternoon, which led to us all sitting together and then deciding to drive to a swimming hole up the mountain. Felix and Milo went wading in the water, but Ian and I took a walk, then found a tree that had fallen across a stream. We sat on it and talked for a while, our legs dangling over the rushing water, and he asked if he could put his arm around me because he was worried I might fall.

"Yes," I said. "But you look less sturdy than I do."

Then he put his arm around me and his lips on mine, in the same motion. Like the kiss was an extra bonus he threw in for free at the last second. It was so random but the second it happened, it felt like something I'd been waiting for.

"Sorry," he'd said. "I just realized how interesting and cool you are, and I couldn't not kiss you."

"That is so cheesy, I might puke," I'd said. "You really will have to keep me from falling."

"Velveeta all the way, baby, and proud of it." Then his face got serious. "Would you want to come back here with me next weekend? We could go for a walk to the falls."

So I did, and we did, and suddenly we were a couple. Everything about it was fast and unexpected. Which now makes me extremely, heartsickeningly suspicious.

Now, Ian takes the *Love Actually* DVD out of my hand and looks at it. "Oh, yeah. The one with all the English people."

It would be so easy for me to stay in this scene with him. We could look through movies and make smart-ass comments, and it would probably come off pretty funny and entertaining. Something Lance and Leslie would keep in the film. Maybe my story could be a love story. And whatever happens with it, at least it's happening.

I picture the suits around their big conference table, watching the next crop of footage. Liking the romance angle.

And then the notion hits. *This moment isn't meant for me.* It's meant for Ian and for Lance and Leslie and also for the money people, and I'm just some kind of device.

I grab the DVD out of his hands, stuff it back in the bin, and march out of the store. Ian follows. Lance and Leslie follow. I look up at them, ready to tell them to ease off, to leave me alone for a few minutes, but the sun hits me so warm as I step outside and the light blinds me a little, like an instant reminder of *here* and *now* and in those two seconds I lose, Ian and the crew have caught up to me.

"Justine! What's going on?" he asks.

Okay, Ian. You want this? You got it. I spin to face him.

"Did you go out with me because of them?" I motion to Lance, Leslie, and Kenny.

"What?"

"The film. Did you do it because you wanted to be part of the film?"

Ian looks horrified. "God, no! What kind of asshole do you think I am?"

"That depends. What kind of asshole shows up in a store he hates because of their overuse of unrecyclable

123

plastic, just because there's a film crew with the ex he dumped for no good reason?"

Ian steadies himself with a long breath in, then out. "I was in the bookstore," he says, pointing across the street, "and I saw all of you go in and . . . I don't know. I was curious." He looks down at the ground now. "I thought it would be fun to be on camera with you."

"And before . . . when we got together . . . ?"

Ian closes his eyes and scrunches up his face, and his body seems to want to be very small. "Look," he says as he opens his eyes and they meet mine. "I'd be lying if I said it hadn't crossed my mind. The film itself, I mean. But it didn't matter one way or another to me. I was like, whatever, about it. I've just always thought you were so cool, in the movies and in real life, and I wanted to get to know you."

"But then you didn't like what you found when you got there."

"I told you that night. I just feel like we were meant to be friends. Can't it be that simple?"

Ian now looks over my shoulder at something far away. Maybe the ridge, where he wishes he could be hiking with a girl who doesn't wear high-tops and complain about her knees.

I don't know how to answer this question of his. Simple for him, sure. Simple for me . . . no. If he had said, *Yes, you got me. I'm an evil schemer who hooked up with you because I thought you were going to be in a movie, then dumped you when it looked like the movie wasn't happening, then started hanging around again when shooting started . . .* I would have been devastated, betrayed, all that. But I also would have something else to blame.

Something else to blame besides me.

"I don't want to be friends with you," I finally say. "It hurts too much."

Ian takes one slow step toward me, then freezes. I guess it's all he dares offer now. "I didn't mean to hurt you."

Now I just shrug, not willing to meet him in that raw place. "I didn't mean to *disappoint* you."

Felix has edged his way onto the sidewalk in front of the store now, and I can see he's in Fierce Protective Friend mode. He doesn't even care that the camera's strayed from him on his Follow Day. "Let's go," says Felix, and takes me by the hand away from Ian. I'm so glad for the assisted exit, I want to wrap myself around his arm.

After we've walked a few storefronts down, I turn to check on the crew. They haven't moved, and they're not shooting us. The camera's pointed at Ian, standing by himself on the steps of the store, staring again at the mountains in the distance. I know, as surely as I know anything, that I will never speak to him again.

NINE

On one of the main country roads that run through town, there's a sign for Hunter Farms. Olivia and I always refer to it as the Cannibal Apple. On it, an apple with a face and arms and legs is holding a smaller, apparently less evolved apple without a face or arms or legs, which has a big bite eaten out of it. "HUNTER FARMS! JUST ONE MORE MILE AHEAD!" says the Cannibal Apple ecstatically in a speech balloon, like this is where everyone on the planet is headed.

There's nothing too special about Hunter Farms. It's

one of several that dot the map around here, doing big fall business with the U-Pick crowds and quietly selling fresh things to locals the rest of the time. But every family seems to latch onto "their" farm, and Hunter has been ours for as long as I can remember. I'm guessing that originally, this was because of Nate and Felix, and our connection through the *Five At* films. In a small town like ours, that's all it takes for lifelong produce loyalty.

It's Friday. Felix has agreed to accompany me to the art house theater one town over, which is something I like to do on weekends, usually by myself, when everyone else is lining up at the mall to see the newest craptacular blockbuster. The crew is meeting us there, which probably explains why Felix was so eager to see a film in Farsi he's never heard of. I'm on my way to get him at the farm, where he still works part-time when his dad needs more hands, like right now during spring tree-pruning season.

I used to feel weird about coming here. Because of Nate. Because he might be around. But Felix always assured me that Golden Boy was never on-site. When I saw the abandoned rabbit hutches behind the farm store, I started to believe it.

What happened to the rabbits? I'm always wondering about this. When Nate traded 4-H for ab crunches, did the bunnies end up as collateral damage? Felix's mom says they were "given away," but that could be one of those euphemisms like "being sent to live on a farm in the country." When an animal is already living on a farm in the country, what lie do you use to pretend something horrible didn't happen to it?

I veer into the circular driveway of the farm store and stop the car on an intentionally random angle, just because I can. In summer, the big doors are open to the road and the ice cream window has a line ten deep and you can't find a parking space, but until then, everything's boarded up except for a small side door with a sign that says, a little too desperately, "Yes! We're Open!"

Suddenly, two people burst through the farm store door: Nate and his grandmother. I've always admired Mrs. Hunter. She dresses like she's forever on her way to a yoga class, and is in the paper every other week as a member of some committee. By contrast, I think I've seen Nate's mom two or three times in the last five years, even though they all live together in the big brick house on the hill above one of the orchards.

Mrs. Hunter is talking to Nate and looks mad. Nate is not talking back and looks haggard. He checks out my car and sees who's in it. But his gaze doesn't ricochet off me the way it usually does. He holds it there. Just staring.

Mrs. Hunter continues talking, her voice raised enough so I can hear a bit through the closed windows. I catch the words *help* and *important*. Nate's still looking at me with an expression I can only describe as *pleading*. It's the distantly familiar version of Nate Hunter, like when a song samples an older one and you can't name it, but you know you know it from somewhere.

I find myself responding to him with a moronic, yet somehow appropriate, shrug. It's enough to count as some kind of exchange. Something passes between us. Then he turns and starts up the gravel driveway toward the house with his grandmother on his heels. I watch him walk. It's not the same walk he has at school.

Not that I notice his walk, of course. I hate him, remember? But just so you know, this walk is the walk of a young boy being nagged by his grandmother about something. It's as if he's curling further into his inner eleven-year-old with every step.

The passenger door of the car opens suddenly and Felix is sliding in. He looks freshly changed, into one of his signature polo shirts and a crisp pair of jeans.

"How was it?" I ask.

"I used to love apple trees," he replies, a little dazed. "No more."

After I pull onto the road, I say, "I just saw Nate being bitched out by his grandmother. I wanted to be entertained by it, but I actually felt kind of bad for him."

"Oh, yeah," says Felix, perking up, a knowing edge to his voice.

"Scoop?" I ask. Felix does not talk to Nate, but Felix's mother talks to everybody.

"Mrs. Hunter wants Nate to spend some time working

at the farm. With, you know. The crew around. Free advertising, and all that."

"Yuck," I say.

Out of the corner of my eye, I can see Felix shrug. "Times are tough. The farm needs all the exposure it can get."

"They're not bugging *you* about it."

Felix doesn't answer. His silence is suspicious.

"What is it?" I ask. "What are you about to tell me?"

"They're not bugging me about it because I've got other things going on." I catch him looking down at his phone. "I got a call from Leslie today."

It's been two days since Lance and Leslie had a big meeting with their producers, and I haven't heard a peep. Which has been kind of nice and kind of devastating at the same time.

"Did they talk about Independent Eye?" I ask.

"They got some notes," says Felix. "Maybe they'll tell you more at the theater. We talked a bit about me. The Independent Eye people talked about me."

The thought of a bunch of cable channel executives sitting around a table, drinking espresso and discussing the five of us like they know us, like they own us somehow, has kept the hair on the back of my neck standing on end for days. Even now, I clench my hands around the steering wheel.

"They're thinking my blog should be part of the online

131

presence for the film, and they'd like to do something with one of my songs."

"Ah, so they know how to get you," I say.

"Well, I don't kid myself with the music thing. I know I'm not that good. Yet. But what I have that others don't is an existing stage. People will see me. Important people, who could actually help me with my career. How else am I going to show my parents I can make a living this way? They want me to find something more . . . reliable. In other words, corporate and mind-numbing and *not who I am*."

I take my eyes off the road for just a second to glance at him and in that second, he appears different. I always thought of Felix's hunger for the spotlight as something desperate and a little annoying, but now I get it. He is chronically unseen, even by his own family.

"You know what it means?" Felix continues. "It means maybe this time, they'll actually care about me. It's always been you or Keira or Nate. Rory and me . . . they never really focused on us because we weren't that interesting. But now, apparently I am."

Felix looks overjoyed. I wish I could offer him any one of a thousand other things to feel this way about: a tricked-out new keyboard, perhaps, or a girlfriend.

"Felix, you've always been interesting," I say. "More than most people."

"Well then, now it's official."

We drive in silence for a few seconds. So Felix is more interesting to them than he was. Does this mean I am *less* interesting? Well, that's no surprise. The best I can do here is be a good friend.

"That's great," I finally say to Felix. "You deserve that."

"I'm so happy that I don't even care that Leslie and Lance are asking us to do what they want us to do." He pauses. "*You* will, though, Justine. You will totally hate it."

He's right. I do hate it. I hate it so much, I'm still trying to figure out how my mouth even formed the sounds of *Okay* that brought me here.

In the corner of the school library, underneath one of the dusty bubble skylights, there's a table where there was never a table. The bookshelves have been moved around to make room for this thing, which was dragged over from another part of the library. It's a larger, taller version of the one we sat at in kindergarten.

Lance and Kenny are tinkering with some lights they brought in, and somewhere, far enough away so we can't see her but not so far that she can't hear everything that's going on, is the librarian, Mrs. Abruzzo. It's after school but I'm sure she doesn't mind sticking around for this.

This. I am the first one to arrive for *this.*

This being all five of us around the table. Nate, Felix, Keira, Rory, and me. Together. Talking, ideally. We'll see.

I wanted to get here early so I could suss out the

situation. The others are probably dallying at their lockers or in the bathroom, but not me. I need to make sure the distasteful thing we're about to do, have all somehow agreed to do, is a distasteful thing I can mentally prepare for.

Felix is next to arrive. He winks at me, hugs Leslie quickly, then moves over to Lance and Kenny.

Rory enters right after him. She looks at me and registers absolutely no reaction, which for her doesn't necessarily mean a damn thing, but still. *Ouch.*

"The folks at Independent Eye aren't completely satisfied with what we've shot so far," said Leslie after we got out of the movie that night. "That one little bit we got with you and Rory was the best. They want you interacting."

Maybe I agreed because I feel so responsible for this turn of events. As for the others? Nate and Felix—no surprise there. Rory, as always, is willing to go along with anything if it makes people happy. And Keira. Well, that's a mystery.

Here she comes now. Nate too. He's got his hand protectively on her back and I feel this instant *Huh?* Of course, they're friends. I know that. But there's something about the way he leans his body toward hers, a graceful curve, that seems truly intimate.

Nate smiles at Rory, who gives him the same nonlook she gave me. He registers Felix and looks instantly, nervously, away. He must see me out of the corner of his eye, but he does not turn.

Yeah, this is going to be a blast.

But it's Keira who surprises me. She bends down to set her leather messenger bag on the floor, and when she stands up, her face is neon-bright with energy.

"Hey, girl," she practically sings to Leslie, and they kiss each other on the cheek. Then Keira turns to see Rory standing on the other side of Leslie.

"Rory," she says warmly, like she hasn't ignored her in the hallway every day for years but is seeing her for the first time in a long while and oh, she's missed her so very much. Rory smiles shyly. Even Rory knows that when Keira Jones talks to you, it's a big deal.

I'm ready for her to ignore me like Nate did, and suddenly my left thumbnail desperately needs to be picked at. But Keira approaches, her arms outstretched.

"Justine, hi," she says, and gives me the quickest of hugs. I'm not sure her hands actually touch my body, but the motion is there, swift and expert, and I'm guessing that's supposed to count. The shadow of our almost-girl-fight in the bathroom that day flickers across her face.

Now there's an awkward moment where nobody is doing anything, and Leslie feels the need to proclaim.

"I can't believe you're all here. In one place! The fact that you were up for this . . . well, it means a lot to Lance and me. And it'll mean a lot to the film and, eventually, the audience."

135

"Do you guys remember where you sat?" Lance asks. "In kindergarten?"

I do, and I know Felix does, but I want to see who else might.

"Yes," pipes up Rory. "It went Felix, Keira, Nate, Justine, and me."

We stand silent for a moment, and then, Rory goes to the table and sits down at one of the chairs. Felix laughs, and Rory looks confused, but his smile is warm and unfiltered as he goes to sit next to her. Then Keira goes to her chair, next to Felix, and Nate moves to the other side of her. Now it's my turn to get on my mark in between Nate and Rory.

Nate does not acknowledge me as I sit. I look around the table and realize Felix is the only person here who doesn't hate me.

"Oh, this is great," says Lance, as if talking to his camera. "The shot is beautiful. Books and posters in the background. Light is perfect."

Now Leslie is leaning in next to me, addressing the group. "I'll ask you some questions, and you can answer me, if you want. I'll be moving around with the second camera. But the point is for you to speak to one another. I may even remind you to do that."

We're all quiet. I'm guessing because the situation is so insane, there are no words.

"Oh, I almost forgot." She grabs a brown paper grocery

bag from the floor and starts to unpack it. There's bottles of juice and sports drinks, and cookies.

"There's no eating in the library," says Rory.

"Special permission," says Leslie.

I can guess what the snacks are for. To keep our hands busy. To give us something to fidget with. If our hands can move, our bodies won't. It looks better. As we reach for the drinks, Nate and I try to grab the same bottle, something pink called BerryLuscious. Our wrists bang and Nate jerks his away like he's been burned. I pretend not to notice and take the bottle for myself.

Kenny's got the boom mic situated and Leslie has taken a position about a quarter of the way around the table from Lance, and I notice the camera's already rolling. I don't think anyone else does yet. They're busy popping open their drinks, unwrapping their cookies.

I'm waiting for Leslie to jump in with one of her questions. But she's silent, watching.

I think they're all hoping the questions won't come. Easier to munch away and pretend this is not actually happening.

Suddenly, a memory pops into my head. Or is it a scene from *Five at Six*? Well actually, both.

Our teacher, Mrs. McGuire, has been having trouble getting the class to settle down when it's time to start working. She's offered an incentive. Each day, the first table to be totally quiet when she claps her hands twice gets a sticker on a chart at the front of the room. Our table, the Green Table, is tied with another table, the Red Table. (Oh, how we hated that Red Table.) We're both one sticker away from getting to go to the Treasure Chest and pick out prizes.

Keira really wants us to win. She wants the plastic princess tiara she glimpsed in there. She has been coaching us on how to be quiet the instant we hear the claps. Rory or Felix tend to ruin it, but we think we have it down.

Mrs. McGuire claps. We zip it up so fast, it's as if we've been freeze-framed. A second passes. Two. Keira has her hand up as a cue to us, to hold it there. Just hold it. I'm sitting on my hands (something the camera picks up as it circles the table). Felix and Nate both have theirs folded in front of them, exchanging glances like they've practiced this at home.

Red Table is completely quiet as well. They've taken a bit longer, though, and we can smell victory as we wait for Mrs. McGuire to complete her evaluation of the room.

Rory has been staring at the board, stone silent. Then she turns around and into the silence, says, to nobody, "I don't like chalk because you can never get it into a perfect point."

Keira shoots out of her chair and yells, "SHUT UP!" Rory starts crying. I wrap my arms around Rory and yell back to Keira, "YOU SHUT UP!" Nate and Felix get up and run to the corner of the classroom.

In the film, Lance and Leslie edited this sequence to

138

build up the tension like a suspense thriller. The moment we all lose it, everything shifts into slow motion. Our faces are stricken with the tragic drama of not getting to pick out crappy little toys from a box.

The next scenes in the film show Felix playing under the farm store counter because he's been ordered to stay out of the way, Nate waiting up for his mom to come home from work so she can read him a story before bed. Rory going with her father and older brother to the local food pantry to pick up canned tuna and beans. Keira being quizzed by her father about geography. Me throwing up in the bathroom the morning of my *Emperor's New Clothes* performance.

There is no narration in the films. Lance and Leslie won their awards in part because you don't need narration. The voice you hear in your head while watching these scenes is, *These kids have problems so much bigger than not getting that last sticker, but they don't realize it.*

Sitting here now, the five of us, I wonder what scenes Lance and Leslie will use to contrast whatever happens around the table. I wonder what I could say or do that will give them something.

I wonder why I can't stop thinking in these terms. Do the others do this too?

Finally, after everyone has opened their snacks and had some time to crunch, Leslie speaks:

"Have you guys watched *Five at Six* recently?"

Everyone nods, except Rory. She shakes her head.

"What do you wish you could tell that kid, your six-year-old self?"

There's the shortest of pauses, then Nate jumps in. "I'd tell myself not to worry so much."

Keira lets out a short laugh, then smiles affectionately at him. "You didn't seem like a worrier."

Nate winks at her. "Oh. I had the weight of the world."

Silence. Then Felix says, "I'd warn myself that I don't know people as well as I think I do." He shoots a look at Nate.

Rory is thinking hard. I'm afraid she's going to say something similar with a glare at me, but instead she just says, "I would tell her what happens in the later *Harry Potter* books."

We all laugh at this, and it takes Rory a moment to realize she's said something funny, and then she joins us. I forgot about Rory's laugh. It changes whatever room she's in. It is the best thing I've heard all day.

Silence again. Leslie looks at me, then Keira. We haven't gone yet.

I'm about to speak when Keira says, "I would tell myself to stop wanting what I'm not allowed to have, and just . . . be . . . present."

She says it matter-of-factly, a big statement but gorgeously simple. Leslie looks at her with such love that I find myself stricken with jealousy.

Now everybody's staring at me. I'm supposed to say something witty and fresh, to slay them with my brutal honesty. To be *Justine*.

What can I say that will trump them all? I go with the first thing that pops into my head and when I say it, I'm not even sure it's out loud.

"I would tell myself that it's all downhill from where you are right now."

Dammit. That came out way less funny and much more self-pitying than I meant it to. Leslie, who has been moving around the table with her camera, stops and lowers it. She looks at me and it's not with the mega-love she gave Keira but, rather, intense curiosity. Like, *Who the hell is this kid and what the hell are we going to do with her?*

After a few horrible moments where everyone gets very busy with their snacks, Leslie says, "Okay, then. That was my icebreaker. I think the ice is broken."

Everyone laughs nervously, but the truth is, the ice is not really broken. Maybe the glaze has been rubbed off a little, so we're not going to slip and fall on our asses trying to cross it, but I don't see so much as a crack.

"So now," continues Leslie, "I'd like you to think of your favorite memory of another person from that film. Or maybe it's not even a favorite, just one that sticks in your head."

Once again, it's Nate who speaks first. "Keira, playing

that board game with her mom and dad." He addresses Leslie when he says this.

"Can you say that again, but say it to Keira? I'd like you guys to look at the person you're talking about."

Nate looks a little chastised, hurt, like he did something wrong, but he flashes Blinding Smile Number Twelve and turns to Keira as naturally as he can. "My favorite memory from that first film is of you, Keira, and your parents. Playing that board game. The three of you in one place at one time, enjoying something."

Keira grins politely, but you can tell this has caused her pain. Physical pain, like her chair has suddenly grown spikes. She can't shift in the seat enough to be comfortable. Finally, she looks at Leslie.

"Am I supposed to tell him thank you?"

"Why don't you tell him about your favorite memory of him?"

Keira turns to Nate without missing a beat. "I remember when you were giving the tour of the orchards. It was so adorable! You were, like, the world's tiniest apple ambassador."

Nate smiles, but there's something behind it. A flicker of sadness. It's fascinating, how they managed to wound each other so easily and accidentally.

Felix has been waiting to jump in, as evidenced by his tapping fingers against the table. Now that there's a pause in the talking, he goes for it.

"Justine," he says, staring at me. "I know everyone talks about the scene where your mom and dad drive you to the hospital. But for me, it's when the doctor comes in and talks to your parents about how they couldn't find anything wrong. You're coloring in bed and the camera stays on you the whole time, and we only hear everyone else's voices. I can still close my eyes and see you sitting there, listening and filling up a whole blank page with orange crayon."

I see Leslie nodding fondly but I don't even glance at the others. I don't want to know how they think of this scene, which took up more screen time than any other scene in that film. Lance and Leslie just kept the cameras rolling and barely edited it.

So now it feels like Felix has tagged me, and it's my turn to say something. I could right-back-at-you to Felix, which he's surely expecting. But where does that leave Rory?

The truth is, all of my favorite scenes from *Five at Six* are with Rory. Rory walking in the woods with her dog, explaining why her father was out of work and the kind of jobs she thought he was most qualified for, like a lifeguard or town mayor. Or Rory and her family holding a yard sale, and Rory having a meltdown when some guy wanted to buy her old stroller, saying she'd need it if she got paralyzed in an accident. At the time, these scenes made me laugh. I'm not sure they made other people laugh. I think they generally made people uncomfortable, because Rory was always looking at the ground and cracking her neck when she spoke.

Then there are the scenes with her and me. The dancing-princess thing. The two of us on a class field trip to a nature center, holding hands as we walk along the muddy trail, behind the rest of the group. In my bedroom, playing Alligator Family—an elaborate situation where I was a mother alligator, and she was my daughter alligator, and I'd just tell her which toys to gobble up. I haven't been able to watch those scenes in years, but I don't really need to. They're running on a loop in my head at all times.

I want to turn to Rory and tell her these things. But I can't.

So I turn back to Felix and a memory comes to mind. I don't think about it too much. I just sort of go with it. "Felix, there's that scene with you and your mom at the supermarket. You're riding in the basket of the cart even though that's not allowed, and you're translating stuff for her because she's trying to improve her English."

Felix's features all sag at once, disappointed and maybe even betrayed.

"What?" I say.

"*That's* the part you remember most from ten years ago?"

I nod, flipping through the film in my head. What else was there? Scenes of him and Nate playing. Stuff on the farm. What does he want me to remember most?

"Great. Just great." Felix pushes his food away and in the space he's cleared, puts his face in his hands. "That's all anybody remembers. Felix with his foreign parents. Felix with Nate. What about all those scenes of me on my own?"

I draw a blank. I can't remember any scenes of Felix on his own. Oh, there was one. In it, he's alone in his kitchen, dancing to Michael Jackson's "Thriller." It's actually a little silly and the one scene in the whole movie that seems set up.

Felix is looking at Leslie now. "It's going to be different this time, right?" he asks. "Like we talked about?"

Leslie lowers her camera and nods. "Yes, Felix. Of course. We told you we would do more with you on your own."

Felix glances at Nate, then at me, embarrassed now. "Okay. I'm sorry about that. I ruined this whole thing, didn't I?"

"No," says Leslie, who then shoots me a look.

"Absolutely not," I add. Not convincingly.

"Shit," says Felix, and before I know it, he's darted out of his chair and is running away from us. Suddenly I'm darting after him: I get past the first bookcase and then pause, turning to see that Leslie has started to follow me with the camera.

"Don't," I practically spit, as if commanding a trained

dog. She freezes and I continue through the library, out into the hallway. Felix is down at the end of it, walking fast.

I call his name, and he turns. "Please don't make me chase you!" I say, and see him smile.

"Camera?" he yells.

"No," I say, as I head down the hallway toward him. He puts his hands in his pockets and watches me intently, and I have to wonder if he's still wishing we could date.

When I reach him, he says, "Sorry about that."

"Who's the diva now?"

"That would be me. So unexpected."

I just shrug.

"It's Nate," adds Felix. "I acted that way because of Nate being there. Do you realize we haven't been in close proximity for more than a minute in years?"

"I'm sure it was not fun," I say, wanting to touch his arm but not wanting to give him the wrong idea.

"Aside from you, he's been the headliner. Even when we were little, it made me jealous that he was on screen so much more than me. Why did everybody notice Nate, when I was right there too?" Felix looks down and rubs his sneaker along one line of a tile on the floor. "Seeing him always stirs up some intense stuff."

"Well, who could blame you for that? After what he did."

"What he did?" asks Felix, raising an eyebrow.

"Yeah. You know. Ditching you as a friend. Remaking

146

himself into the Nate-tastic incarnation he's become."

Felix stares at his sneaker for another long moment, then lifts his head. "Right."

He takes a quick breath and I get the sense he's about to say something else, but we hear the library doors open down the hallway and Leslie appears.

"Will you come back?" she calls.

Felix and I look at each other.

"Give us a minute," I yell, and grab his hand. I pull him around the corner to a water fountain nook, where Leslie can't see us.

"We should go back."

"I have a feeling they got what they wanted. They got something exciting."

"You don't understand," says Felix. "They're planning to focus on me this time. I don't want to jeopardize that."

"Just tell them what you told me, about Nate. They'll want more time for you to talk about it all."

Felix thinks for a moment, a flash of panic in his eyes.

"I'm not sure I want to."

"Why not?" I ask. It seems obvious to me. Nate looking bad. Nate's image, smudged. I like that.

"It's complicated." Felix peers back around the corner toward the library. "I can't go back there. Not today." He takes a deep breath, then reaches out and grabs my hand. "Will you leave with me? I can call my cousin for a ride. If we take off together, it won't just be me they're mad at."

"You can say I made you do it. They're permanently annoyed with me anyway."

"Deal," he says, taking my hand and pulling me toward our lockers. "Let's get our stuff and then get lost."

Merengue music from a stereo system fills the backyard of Felix's parents' house, and because of this, nobody can stop moving. Technically, officially, it's a birthday party for Felix's younger brother, Gabriel. But there are more adults than kids here because they've invited every family member within a sixty-mile radius. So there's a lot of people and a lot of food and a lot of noise. An elderly aunt and uncle start dancing an elaborate Latin ballroom routine and a circle forms around them to watch.

Felix doesn't join the circle. He's busy carrying his brother's newly gifted toys, armload by armload, into the house. He dumps some of the toys on the sofa and collapses down next to them.

There's a cut to Ana entering from outside through the sliding glass doors in the kitchen. "Felix, you're not going to stay in here again, are you? The cousins will think you're rude!"

"I talked to them. I ate those beans Naomi always makes." Felix turns to the camera and pretends to put his finger down his throat, just so we know what kind of sacrifice that was.

"It's your brother's party and he'll be very upset if

you're not celebrating with him!"

"Mami, he's like high on sugar and running around with that new squirt gun. He doesn't give a crap where I am."

"Don't curse at me!"

Felix looks at the camera again and shakes his head, rolls his eyes.

"Ten minutes!" *snaps Ana as she leaves to go back outside, a bag of ice in her arms.* "You come out in ten minutes!"

Felix waits until she's gone, then starts shuffling through his brother's loot. He's looking for something in particular, and when he finds it, he smiles wide. It's a kid-size electronic keyboard, packaged so you can play it without removing it from the box. Felix glances over his shoulder to make sure nobody else is around, then starts fiddling with the keys, stringing them together one by one into aimless melodies.

Another cut. Felix has been asked a question. We can tell because his brow is furrowed in concentration.

"I'm not embarrassed by my family," *he says.* "I wish I could relax and have fun like they do. I just . . . sometimes I don't know where I want to be. When I'm hanging out with Nate at his house, I never feel like I belong there. Then when I'm here with everyone, I don't really fit in either. So it's hard."

The camera stays on Felix as he continues to mess

around with the toy keyboard.

The next thing we see is Ana coming back into the room, calling Felix's name. But he's gone. One final shot of the scene shows us Felix sitting cross-legged in the bed of his dad's pickup truck in the driveway. He's playing something on the toy keyboard, but it's completely drowned out. His fingers move and his head sways and he seems to be in a good place, but all you hear is his mother shouting and music he didn't make.

Lance and Leslie got some heat for how Felix was portrayed in *Five at Eleven. Of course, the one kid who's a full ethnic minority gets reduced to a supporting character,* people complained.

It was much smaller heat, just a puff of warm air really, compared with the criticism over that scene with Keira and questions about footage of Nate. The scenes everyone loved and laughed over were mine. Rory came across as odd but charming and memorable. But there was Felix, with his own quiet story in the background.

I realize now that by starting his blog, Felix took it upon himself to continue telling it.

TEN

eslie calls me on Saturday morning. They're not shooting today. Lance's back is killing him and Kenny's got a family commitment, and she sounds almost happy about it.

"I'm going to check out the Walkway Over the Hudson while I'm unencumbered," she says. "Do you want to come with me?"

I remember when I was eleven and Leslie took me bowling. Just her and me. It made me feel Chosen. "Sure."

An hour later, Leslie and I are driving east from town in her rented SUV. She's wearing black yoga pants, hiking boots, and a faux-fur leopard-print hoodie. This is a departure from what I now realize is her "shooting outfit" of jeans, boots, long-sleeved tee, and a fleece vest. What she's wearing now seems more casual, yet still carefully arranged.

"I'm so glad you were able to do this with me," says Leslie.

"Was I the first person you called?"

"You mean, out of the five of you?" She looks sideways at me, a little pained. "Well, yes, you were the first person. If you hadn't been able to come with me, I may have called someone else. Or maybe I would have come alone. It's hard, being here without any friends around." She glances at me again, and when she does, I catch a glimpse of myself reflected in her aviator-style sunglasses. "But I consider *you* a friend."

I know I'm supposed to say *I think of you as a friend too*, and then I remember all the things they wanted me to say on camera and I never did, so I go ahead and say it. Leslie smiles but keeps looking at the road.

We grab the last open spot in the Walkway parking lot. Before Leslie gets out of the car, she reaches into the backseat and grabs a camera bag along with her purse.

"I'm just going to get some B-roll while we're here. You don't even have to be in the shot. In fact, I don't want you to be. Okay?"

I nod, but can't help feeling disappointed. I'd imagined our walk to be camera-less, but now it's like she's invited along a friend I can't stand.

We walk past some food trucks and a display detailing the origin of the Walkway—how it was an abandoned railroad trestle over the Hudson River until they raised a gajillion dollars to turn it into a pedestrian bridge. Leslie shoots the display for a few seconds, then moves on. We walk a little farther, and once we're out on the bridge, under the wide, clear sky and over the shimmering river, Leslie takes a deep breath.

"Oh, I miss this kind of water," she says, moving to the railing and leaning over.

"You've got the ocean in Los Angeles," I say.

"I don't like waves. They're loud and always seem angry. Plus there's all the *stuff* like seaweed and jellyfish. No, I'm a lake and river kind of girl." She takes out the camera, shoots for about a minute, panning from one side of the river to the other. A commuter train moves along the eastern bank, a silver snake against lush green. "You know, when I was a kid, we had a summer house on one of the Finger Lakes. I waterskied all over that area."

"Where did you grow up?" I ask, trying to remember if that was in her bio.

"Connecticut," she said.

"I know so little about you," I say, "while you know so much about me."

Leslie considers this. "True. What do you want to know?"

153

I think for a moment. "What were you like in high school?"

Something not-so-happy travels across her face. "I was a total jock. Field hockey and volleyball."

"Were you good?"

"Very."

"I totally wouldn't have guessed that, but now that I think about it, it makes a lot of sense."

Leslie smiles now. I didn't mean it as a compliment.

"You probably had a million friends," I add, not wanting this conversation to end.

She laughs. "Hey, that's one of *my* tricks. Asking a question without it being a question." Then she grows suddenly quiet, her forehead falling so easily into the shape of her frown line, and looks down at the camera. "I don't know why I never thought to do this before."

Now she holds up the camera and offers it to me.

"What are you doing?" I ask, even though I totally know what she's doing.

"Here. Take it. You know how to use it?"

She pushes the camera into my hands and my hands accept it. It's actually lighter than it looks.

"I've never used one this big," I say.

"It's not much different than your average home video camera. Except you should use both hands to keep it steady. You see the record button and the one for pause?"

I nod. "Then the T and W for tight and wide? That's for

zooming in and out." She reaches over to close the small LCD display screen that swivels out of the side of the camera. "Use the viewfinder, not the display. The display is easier once you get the hang of things, but I find that the viewfinder is more . . . pure."

I run my thumb over the buttons. "What do you want me to shoot?"

"Me. Ask me that question again about my friends."

I look at the camera, then back to her nodding. She seems really intent on this, almost urgent. Well, okay. I press record and point it at her, then use the viewfinder to frame the shot so there's some hills in the distance over her shoulder.

"You must have had a million friends in high school. . . ." I say.

"My teams and I were tight," replies Leslie, looking uncomfortably at the camera. "But it was actually kind of isolating. Kids who weren't on the teams were too shy to ever talk to me."

"Are you still in touch with them? Your team friends?"

Leslie pauses. "No."

A woman walks into the frame behind Leslie, then realizes she's in our way and moves. But she hovers nearby, curious.

"Really? You don't keep in touch with a single high school friend? Even online or something?"

"No," says Leslie. Even more firmly.

"They don't come find you? Even after the movies were out and you won the Oscar?"

"I went by my middle name in high school, and then I took Lance's last name when we got married."

This is really interesting to me, but it's also interesting how this woman is watching us. She's about my mom's age, with one of those short haircuts that can best be described as *efficient*. Another woman, holding a guide-book, joins her now. They both have purple fanny packs and unnaturally white sneakers.

"Oh," the first woman says in a thick accent when she realizes she's diverted my attention from the camera. "I don't want disturb you. We are walking from that side"— she points to the far side of the river—"to that side. Can you tell us we should go all the way? What is over there?"

"Just some food carts," says Leslie, her face lighting up into helpfulness. I don't press pause on the camera. "There's no real town like there is on the side you came from."

The woman turns to her friend and says something in a language I don't understand. It has sharp edges and catches in her throat. Leslie touches my wrist. When I turn, she points to the camera, then nods toward the women.

I pan over with the camera to get them into frame. It feels really rude. Intrusive. But looking at these women through the viewfinder, their conversation takes on a totally different feel. Like this is a story, somehow. While they're talking, one pulls a guidebook out of her fanny pack and starts flipping through it nervously, front to back, back to front. I press the T button to zoom in on her fingers. It's jerky at first, but then smoother. I zoom out. Back in.

"Okay," says one of the women. "We go back the way we came. Thank you!"

"Good luck with your movie," says the other.

I shoot them as they walk away, talking again in their painful-sounding language. I'd need a throat lozenge all the time if I spoke what they're speaking. They pass a sign that says, "Mental Health Hotline." I zoom in on that. There's a phone receiver hanging on it and some writing. A message for anyone contemplating a bridge jump into the Hudson as a way out.

"When you're shooting," says Leslie, watching me, "you never know what's going to be interesting and what isn't. Sometimes you don't even know until after the fact."

I nod, keeping my eye on the viewfinder. Leslie is trusting me, instructing me. It feels genuine.

We're quiet like this for a bit, until Leslie's cell phone rings. She pulls it from her bag and checks the caller ID. "Hey, babe," she says, then mouths the word *Lance* to me.

I move away from her, closer to the Mental Health Hotline sign so I can read the words on it. "Life Is Worth Living," it says. "There Is Always Hope. Please Call." I don't go so far away, though, that I can't hear her conversation.

"The Walkway is incredible," says Leslie to Lance. "We'll come back when you're feeling better. What's up?"

She paces and listens. I pan across the width of the bridge, shooting whatever I see. A family on bikes. Two men running in tiny tight pants. One woman walking a whole mess of mismatched dogs.

"I don't understand," says Leslie. I look away from the camera at her, and at that exact moment she looks back at me, then moves farther away so I can't hear her anymore.

But I can see her, and I just keep the camera on her, zooming in on her face as she frowns and shakes her head and sighs. It doesn't feel intrusive at all. It's just another story. When she notices me shooting her and turns her back to me, well, that's when the story starts to get good.

After a few minutes, she turns and walks back to me, tucking the phone deep into a pocket of her vest. I keep the camera on her, not ready to look at things without it yet. Her face is sagging like it can't hold the weight of whatever she's thinking about.

"We have to go," she says.

"Bad news?"

She smiles, but sadly. "Hopefully not."

"Will you tell me?"

Leslie winces. "Eventually."

"Why wait?"

She stares out at the river, looking more depressed by the second. "No point in putting it off, I suppose. Let's walk over to the side so we're out of the way."

Yeah, this can't be good.

When we get to the railing, Leslie reaches out and takes the camera from my hands. I force myself to uncurl my fingers, let her reclaim it. She clutches the thing to her chest and gazes at the water, sighing deeply in preparation for something.

"We had a long conference call with our coproducers last night," she finally says, avoiding my glance. "You know, they've seen a lot of the footage so far. We've talked about our general vision for this film."

"You have to have a vision?" I ask. "I thought your vision was as simple as showing people what the five of us are up to now that we're sixteen."

Now she turns and meets my eyes. "Well, there has to be an arc. You start the film at one point and end at another. There's a little high point of drama along the way. And we lucked out with the first two films. There were arcs. For better or worse, they happened naturally. But this time . . ."

"No arc," I say.

"Not yet. We've had some . . . ripples, shall we say. But they're not coming out on their own." Leslie searches the distance again. "I'm sure if we could have extra crews and follow you guys around for months, the stories would emerge. But we don't have those luxuries. And it seems like these ripples only happen when certain people get together. Like that scene with you and Rory, or in the library with Felix and Nate."

I'm starting to see where she's going with this, and it scares me.

"Last night, one of the Independent Eye people suggested the idea of asking the five of you to participate in a special kind of *experience*. Together."

"That sounds gross and sexual," I say.

"Not gross and sexual," says Leslie calmly, and now she reaches into her backpack and pulls out a folded sheet of paper, opens it. "Team-building," she reads. "Self-realizing."

She shoves the paper toward me and I take it.

"Lance called just now to tell me that the head of production loves the idea and is insisting we make it happen."

I unfold the paper. It's a printout from a website. "AIKYA LODGE YOUTH RETREATS," it says, above a photo of a smiling boy and girl holding menacing-looking papier-mâché masks, covered in sticks and feathers. I remember Josh Gordon made one like that in fifth grade art class. They sent a note home to his parents about it.

"I know what you're thinking," says Leslie. "This is not what we're supposed to be about. This is fabricated and fake and not observational documentary at all."

I might have been thinking that.

This is where Leslie starts to lose it. She takes a deep breath and it comes out in short, shuddering bursts. Her eyes well up. "I cried when we hung up from the conference call," she says. "It's that far from what we originally planned. But we're sort of . . . trapped. We need the Independent Eye backing, and we need the distribution. Lance says he agrees with them. Lance says he'd rather make no film at all than a film that doesn't add anything to your stories."

"What do *you* say?"

Leslie pauses and seems to be really putting together an answer for me. "I say, if we have to do this, let's find a way to make it different. Not like some trashy TV show but . . . meaningful."

"And what happens if we don't want to take part?" I ask.

"Honestly? I haven't thought about that yet. I'm hoping I won't have to. And if you agree to do it, you know everyone else will too."

Is that true? Felix will say yes if I do. So will Nate and Rory. That leaves Keira. Why Keira would go anywhere with these guys, let alone to a lodge in the woods, still baffles me. But she keeps showing up when they ask her to.

So. Me. Why am I not repulsed by this idea? Why am I picturing Felix and Rory and Nate and Keira and me at this creepy-sounding Aikya Lodge together, with just the cameras, and not hating it?

"I'm sorry, Justine," says Leslie, dabbing at her eyes with a fingertip.

"You probably should be," I say, forcing a smile. "But I think it's going to be okay."

ELEVEN

Everything happens quickly after that. As predicted, once I agreed to go to the Aikya Lodge, the others did too.

"Whether we want to admit it or not," said Felix about the whole matter, "we're too invested to bail now."

This "experience" is scheduled for the following weekend. We're supposed to arrive on Friday at 5:00 p.m. and get picked up Sunday at 5:00 p.m. The exactness of forty-eight hours is important, somehow. They haven't told us much. They just gave us a list of what to pack.

Dad drives me along the roads that cut what seems to be an excessively winding path up the mountain. We're stuck behind a car that has two bikes strapped to the back, and in front of another with a kayak on its roof. Most people gain this altitude for the sake of fun, but not us.

"Will you call me tomorrow and let me know how it's going?" asks Dad. We've been silent up until now.

"We had to leave our cell phones at home," I say. "But if you want, I can ask Lance or Leslie to report in."

My father considers that for a moment. "No, that's okay. I don't want to be a pain. As long as there's a way for you to reach us." He glances at me. "You seem rather non-resistant about all this."

"Is nonresistance the same as acceptance?" I ask. "Because that's how I see it. I'm accepting. You signed away my life ten years ago. I have to make the best of it."

He takes his eyes off the car in front of us for just a second, so he can get a confused look at me, then turns back. I guess it's not fair I brought this up while he's driving. "Is that really how you feel?"

"Yes. No. I'm not sure."

"Well, damn," he says, his voice growing soft.

"I understand that you didn't really know what it would mean."

"Why?" he asks slowly. "What does it mean?"

I shrug. "That it would change me. That instead of my life shaping a film, a film would shape my life."

164

Dad is quiet and I can see him swallow hard. After a few seconds he says, "We didn't consider that. But I guess this time around, I've noticed. I just didn't notice that I was noticing."

My dad. The pediatrician who can tell in an instant if a kid has, like, lactose intolerance, but can't see that a decision he made a decade ago has altered his own child forever.

"I'm sorry for that," he continues. "But let me ask you this. If you could, knowing what you do now, would you undo it? Would you time-travel and stop us from signing that first contract?"

The line of cars has slowed, as it always does leading up to the state park entrance, and my mind slows with it. That is a truly excellent question he's asked me. I can't answer it lightly.

"I'll let you know after the weekend," I finally say, and he laughs.

After we pass the park, the other cars have peeled off and we're on our own, pointed ever-so-slightly downhill now as we reach the other side of the ridge.

"There. That's it," I say. Nailed to a tree up ahead is a wooden sign that reads "AIKYA LODGE" in letters so ornate, you'd have no idea what they said if you didn't already know. Dad turns down the road, which very quickly goes from paved to pebbles to dirt. Another minute and we pull up to the lodge. It's all wood and looks like something you'd see in Frontierland at Disney World. I'm instantly suspicious.

"Nice," Dad says. Lance and Leslie's SUV is already parked there, along with another car I don't recognize. We get out of the car and I pull my backpack from the trunk.

"I'd like to walk you in," he says. "Is that allowed?"

"I'm allowing it," I say, and smile at him to let him know the conversation we just had made a difference. We walk up the steps to the wraparound porch and a pair of oversize double doors. Ridiculously oversize, like giants live here.

The door opens and a woman steps out onto the porch, her face eager, expectant. She's willowy tall and wears a T-shirt with a long denim skirt. It's been a while since I saw someone pull off a long denim skirt like that, and I have a feeling this person will be impressive.

"Hello, there! You must be Justine! I'm Pam." She doesn't look like a Pam. "I'll be leading the workshop." We shake hands and hers is bony, ice cold. She does the same with my dad and then ushers us into the foyer of the house.

The first thing I see, to the left off the foyer, is a huge room with an enormous stone fireplace, reaching to the top of a cathedral ceiling. Three low, almost shapeless couches form a semicircle across from the fireplace, and a large Oriental rug covers the floor in the space between.

"Just put your bag down here," says Pam, pointing to the base of a staircase. "I'll show you to your room in a minute."

"Are we the first ones?" I ask.

"Everyone else is in the kitchen."

And now I can hear the *vump-vump vump* of something being chopped, and a clang of metal utensils. Pam brings us through the fireplace room and into the biggest kitchen I've ever seen. It seems built for Paul Bunyan, if Paul Bunyan watched a lot of Food Network shows and really loved to cook.

Nate and Keira stand at the massive kitchen island, cutting vegetables. Rory is stirring something at a six-burner stove. Lance floats nearby with the camera, and Kenny holds the boom mic in between two stained glass chandeliers hanging from the ceiling.

Leslie stands in the corner, biting her pinky nail.

"And here's Justine," says Pam, introducing me onto this very strange stage.

Leslie comes over and gives me a hug, touching her cheek to mine for a long second, not saying a word.

"This is my favorite icebreaker," says Pam. "Putting people to work in the kitchen together. Together, we're making stew. Together, we will eat it." I have a feeling she says this word, *together*, more than will be humanly tolerable.

Nate and Keira look up briefly at me, then back down,

and I see that the food-prep is a good way to avoid making eye contact. Rory glances up in my direction and actually meets my father's eyes. He smiles at her and she smiles at him, ever so briefly, before turning back to the stove.

I feel Dad's hand on my shoulder. "Everything good here?" he asks softly.

"You can go. I'll see you on Sunday."

"I would say have fun, but I have a feeling that's not quite appropriate." He rumples my hair, probably wanting to kiss me on the cheek but also not wanting to embarrass me, and then he's gone, back through the great room. I hear the front door open, then close.

Turning back to Leslie, I ask, "Felix not here yet?"

"Running late, apparently," says Leslie. "Let's get you settled in."

She takes my hand and leads me back toward the foyer, and I catch a glimpse of Pam giving Leslie a dirty look. I can already see the friction: two women, both with agendas to follow. This might end up being really fantastic.

Upstairs, there's just one long hallway with several doors. We turn into the second one, which is a smallish room with two sets of bunk beds and one tall faux-rustic wooden dresser with four drawers. "The girls are in here. You and Rory and Keira."

"We're sharing?"

"Part of the workshop."

This had totally not occurred to me, that I might be

sharing a room with two people who dislike me. Was that in the brochure? Could that have been on the packing list, under *comfortable pants* and *slippers*, a note along the lines of, *Be prepared not to sleep because you'll feel the hostility of your bunkmates thick in the air like humidity?* Also, maybe they could have added some practical tips like: *Bring some Beano in case you have gas during the night and don't want anyone to hear.*

There's a large but sleek black leather bag on one of the lower beds. Surely Keira's. On the other, a stuffed brown and white horse rests against the pillow. Misty! Rory's horse. Rory's horse, which I know so well, and the sight of it would fill me with a long unspooling of memories, if it weren't looking at me suspiciously.

"I guess I'm on top somewhere." I look at Leslie. "Where are you sleeping?"

"Down the hall, with Lance. I have to sleep on a top bunk too, if it makes you feel any better."

"Nate and Felix?"

"Right there." She points to the door across the hall.

"Just the two of them?"

"Uh-huh." She looks at me nervously. So she knows how epically unhappy Felix will be about this. Then Leslie lights up with a smile, turned on like a switch, and chirps, "Can you believe Kenny gets a whole bunk room to himself?"

* * *

169

I know it's hard to screw up the process of taking a fresh loaf out of a bread maker and slicing it, but damn if this isn't the best bread-slicing job I've ever done. The pieces are perfectly shaped. I'm not sure people are sufficiently appreciating that, as they grab theirs and dip them into the stew. *The stew!* That's all we can talk about, because it keeps us from having to talk about anything else.

"Exactly the kind of meal you should eat at a big wooden table," says Felix. His dad's pickup truck deposited him and his keyboard a few minutes before the food was ready, and Felix only had time to mumble apologies about a problem at the farm before sliding into a seat. He has not yet been upstairs.

Lance, Leslie, and Kenny have postponed their stew enjoyment so they can shoot us eating.

The table is round and, again, mammoth-sized. So much that we're able to spread out and it feels like we're not actually sitting next to anybody but just vaguely sharing a universe with them.

"Usually, there's more people eating here, right?" I ask Pam.

"Yes. Our standard group is about a dozen. Then I have a coleader here."

Silence. This is where we'd all check our cell phones, if we had them. I'm already feeling the tug of something missing, like a phantom limb, and I'm sure everyone else is too. Keira keeps reaching for the front pocket of her jeans, then stopping herself. But there's a decent chance the outside world is, in fact, still there and surviving without us.

"This is a good time for me to go over what we'll be doing during the next twelve hours or so. I don't like to plan further than that."

More silence. We're even chewing quietly. It's driving me crazy and yet, I'm doing it too.

"After dinner, we'll wash up, then build a campfire out back for a facilitated activity. Then bedtime, because we'll be up early for breakfast and an outdoor excursion."

"Outdoor excursion?" asks Nate. "Is that a fancy word for a hike?"

"It's a fancy word for bouldering, if you must know."

"Cool," he says with a grin. "I like bouldering." None of us agrees with him.

"After that," continues Pam, "well, we'll cover it when the time comes."

"Aikya Lodge," says Keira randomly. "It sounds Japanese."

"It's Sanskrit," says Rory, her mouth full of bread. "I looked it up."

"That's right," replies Pam. "It means *unity*."

Dead air again. Pam looks to Leslie.

"Pam," says Leslie, "why don't you tell us about your background and how you started the retreats. This is a more natural setting than an interview later."

Pam nods and seems relieved. The story of her life is more detailed and less interesting than I imagined, but it fills up the rest of dinnertime. I play my part, listening carefully while wishing I were somewhere else—in the Bahamas, perhaps, or getting a root canal.

When we're all done eating, we clear our own plates and Pam asks Rory and me to do the dishes together at one sink, Felix and Keira at the other. Nate gets to wipe down and sweep up.

The routine of the dishes task—she washes, I dry— keeps Rory and me focused on something other than the awkwardness between us, and I wonder if that's part of the plan. We don't even have to talk, but I can't help myself.

"You brought Misty," I say, as she hands me a dish. I enfold it in a towel, gently, because these dishes look expensive. I don't want her to think I'm making fun of her, so I add, "It was cool to see her again. She looks pretty good."

"She got restuffed recently," says Rory in her deadpan. "And washed. And her eye fixed." She stops washing for a moment, then glances sideways at me and starts again. "Did you bring Angel Dog?"

Ah. Angel Dog is a black stuffed poodle wearing a fairy costume that I won at the county fair one year. My dad paid off the carnie at the Clown Head Water Balloon race so it was only him and me playing, and he let me win, and I pretended I didn't know that. Rory was with us, and within minutes she had planned out an elaborate future for our favorite stuffed animals. Angel Dog and Misty were going to shack up in a purple castle somewhere and have androgynous horse-dog babies. Once, I suggested that Angel Dog may not be down with interspecies romance, and Rory freaked out about that. I had questioned her vision, and she couldn't deal; it was a pattern that had repeated itself so many times during the course of our friendship.

"No," I say. I don't add that Angel Dog is lost-on-purpose somewhere in our basement playroom.

Rory is silent and still for a moment, staring warmly at the dish in her hand. "That's a shame," she finally says, and resumes her washing. "It would have been good to see him again too."

I look up and see the boom mic hovering above us, and the camera, which has caught this whole exchange. Leslie is not biting her pinky nail anymore.

TWELVE

A re you kidding me?" asks Felix, standing outside his room, still holding his backpack and keyboard case. I've accompanied him up along with Pam, Leslie, and Lance, but the others are downstairs. "Nobody told us about this!"

"This is part of the program," says Pam. "Besides, we don't have the space to give everyone a private room. Kenny and I each have one and that's only by default."

"Can I share with Kenny?" says Felix, brightening, ignoring the irony that it would be less awkward for him to share a room with Kenny than with Nate. I look over at

Lance, who clearly wants to help talk Felix down but also doesn't want to stop the camera for even a second.

"Just by virtue of this objection," Pam says evenly, "I'm thinking that it's important for you and Nate to share a room. This is why we're here. You don't have to talk to each other. You just have to sleep. Share some space."

Something occurs to me and I turn to Leslie. "Are you guys going to shoot in the rooms?"

Leslie looks at Felix, who returns the look imploringly, and says, "No. Not tonight at least. Tomorrow, maybe, for just a few minutes. If everyone's okay with it."

"If everyone hasn't left by then," mumbles Felix, and he picks up his bags.

"Keep your keyboard for now," says Leslie. "We'd like you to have it at the campfire."

Felix's reaction starts off as a glare, then morphs into a caged-animal thing. Like he wants to heave the keyboard case at someone's head but knows he shouldn't. So now, he just nods, tosses his backpack into the room, closes the door, and walks way too slowly downstairs with his keyboard.

Nate, Keira, and Rory are waiting on the couches in the living room, and even with the size of the house, I'm sure they've heard everything. Nate stares at the ceiling when Felix walks in but lowers his eyes when I enter. Those eyes, so deep green, meet mine and hold me there for a second. There's something in them that looks and feels achingly familiar. Something personal. A memory, maybe.

Or a reflection.

A few dozen yards from the house is the campfire ring, a small circle of small stones inside a larger circle of larger stones. Low canvas chairs fill the space between the two circles.

"Wood's over there," says Pam, pointing to a shed. "Who knows how to build a fire?"

We're bundled up in jackets, hats, gloves. It's chillier than I expected, on the mountain at night in May. I'm just hoping there will be marshmallows involved at some point.

Felix walks to the shed, grabs as many pieces of wood as he can, then glances back at Nate, the only other guy here who doesn't already have something in his hands. Nate takes the cue and goes to the shed. Felix steps aside just as Nate gets there. Now Keira moves in behind Nate to get some wood, and I feel lame so I follow suit. Rory just bends down and pets one of the rocks.

"Are these naturally shaped like this?" she asks nobody.

Then Felix is directing us to put the wood in certain configurations, and I can see that Nate sort of has his own ideas but is afraid to contradict him. Leslie, Lance, and Kenny get to stand in the background, not helping. Observing. Leslie's got her camera and is shooting us from a different angle. Pam is arranging the chairs, taking away all but six of them, moving them closer together so they're clustered around one side of the ring.

"Lighter?" asks Felix proudly. We've made a pile of wood that seems intricate yet haphazard. Pam hands him a box of matches and he snickers. "Of course. This is not a Cortez family bonfire."

"Just be glad we don't have to rub two sticks together," I say.

Pretty soon, the fire is going. Pam has grabbed the middle chair and I score the one next to her. Felix sits next to me and I feel padded. And now, the heat from the flames drifts toward me, the smell that is family camping trips from before my parents split up, and Girl Scouts from when I was enthusiastic about things. Through the flames, I see Nate's face on the other side of our *C* of canvas chairs, deep orange reflected on his cheeks and hair.

We all stare at the fire for a while. It's hypnotic and, again, keeps us from making eye contact.

"What is it about a campfire?" asks Pam, and I recognize that teachery way of asking a question that's crafted to sound like she's just wondering. But she's not wondering. She knows exactly what she wants to hear.

"Warm," says Felix at the same time that Keira says,

"Beautiful," and they exchange a quick, embarrassed glance.

Leslie moves around the circle with her camera, while Lance and Kenny stay put behind Pam.

"Universal," says Pam. "I like to think a fire connects us to our history as humans. Our ancestors needed it so they wouldn't die of cold, so they could cook their meat. We don't need it for that anymore, but we're still drawn. So I'd like to ask you each to share a memory of fire. It can be anything."

There's a pause, and then Rory says, her voice clear and even, "When I was eight, my next-door neighbor's house burned down."

Nate turns to her. "I remember that. The Schneiders, right?"

"They were so mean to me. I was glad they had to move."

Now it's Nate's turn to talk about when they burn brush at the farm, and then Keira mentions reading in front of the fireplace. Felix recalls the fire-eaters at the circus, which seems a little forced, like he's trying to come up with something different from the others. When everyone's spoken but me, I've had enough time to decide on the most interesting fire memory I've got: the time Olivia taught me how to put out a match with my fingers, but purposely left out the part where you lick them, so when I tried it, I got burned.

"Literally and figuratively," I say, and everyone laughs, and this makes me happier than I care to show.

"Okay," says Pam after we all settle again. "I've got an activity I want us to do together. It's one of my favorites. I'd like each of you to think of one true fact about yourself, and then one lie. The rest of us will try to guess which is which." She pauses dramatically, as if we're supposed to react, but nobody does. "Don't be obvious."

"So we're trying to trick one another?" asks Keira.

"Not trick. Just . . . challenge. Maybe surprise." Pam looks at Nate. "Even if someone knows you very well, try to come up with something they won't figure out easily."

I've got a question: "Does it have to be something profound, or really any kind of information, like *I'm wearing day-of-the-week underwear?*"

Pam laughs, but it sounds more charitable than genuine. "I suppose the fact could be as big or as small as you're comfortable with. But that's not necessarily the idea."

The fire crackles. No one volunteers to go first.

"I don't call on people," says Pam, "unless I absolutely have to."

I'm kind of curious to see what *absolutely have to* looks like, but Felix pipes up. "I've got one." He pauses. "I hate Milk Duds. I think they're slimy and disgusting. And, um . . . I personally wrote a bunch of online user encyclopedia entries for the *Six* and *Eleven* movies.

Rory, fascinated, asks, "Is that true?"

"You tell me," replies Felix, lifting his eyebrows.

"Oh . . ." she says. "Hmmm."

"I can't believe anyone hates Milk Duds," says Nate. "If you could chew happiness and get it stuck in your teeth, it would taste like that."

I happen to know Felix loves Milk Duds, and if Nate remembers too, he doesn't let on. Rory and Keira vote that the truth is the Milk Duds thing, and Nate votes for the online encyclopedia. I do too, although I feel like I'm cheating. The encyclopedia is news to me but makes perfect Felix-sense.

When it's time to reveal the answer, Felix just says to Lance and Leslie with raised eyebrows: "You guys should probably be thanking me. I corrected a lot of wrong information on those pages." They don't look like they want to thank him.

"Felix," says Pam. "I like how the truth you came up with is something to do with the bond you all share." Felix looks at the ground. For someone so desperate for approval, he's not good with compliments. "Okay. Who's next?"

Keira holds up one long finger, and Pam nods at her. She stares into the fire for a few moments and then says, "I like to pretend I have migraines. Sometimes I'll do it at school when I need a break, and I make sure the nurse tells my dad. Because my mother used to get them all the time and I know he's afraid I might have the same, uh, issues as her. It's like a little weapon for me, for when I'm mad at him for pressuring me into something."

This sounds alarming and she must realize that, because she quickly adds: "For instance, agreeing to do this film, just so we could show the world how *okay* we have been." She stops, then starts again. "Also, my girlfriends are like sisters to me and I would never, ever think of them as total bitches."

Keira says all this matter-of-factly, almost reciting it while gazing at the flames. My eyes go to Nate, who is regarding her with protective worry, but there's something off about it. It's not even brotherly. It's more . . . paternal.

I'm guessing we're all taking a moment to process the same thing here, that Keira has sneakily told us two very personal truths and zero lies. No earths have been shattered by the revelation that Keira thinks her friends are bitches, because they are, but it's a relief to hear she agrees.

"I'm sorry you feel that way about your friends," says Rory. Nobody is doing the voting thing.

I'm focused on the irony of the headache fact. It's the flip side of my situation, but feels strangely similar.

"I still get stomach cramps all the time," I say suddenly, forgetting that we were supposed to guess at

Keira's statements or whose turn it might be next. "I hide them from my parents. So you and I, we're kind of like opposites."

Now, Keira's eyes unlock from the fire and shift to me. To mine. In an instant she's the same Keira she was five minutes ago, but also the Keira I remember from kindergarten, and a totally new and unfamiliar Keira as well. One with a dark side.

I guess we all find our little ways to stay in control.

Keira seems about to speak to me, *to me*, her face soft and her jaw slack, when Rory says, "You have to say a second thing, Justine."

Everyone else is looking at me expectantly. "Okay. Um. I am, in fact, wearing day-of-the-week underwear. But just to be a rebel about it, I never wear the right day."

The other kids and the crew laugh. Again, it makes me so happy. This time I'm not afraid to show it.

Pam, however, sighs and actually rolls her eyes, which seems very un-Pamlike. "This would be a really great activity if you'd take it seriously."

"*I* took it seriously," says Felix.

"Me too," adds Rory.

"I know you did," says Pam.

"It's late," says Leslie, finally piping up. "They've been at school all day. Why don't we try again tomorrow, now that we've all got the hang of it? Nate and Rory, you don't mind, do you? You didn't get a turn."

Nate and Rory shrug. Pam gives Leslie a sharp glance. Leslie sees that glance, and raises it one proprietary suggestion. "But I would like to wrap tonight with Felix doing a song. It's a campfire and all, and he did lug his keyboard all the way out here. Felix, that still cool?"

Felix nods, but not with the enthusiasm I would have expected from him at this request. Nobody ever *asks* Felix to sing, even if this isn't an ideal situation. Still, he takes the keyboard out of its case, rests it on his lap in the canvas chair. Turns it on. Waits for Leslie to find a good spot with the second camera and finally takes his cue.

He plays into the night and I learn something else: When you're outside on a mountain with nothing but infinite sky and stars and rising campfire smoke above you, when you're in a situation where everything is screwed up but also seems utterly natural, even Felix's hesitant chord changes and reedy vocals sound exquisite.

I'm sitting with Felix on one of the couches in the great room. Nate, Keira, and Rory have gone upstairs. My skin, clothes, and hair smell like campfire and I can't stop sniffing them.

"I'm counting to five hundred," says Felix. "That should give Nate enough time to get settled into bed."

"I may have to go to a thousand," I say. "You know. Girls."

We're silent for a moment, listening to the shuffling sounds coming through the ceiling. The back door opens, then footsteps through the kitchen and into the great room. Pam.

"You two okay?" she asks, taking off her jacket.

"That's a relative term at the moment," says Felix.

Pam laughs. "This will sound cruel, but that's actually the kind of reaction I like to get."

She gets paid to make people uncomfortable, to force them to do and say things they don't want to do or say. The people are supposed to be glad about this. It seems like a line of work worth pursuing.

"We do have a strict lights-out policy here," says Pam, removing a notebook and pen from her jacket before hanging it on a hook in the foyer. "So how about, five minutes and you guys are in your rooms? It'll be an early start tomorrow."

Felix and I just nod, then watch her climb the stairs, her notebook and pen tucked under one arm. We sit in total silence now, Felix running his finger in strange patterns on the couch, making the microsuede change grain back and forth. I pick at a mysterious scab-dot on the back of my left hand. Gradually, the shuffles from upstairs die down, and then we hear Pam call from the top of the stairs, "It's time," and we rise.

Once we're up in the hallway, I hug Felix goodnight and watch him disappear into his room. When I open my own door, the room is only half-dark. Rory is in bed, clutching Misty and reading with a flashlight. Keira's bed is empty. The bathroom too.

"Where's Keira?" I ask Rory.

"Not sure," she says, not looking up.

I grab my sweatshirt and pajama bottoms out of my backpack, along with my toiletry case, and disappear into the bathroom. Once I'm changed and washed up, I return to find Rory's eyes closed, her mouth open, the flashlight still on but rolled down into the bed so it's shining on her face and looks very dramatic. I watch her for a moment. *I can stare at her right now. I can really stare.*

Her features have changed a bit since our sleepovers, the nose longer and chin pointier. Those nights when we whispered in the dark until one of us passed out first and it was always her. "I'm not asleep," she says suddenly, not opening her eyes. Scaring the shit out of me.

"Okay," I say.

"Why are you standing there? Are you watching me?" Eyes still closed.

I don't know what to say to this, so I just turn around and leave the room, mortified.

I hear murmurs down the hall and light glows from under the door of Lance and Leslie's room. Where is Pam and her lights-out policy enforcement? I inch closer, floating heel to toe on the wood floor, mentally chanting *no creak no creak no creak.*

The murmurs are a little clearer now. I press my ear to the wall.

"That's all we could find so far, and we're not sure she still lives there," Lance is saying softly.

"But you must have a cell phone number or something!" It's Keira's voice.

"It's not that easy." Leslie.

There's a pause. "But you'll check out the address?"

"We told you we would, and we will." Lance again.

Suddenly there is movement in the room and I panic, darting back down the hallway and through my door. I hear another door open, then close, then footsteps. Within moments I'm up on a top bunk, burrowing under the covers like something small and hunted.

Keira enters the room quickly but then freezes, switches gears to close the door slowly and silently. She moves to the bed and climbs in, and it shakes a bit. This is when I realize that in my haste I've chosen the bunk above hers, and wonder what she'll think of that.

We told you we would, and we will.

It all makes sense now. Keira agreeing to do this film. Agreeing to do whatever they asked of her, in exchange for something.

She's lying underneath me, and I listen to her turn over and sigh. It's like her pissed-off energy is radiating upward and then there's the weirdness of her knowing I picked her bunk, and the extra weirdness of my

187

knowing her knowing. I don't think there's any way I'll sleep.

But it's been a long day. Eventually, I'm dreaming that Felix has just told me he's leaving to play keyboards on tour with Michael Jackson in heaven, and I'm begging him not to go.

When I open my eyes to a streak of unfamiliar light on the ceiling above me, I have no idea where the hell I am. Someone is knocking hard somewhere. The door.

To the room I'm in. With Keira and Rory. At Aikya Lodge and oh yeah, life blows.

"Time to get up!" Pam's voice. "Everyone dressed and in the kitchen for breakfast in fifteen minutes! Comfortable clothes and sneakers, please!"

From across the hall, we hear a loud yawn from one of the guys, a roar that's got the funny of a monkey and the scary of a lion, and it goes on way longer than you'd think possible. I bust out laughing.

"That's funny?" asks Rory, sitting up and looking at me. "Yes."

She nods and then, staring across at Keira's bed, frowns. Glances up at the bathroom door, which is open.

"Keira's already up," she says.

I peer over the edge of my bed to verify. "That figures," I say.

188

I climb down and after Rory has retrieved her clothes from her drawer, I grab mine and move into a corner, turning my back to her. I glance over my shoulder to see that Rory is standing naked in the middle of the room, slowly getting dressed.

Downstairs, Lance, Leslie, Kenny, and Pam have already eaten breakfast, which is oatmeal and fruit and eggs and bagels. Lance has a camera on the tripod in the corner.

"Load up," says Pam. "You'll need the energy."

Nate comes down next, his hair uncombed, his eyes shaped differently than usual. He's wearing his swim team sweatshirt and olive green cargo pants and black work boots, like a recruit for the prepster army.

After another minute, Felix appears. He looks even less rested than Nate.

"Is Keira on her way?" asks Pam.

"I thought she was already down here," I say, scanning the room again to be sure. No Keira.

Pam plunks her coffee mug on the counter and marches through the great room, then up the stairs, calling Keira's name. It echoes through the house. *Keira? Keira? Hello? Keira?*

Now Pam is downstairs again, pulling on her jacket and opening the front door. Lance and Leslie look at each other, a little bit of panic. Lance moves to the camera

189

and takes it off the tripod. He's got a perfect shot as Pam comes back inside, moves quickly into the room, her face completely drained. She looks right at Leslie, then takes a deep breath and delivers news.

"Your car. Is gone."

THIRTEEN

Turns out, Lance is a pacer. I wouldn't have guessed that.

He's treading the wide planks of the kitchen floor back and forth, back and forth, while he scratches the same spot on the back of his head. It all seems a little overdramatic. Maybe he thinks that if he keeps moving, he won't feel like such an idiot.

Because during the night, Keira managed to sneak into their room and steal their car keys, both cell phones, and Leslie's wallet.

I'm a little shocked and a lot—so much that I can't even contain it—impressed.

"Who'd have thought?" I say now to Felix. We're sitting on a bench on the front porch. It's warm, so the door is open and we can hear everything that's going on at the back of the house. Rory sits on the steps in front of us, reading. We've been rather forgotten at the moment. It feels like a wide crushing pressure has been lifted off my chest, and the sun is shining and this weekend is turning into something pretty terrific.

Felix has his keyboard on his lap and plays a few random, distracted chords in a melancholy key. "Keira's always had a lot going on below the surface."

"Yes," says a voice to our left, and I turn to see that Nate has stepped onto the porch. As the resident expert on the subject in question, he had been asked to remain in the Holy Shit Keira Is Gone headquarters. Here, the light hits his face but doesn't brighten it; it's drop-shadowed with worry. "She does have a lot going on."

"Any news?" I ask.

Nate shrugs and leans against the porch railing, facing us but focused on the side of the house above our heads. "They finally got ahold of her dad. He said he had a voice mail message from her, telling him she was okay and she wanted to be left alone for a day or two, and to ask that nobody come find her unless they hadn't heard back from her by Sunday night."

"That sounds incredibly thought out," I say.

"That's Keira," says Nate. "She plans."

192

"Did she say anything to you about where she was going?"

"No," he says, his head drooping. "But Leslie said something cryptic about knowing where she might have been headed."

I've been thinking about the conversation I heard last night, trying to make sense of it. It sits like a tiny sparkling something in an inside pocket of my jacket, and I need to show it off.

"They had some kind of information for her," I finally say.

Nate's head snaps back up and looks straight at me like suddenly, miraculously, I matter. "What do you mean?" he asks.

"She was in Lance and Leslie's room last night, and I overheard her talking to them about finding an address for someone, and she was pissed."

"Her mom," says Nate after a pause.

"I figured."

He thinks about that for a moment, then shakes his head with I should have known heaviness. We're all quiet again. Rory has stopped reading and is staring out at the woods. Felix has stopped trying to find the world's saddest chord. From inside the house, Leslie's voice is rising and Lance's voice is rising with it, and it sounds like they're performing a bad operetta.

Finally, I can't stand the silence so I state the obvious.

"Keira went to find her mother."

"It would seem," says Nate.

"When was the last time they saw each other?"

"Not since, you know, that day. But Keira told me she'd gotten a few letters from her, over the years. Nobody was even sure where she was living these days."

"If Keira's driving to the last address, it can't be too far away."

"True," says Nate, who seems microscopically comforted by this idea.

"I bet it's killing L and L that they can't go along and shoot," I add.

Nate puts his head in his hands. Felix and Rory continue to say nothing. I try to see what this means for the rest of us and keep talking. "If she doesn't want help, if she's got money and transportation and a way to get in touch, then why are we worried about her? We can go home and the rest of our weekend is saved, and we'll hear about it all later."

Nate shakes his head. "But if she does find her mom, who knows how that will go down. And then she's alone. . . ." He pauses, maybe playing out a mental scenario, then adds, forcefully, "I have to find out where she went." And I realize he's in love with her. They may not be a "couple" or public about it and maybe she doesn't even feel the same way, but it's like a title card with big red letters inserted into the scene: *KEIRA*

MEANS THE WORLD TO NATE.

I keep returning to the facts. They're all I can offer. "Lance and Leslie know where she went. They gave her whatever info she has."

Now Nate gives me this look of pure *duh*. "They'll tell us."

"I wouldn't bet on it."

"That's right," says Rory, now standing up to join us. "They won't tell us. They're going to make us stay here and talk about what happened, and then we'll still have to do the bouldering thing, which will actually be easier now because there's an even number."

"How do you know this?" asks Nate.

"Because while you guys have been talking, I've been listening to every word they're saying in there."

We all freeze and listen. It's just murmurs now.

"Wait for it," adds Rory. "They'll be out here in a second."

So we do. And they are.

Pam looks paler, if that's even possible. Leslie's eyes are red and she's clearly been crying, and although this thing has seemed mostly amusing to me so far, it hits me how this must hurt her. How she must really care about Keira and maybe even about all of us. It's very possible that she's a much nicer person than I am.

"Hi, guys," she whispers, her voice catching, and Nate does something unexpected: he wraps her in a hug.

Lance, who's holding the camera, regards them with something that's half-jealousy, half-remorse, like *Well, shit, I should have thought about hugging my own wife.* But then he snaps out of it and says: "The thing about making a documentary film is that these things happen, and you can see them as a setback, or you can see them as a kind of gift." Leslie and Nate both give him a dirty look and he adds, "Assuming, of course, that nobody gets harmed."

"So you still want us to do the bouldering," I say, as if I'm so smart that I already figured that out and did not benefit from Rory's mutant eavesdropping skills.

It's Pam who answers. "Yes, we do. It'll be a little different than I originally planned, because now there's just four of you, and we can break into two teams."

"In the meantime, we'd like to talk to you about Keira leaving," says Lance.

On cue, Kenny steps out onto the porch with the boom mic. It's all so seamless, I wonder for the blink of a second if this was set up and they asked Keira to leave. Right now nothing seems impossible.

"Can I go in and grab my sunscreen first?" I ask, and don't wait for an answer before darting inside and upstairs. I walk into my room—the girls' room—and sit on Keira's bed. She was here, thinking. Fuming. Planning. The dark and the quiet, making everything seem worse than they really are because they always do. How she was sleeping in a room with two girls she's known for ten years but doesn't know at all, and maybe felt more alone than she possibly could have anywhere else.

Nate's voice in my head. *I have to find out where she went.*

Keira's face now. Her face from that scene five years ago, of pure and open devastation. Then her face at the campfire. A face that is secrets and hiding and total fear that anyone will find out what you are really thinking and who you really are.

And maybe there's some kind of brilliant-plan mojo coming off Keira's bunk, because suddenly I have one.

The boulders waiting to be bouldered lie just a mile into the woods, a medium-size rockface set into a steep hill. It's a pretty spot even if it does make me think of Ian. Nearby, we can hear a creek rushing and a waterfall.

"I had no idea it was going to be this loud," says Lance. "We'll have to mic them two at a time."

"That's fine," says Pam, removing the crash pad strapped to her back and laying it on the ground. "Because they're going to climb two at a time." She motions to a little circle of logs I hadn't noticed yet, and we take that as our cue to sit. Felix and I share one, and I enjoy watching Nate decide whether or not he's going to share with Rory or find a spot on his own. Without Keira here he seems floating, untethered. After a few awkward moments, he sits next to Rory. I like this pairing. For the purposes of the film, it will be interesting. Not that I'm thinking about the purposes of the film.

Once Lance and Kenny have chosen a spot, Leslie again shooting the second camera, Pam continues.

"This is my favorite part of the programs I do," she says, looking up at the trees. "Climbing a rock seems like such a simple, even silly thing to do. Why do it? Isn't that for little kids? We'll talk more afterward but for now, let me say that this activity is all about teammates being conscious of each other. There's no winning or losing. There's just . . . doing."

"Winning and losing not there is," says Felix in his Yoda voice. "Doing, there is just."

A burst of cackling laughter from Rory. No doubt in her mind about *that* being funny.

Pam smiles too, and then says, "Rory, why don't you partner with Felix?" She looks at me. "And Justine, you'll be with Nate."

What? No. That's not right. I need to be with Felix. *Felix.* So I can talk to him about my idea.

I glance over to Leslie, who meets it with a raised eyebrow and a sideways smile. Dammit.

"Who wants to start us off?" asks Pam, and Nate holds up a finger like Keira did last night. Before I know it, Kenny is coming at me with a lavalier mic and I'm avoiding looking at Nate and now we're at the base of the rock and Pam is talking again and the camera is rolling.

"I call this Plus One. One of you climbs first, maybe four moves up the rock. The other one has to watch exactly where the footholds and handholds are. Then it's that person's turn to climb the same sequence, but you're going to add one more. Then the first person goes again, and adds one to that. You have to pick a move that you know the other person can do. Help each other, remind each other of the sequence. The goal is for both of you to make it to the top with the sequence you've come up with together." She turns to Felix and Rory. "Now, you two need to go someplace where you can't see them. We don't want you using the same moves when it's your turn."

Felix and Rory glance awkwardly at each other for a moment, then Felix motions Rory in a direction away from us. They quickly disappear into the greenery.

Nate does some swimming-type stretches, circling his arms so he looks like a little boy pretending to be a helicopter, then bends back the palm of each hand. I assume this means he's going first. And now he looks right at me with those green eyes.

"How easy do I have to be?" he asks.

Totally insulted and not thinking straight, I say, "Not easy at all. I've done this." At day camp, years ago.

He nods, and I wonder what I've set myself up for.

Nate hoists himself onto the face, putting a foot not on the obvious first hold, so prominent it's like the rock has a front stoop, but rather a few inches higher in a small bump. And I watch him.

He climbs until he's put his hands or feet in three more places, then turns and says, "Got that?"

"Yep," I say, although I've never said "yep" like that in my life.

Instead of climbing down, he launches himself off the face of the rock and into the crash pad. Stands up, dusts himself off. It's my turn to go.

"Put your right hand over there," he says.

I look down and snap, "You don't have to say anything until I ask you to."

"Okay, okay. Just trying to help." He holds up his hands in defense and starts backing away.

Next move. I close my eyes and see it in my head. Then I put myself there. The next one is harder. I have to stretch one hand all the way out to my right, even though there's a hold closer than the one Nate used. His arm is longer. That didn't occur to him. I take a moment to figure out how I'm going to make it work, and out of the corner of my eye I see movement. The crew changing position, getting closer. Fantastic.

I will be damned if I don't reach this. Not on my first turn.

And somehow I become more elastic and make myself long and my fingers touch the edge of the hold and then my palm is there and I've grabbed it. It's just a tiny little bump in the rock, but I grip it like a lifeline.

"Yes!" says Nate, and I jerk my head down to look at him. He seems surprised by his own positive encouragement.

The other three moves are easier. I pick my fifth move, the move Nate will have to replicate. I decide to get him back by adding a foothold that's actually a little too close to the one I'm already on. It's a little tricky for me, but it might set him off-balance.

"Awesome work, Justine!" says Pam. "Can you jump down?"

If he did it, I can do it. And I do. The letting go is the hardest part. The landing is soft and actually fun.

When Nate gets back on the rock, he has trouble remembering the second and third moves so I talk him up the rest of the sequence. He doesn't complain; surprisingly, he just accepts my help, then adds another move that I can barely see since he's almost at the top already. When he falls back down to the pad, he lands a bit wrong and lets out an "Oof."

"You okay?" I ask.

"Side impact," he mutters, then looks up at me from the pad and grins.

When I'm on the rock, I have no trouble with the first three moves and then my mind goes blank. I just look at him, and he tells me where to go next. By the time I get to my add-on move, I'm practically at the top. All it takes is one well-chosen grab at the ledge and I'm up. I will do this.

"Yes!" shouts Nate when I finally grip a hold and pull myself to the rock's "summit." I look down to see Nate pumping his fist, Pam beaming, both camera lenses staring up at me with their gaping, empty eyes. Now Nate has to make it up the rock with no help from me below, and he does. Quickly. Like now we've unlocked some formula for doing this. Got a mountain that needs climbing?

When he pulls himself up to where I am, I instinctively reach out a hand. Instinctively, I'm guessing, he takes it, and now we're standing next to each other, face-to-face, eye-to-eye, on top of a rock in the middle of the woods and somehow, it does not seem at all preposterous.

Pam claps. Leslie claps. Lance nods emphatically. Off in the distance, I hear Rory's and Felix's voices mixing in with the hum of the creek.

"You can actually walk around that way, and just come down the hill over there," says Pam. "Or, of course, you can jump again." Nate peers over the edge of the boulder to the crash pad, sizing up the drop. Then he shakes his head.

"No need to undo the success here. I'm taking the easy way down."

When we've followed Pam's directions and we're back on the ground with everyone, Leslie comes over and puts her hand on my shoulder.

"That was so cool," she says.

I just take off my mic and hand it to her.

"Why don't you guys go find Rory and Felix and tell them to come over."

I walk ahead to the spot where we last saw Rory and Felix, and I can hear the rustling behind me that means Nate is following. When we get there, however, we find no trace of them.

"Felix?" I call.

"Over here!"

I follow the sound of his voice, toward the creek, and peer down to see him and Rory sitting together on the bank, each holding a stick and poking the water, as if they're trying to stop it. Nate is right behind me.

"You guys are up," I say. I can't tell if they've been talking or not. Felix looks a little relieved to be rescued from the situation.

"How was it?" he asks as he climbs up the bank.

I look back at Nate and we exchange a look. "Not bad," I tell Felix. "You'll do fine."

"Ha," says Felix. He pauses to wait for Rory, and when she catches up to him, not even glancing at either Nate or me, they walk off toward the others.

Nate and I watch them go for as long as it gives us an excuse not to look at or talk to each other.

"Felix has never done any bouldering," I say when they're finally out of sight.

"He's afraid of heights," says Nate, and steps down toward the creek, sitting in the same spot Felix just occupied.

"He is?" I ask, following him, but I don't sit where Rory sat. I pick another rock, on Nate's other side, farther away. "I didn't know that."

"Well, he used to be, at least. When we were little I could never get him to climb anything." Nate shakes his head. "I'm really surprised he's going along with this, but I guess he wants to save face."

"They told him he'd be the . . ." I don't want to say *star*. "Focus. This time around."

Nate frowns a bit, seems disappointed. Hurt, even. "I didn't know that."

We're silent for a moment. Nate and I have found a way to interact: Talk about other people, not ourselves. Where else can I go with this?

"Are you worried about Keira?" I ask.

"Yes," he says flatly.

The expression on his face, the expression that's still overwhelmingly protective, gets to me. And then I realize that Felix is not the person I should be talking to about my idea. It is Nate.

Should I do this? Suddenly I'm just way too curious to see what would happen if I did.

"I was thinking," I say slowly after a few seconds, "that I would go find her."

Nate turns to me, eyebrows raised. "She said not to."

"She said that to her father and Lance and Leslie. She didn't say it to us."

He pauses, realizing this is true. "*You* would go find her?"

"Me, and Felix."

"You weren't going to tell me about this?"

No, I wasn't. Isn't it obvious why?

"I didn't think you'd be . . . interested. You seem very committed to doing everything they want you to."

Nate's shoulders droop a bit. I'm right, I guess. "I'm interested," he says. "For Keira's sake."

"Okay." I flash on the image of Nate and me together in search of Keira. It doesn't seem possible that this could actually take place.

"But how do we know where to start?"

"I've got that figured out. I just need to get to the house before they do so I can use the phone." Silence again. We watch the water.

Finally, casually, Nate says: "I've got just the thing."

Half an hour later, we're all ready to head back to the house. Rory and Felix took much longer with their climbing game, and Felix returned looking disgusted with himself. Now we're supposed to make lunch together in the enormous kitchen, and eat it together, and process everything from the morning and talk about it in a string

205

of golden cinematic truths.

I plan my timing carefully. Right after Leslie removes the battery on her camera to replace it with a fresh one, I start grabbing my stomach.

"Are you okay?" asks Leslie.

"Yeah, I'm just getting some cramps. I'll be fine."

Two minutes later as we start to walk, I stop dramatically in my tracks and clutch my stomach again, try to seem panicked. I feel Pam's hand on my shoulder. She looks pretty ridiculous, with the big crash pad on her back like she's dressed up for Halloween as a giant bar of soap.

"Justine, what's wrong?"

"It's too embarrassing," I say, waving her off.

"If you're feeling sick, you need to tell me."

"I . . . just, uh . . . I really have to get to a bathroom. Is there an outhouse nearby or something?"

Pam shakes her head. "We'll be at the lodge in ten minutes. Can you make it?"

"I think so . . ." Then after a pause, I grimace. "Maybe not."

I mean, really. This is Oscar-worthy fake diarrhea.

"Do you want to run ahead?" Pam hands me a key on a beaded keychain. "Go, go. We'll see you in a few."

I nod quickly, gratefully, grabbing the key and then taking off, ahead of the others, not even looking at Nate, as fast as I can. All I can think is, *The phone, the phone, the phone. Please let her pick up. Please let her pick up.*

FOURTEEN

When we come downstairs from changing into clean clothes, Pam has laid out a make-your-own-sandwich spread. I'm not sure how we're supposed to bond over deli turkey and half-green tomato slices, but whatever. Lance has the camera set up on the tripod and Kenny's already positioned with the boom mic.

I'm wearing two tees—my vintage black *E.T.* shirt on top of a long-sleeved plain white one—and my jeans are tucked into my high-tops because, for some reason, this makes me feel more prepared.

What the grown-ups don't know is that I've done more

than change. I've packed. Nate too. I build myself a huge sandwich. *Eat up. You have no idea when you'll be able to grab some food again.* Nate and I exchange a glance and I know he's doing the same thing.

The clock says 1:04. She could be here any minute.

Rory sits down first, with her plate full of food items carefully arranged so nothing touches. I notice she's changed into an outfit that looks funkier than she probably planned: a ruffled turquoise blouse and deep purple track pants. She's got the turkey and swiss cheese rolled up and aligned parallel, an inch apart. One tumbles toward the other as she puts the plate down, and she takes a moment to even them out again.

I sit two seats away from her at the big round table and Felix joins me.

"How are you feeling?" he asks.

"Better. Thanks."

"To be honest, I'm kind of glad that happened to you because now nobody remembers how awful I was on the rocks."

"Good thing they got you on film, then," I say. I mean this as a joke, but Felix drops his sandwich onto the plate and sighs. I guess he's officially reached the point where he forgets the cameras are there. I've never been to that point myself.

After we're all situated, Pam sits down with a glass of water and no food. I have not yet seen this woman eat.

"So. Reactions to the bouldering activity? What sticks in your head?"

"My fingers hurt," says Nate. "I forgot about that feeling."

"We would have expected you to climb with confidence. Because you're an athlete. Did you feel those expectations?"

"Yeah, of course," says Nate. He gets a faraway look. "I'm used to those expectations."

"What about you, Justine? You had a moment on the rock where you looked . . . surprised."

"I was," I say.

"Can you elaborate?"

"I surprised myself."

"Why? Didn't you think you could do it?"

And then, right at the moment when I need it, I hear a car in the driveway.

Pam frowns, then looks hopefully at Leslie, who returns the look and passes it over to Lance. Leslie rushes to the window and when the hope turns into confusion, I know this is my ride.

I get up, fighting the urge to wrap my sandwich to go, and glance at Nate with meaning before leaving the room. I can hear him follow and then, when we reach the foyer, he turns to run upstairs.

"Justine?" asks Leslie on our heels.

I'm at the front door now. Then I'm out the door and onto the porch. The car sits in the driveway.

"Hey!" I shout.

"I almost didn't find it," says Olivia as she rolls down the window.

"Give us a minute," I say, and run back inside, leaving the door open. Nate is flying down the stairs two at a time, holding his backpack and mine.

Now Leslie and Lance and Pam and Kenny are standing in the foyer, with the exact looks on their faces that I had imagined. Lance still has the camera running and Kenny positions the boom mic. It's like I scripted this and now we're acting it out.

Rory and Felix are coming up behind them now, Felix chewing a mouthful of food.

"What's going on?" asks Leslie slowly.

"We're off to find Keira," I say, as no-nonsense as I can.

"What? No. I don't think that's—"

"You'll tell us where she went," interrupts Nate.

Leslie looks at him, stung. Completely betrayed. "How do *I* know where she went?"

"Please," he says. "You know. You struck a deal with her. Now we'd like you to strike a deal with us."

Lance and Leslie exchange a look, then turn to us with the raised eyebrows and tilted heads of *Go on*.

"We'd like you to give us the same information you gave Keira," says Nate, now sounding as friendly as if he were ordering a box of cookies from a Girl Scout. "About her mom."

Leslie looks at me and I nod. It feels a little weird having Nate say this, since I'm the one who thought of it, but I have to admit it sounds better coming from him.

"What's the alternative?" asks Lance.

"We leave anyway, and we drop out of the film completely." Nate pauses, looking at his hands for a moment. It's so obvious, even voiced by Nate, that this bargaining chip was my brainchild. "But if you give us some help here, we'll come back, and we can talk about our experience, and maybe you'll still have a story to tell."

Now, I let myself glance at Rory and Felix, who I have kept as blurs in my peripheral vision. Rory seems fascinated, her mouth open a bit, like she's transfixed by a TV show. Felix. Well, Felix's features have hardened into something decidedly un-Felix.

Leslie leans heavily against the staircase banister and opens one palm. She seems quite taken with it for a moment, as if she forgot what her own hand looks like. Lance is shooting her with the camera. "This has gotten so crazy," she says. "I don't understand why." She looks at Nate with a resolve I haven't yet seen. "It's important to you, that you find her. Right?"

Nate raises his eyes to the ceiling, takes a deep breath. "Yes."

Leslie turns to Lance and shrugs, then says simply: "We need to let them go." It could mean so many things. She straightens up. "Let me get a pen and paper."

As Leslie walks back to the kitchen, Felix steps up to me. His cheeks flushed. "You and *Nate?*"

"I didn't plan that. I'm still in denial about it." Then, an idea. "Do you want to come?"

Felix looks at Nate and their eyes bounce away from each other. Felix shifts his gaze to Lance and the camera. "No. I need to . . . be here."

"I'm not sure how much *here* will be left after we're gone," I say, but Felix shakes his head sadly.

Leslie comes back into the foyer and hands Nate an envelope. "That's everything we gave her. I'm going from memory because all my notes were in my phone and Keira has that, but it's the best I can do."

"Thank you," says Nate sincerely.

"I'm sorry this was such a disaster," says Leslie.

At that, Pam gives her a dirty look. "Nothing is a disaster once you have time to reflect on it. I'm sorry this workshop wasn't fruitful in the way we'd all hoped."

I'm tempted to say something trite like *Oh, it was, I really feel like I grew,* but what's the point? Instead, I just take my backpack from Nate and step onto the porch.

"Wait!" yells Rory. She's walking slowly down the stairs. I had no idea she'd even gone up there. She's clutching Misty to her neck, looking unsure of herself, forcing one step in front of the other toward us. "I want to come too."

"Rory," I say, "I don't think—"

She stops cold. "You don't think what? You don't want me along?"

For two months, I've been hoping for a situation where Rory actually wants to be in my company. Why am I discouraging her?

"There's no real plan here. No schedule. No routine. Can you handle that?"

Her eyes widen for a moment, but her body gets more rigid with what seems like resolve.

"I want to be part of whatever you're doing."

She forces a totally practiced smile that I'm sure she's run through in a mirror countless times, and it suddenly seems impossible that we could leave Rory behind. Of course, she needs to come with us. Besides, she's useful when it comes to certain things, like getting unlost.

"Okay," I say. She walks past me to Olivia's car, gets into the backseat, slams the door shut. I see Olivia turn to say something to her.

Now Nate is moving down the steps to the car, leaving me to face the crew and Pam and Felix alone. Felix is staring at the stripes on his polo shirt, his hands shoved into his pockets.

"I know this changes everything," I say, but I'm not sure to whom.

Felix takes a deep breath and then, without raising his head to look at me, walks swiftly in the direction of the car. We all watch him climb into the backseat as Rory and Nate slide over to make room.

There is nothing else to say. Pam has a disappointed-schoolteacher thing going on. Lance and Kenny have the camera and mic on Leslie as she sags against the banister again. Turning away from all of them is so easy, yet so difficult. I do it quickly and walk to the car.

Rory, Nate, and Felix accordioned into the backseat together look uncomfortable in every possible way. How funny that they've left me to ride shotgun, like they trust me to be in charge here. Like I know how to lead them. I slide in and give Olivia a kiss on the cheek.

"Thanks for coming."

"As if I would miss this."

Olivia starts the car and begins to back out.

"Wait!" shouts Leslie. She's running down the front walk.

"Should I keep driving?" asks Olivia, and I nod yes. We need to get out of here.

"Just a second!" yells Leslie again. "Please!"

"Okay, stop," I say, and Olivia slams on the brakes. There's something about Leslie's face now, a rawness in her voice. When Leslie sees that we've actually stopped, she holds up a single finger as a sign for us to hang on, then rushes back into the house.

"I would *love it* if she went in to get us some money," says Nate.

But when Leslie reappears, hurrying toward the car, she's carrying a canvas case with a long strap. I've seen it before.

It's her camera bag.

She circles around the front of the car and when I see she's headed for my window, I roll it down.

"Here," says Leslie, breathless. She shoves the bag through the window and I take it.

There are a few things I could ask here. Such as, *What do you want me to do with this?* Or *Why* or *How* or *When?* But the weight of the bag in my hand, the way it feels like I've just had a severed arm reattached, makes those questions redundant.

Leslie stands back from the car and in lieu of a wave, shoots us the most bittersweet look I have ever seen. It almost makes me want to invite her along for the ride. But she is not one of us.

"Now?" asks Olivia, slapping the leg she's got on the brake.

"Now," I answer, and the Aikya Lodge begins disappearing from sight.

Information that we do actually have:

1. Keira's mom's last known address was in Manhattan on West Forty-Seventh Street.

Minor technicalities we have to work around:

2. The fact that she is probably not living there anymore.
3. The fact that we have no way to contact her.
4. The fact that she may not even be using the same
   , name.

But first things first. We're on our way to Nate's so he can sneak into his house and get his wallet and phone. Then he can call Keira at Leslie's number. If Keira sees it's him, she may answer. At least, this is what he believes. I'm not so sure.

Nate is driving now. I don't know why Olivia seemed eager to hand him the keys to Sob; she's never let me drive it, and I got my license a few weeks before he did. But I'm too grateful to be annoyed right now, because when we dropped Olivia at the library on campus, she handed me all twenty-three dollars of cash from her wallet.

I'm still in the front passenger seat, and I've got the camera rolling so I can shoot Mountain Ridge as we rumble through it. The tenements disguised as off-campus student housing, the achingly cute historic buildings converted into chic restaurants. I pan across the three competing artisan craft stores on Main, and the shop with all the tie-dye clothing displayed on the sidewalk, like it puked the 1960s right into the street.

I turn to the backseat and point the camera at Felix.

"You've done that, like, ten times already," he says grumpily. He's sitting with his arms crossed, pressed against one door, as far as possible from where Rory has Velcroed herself to the opposite side. We survived the drive down the mountain thanks to Nate, who distracted us from the palpable layer of *What the Hell Do We Do Now?* in the air by recounting the entire weekend to my sister, while I shot him and tried to keep the camera still and also not get nauseous. Now I stop the camera and nestle it into my lap. I don't want to overdo it.

We drive south from town and pass the Cannibal Apple sign. A minute later, before we get to the Hunter Farms store we all know so well, Nate turns down a dirt road I've forgotten was even there. We bump our way past some outbuildings until we reach the back of his house. I've seen it from the road and the orchards, but never this close. It's set deep onto the property with a view of the mountains, and has always seemed like something out of a movie set.

Nate pulls the car up to the back door alongside a beat-up sedan. "Looks like only my mom is home," he says. "This should be easy. Keep it running."

Keep it running, like this is a getaway car. Then Nate is quickly gone, into the house. I turn to look at Felix. He's staring at the place with what I can best describe as reluctant longing.

"When was the last time you were inside?" I ask.

"Can't remember," he says, shrugging extra casually. "It was years ago."

For a minute, we're silent. If we had our cell phones, we'd be messing around on them to momentarily check out of this situation. But I'm getting used to that feeling of being stuck in the here and now.

We hear something slam somewhere, a truck door perhaps. Felix and I both slouch down in our seats. Rory looks at us, puzzled, then follows our lead.

"Wait a minute," I say. "Why are we hiding?"

"*I'm* hiding because my dad could be around," says Felix. "*You're* hiding because you have a lot of guilt about starting this thing and it's making you jumpy."

I'm about to ask him to elaborate when Nate emerges from the house, gingerly closing the back door, then running on his toes to the car. He slides in, throws the gear shift into reverse, and in seconds the Hunter house is becoming a distant icon again.

"Done," says Nate simply.

"Nobody saw you?"

"Nope," says Nate. "But they've contacted our families by now, don't you think? We should call them ourselves to do some damage control." Nate hands me his cell phone and turns onto a road that will lead us quickly to the thruway. "I want to get moving but we can stop at a rest area later, and then I'll try Keira."

It feels weird to be holding Nate's phone. I instantly

think about how much time it spends in Nate's pocket, and then try to unthink that.

"You seem to have this all figured out," I say.

"Well, you got us out of Aikya Lodge. I figured, the least I can do is fill in some gaps." He smiles sideways at me.

"So what's next, Captain?"

"We can be in the city in two hours. We'll meet up with Keira, take it from there."

"Have you ever driven in the city?"

Nate's smile vanishes. I see his upper arms tense under the fabric of his forest green T-shirt. "No."

"Have you ever even driven on the thruway?"

"A few times. With my grandparents in the car. Just chill, okay? I can be a rock star driver if you stop making me nervous with questions about it."

"Can I make you nervous with questions about something else?" Nate warily lifts his eyebrows. "What if we can't find Keira before tonight? Should we just come home?"

Truth is, I'm embarrassed that I'm asking all this now instead of anticipating it from the beginning. I was focused on getting out and had faith that the rest would fall into place.

"I've got someone to call, if it comes to that. Remember Dylan Boone? He graduated two years ago? Now he's at NYU."

219

Dylan Boone, another swim team star.

"Is he the one who came out of the closet, like, two days after he left Mountain Ridge?"

"Surprising absolutely no one," says Nate. "He's a good guy. We've kept in touch. I'm sure we can crash at his dorm room if we have to."

Dylan Boone, who could have gotten an athletic scholarship to any college he wanted, but chose to go to school in Greenwich Village. It gave me a new respect for him.

"Who waits until they leave Mountain Ridge to come out anyway?" I wonder aloud. "I mean, honestly. We have our own Pride parade."

Nate and Felix shrug. After a few moments, it's Rory who speaks.

"There are a million reasons, Justine," she says matter-of-factly, and suddenly I feel this surge of *holy shit*. Is Rory a lesbian? If she is, she's done a genius job of hiding it, because we used to talk about kissing boys all the time. Rory was almost scientifically obsessed with this, creating what she thought was a hyperrealistic set of fake lips involving a balloon and hair gel. It would have been perfect if not for the taste of rubber.

In the stiff silence that follows, I dial my mother. When she picks up and I say, "Hey, Mom," and she says, "Justine," in that way that really hits hard on the *S*, I know she's already spoken to Leslie.

I tell her the facts and only the facts: I'm fine, better

than fine, and we're going to the city and we'll be back tonight or tomorrow and this is Nate's phone but don't call it unless there's a really, really good reason to.

"Okay?" I ask. There's no answer. "Okay," I say then. Not as a question, but as a good-bye.

I hang up and offer the phone to Felix, who shakes his head. "Not ready yet," he says. "Ana will be running the Dominican Curse Marathon by now."

But he takes the phone and hands it to Rory, who starts dialing.

Olivia has only two caseless CDs in her car and they're both awful, but Nate has thought to grab not just his phone and charger but also the cable to plug it into the stereo system. His seamless integration of Road Trip Entertainment into our quick getaway—impressive. Once we've gone through the tollbooth at the Mountain Ridge exit and are headed south on the thruway, Nate hands me the cable.

"There's a playlist on there called Away Meets," he says. "I listen to it on the team bus. It's a good place to start."

I start scrolling through his phone, pretending to be looking for the playlist but really just checking out his music library. Nate's taste falls squarely in the Not Bad to Incredibly Incredible range.

"The soundtrack to *Grease?*" I ask. I expect him to be embarrassed, but he just smiles and shrugs.

"I'm a T-Bird at heart."

I laugh, but Rory and Felix don't join me.

"Actually, it was Felix who first got me into that movie. Remember, dude?"

Felix looks out the window, presses his nose to the glass so it goes crooked and reminds me of a Picasso painting. "Yeah, I remember."

The pain evident on Felix's face brings me back to reality. Nate hurt him, so bad he had to bait new companions with apple cider donuts.

I turn back to the phone, find the playlist Nate's talking about, and press the play button. The music fills the car, seeps into the awkward empty spaces between the four of us. It feels a little like oxygen. I can breathe more easily. So I take out the camera and start shooting again.

Here are the familiar landmarks that mean we're headed away from home, south toward something interesting. A horse farm. A billboard advertising a nearby water park, which stays up year-round and always depresses me in winter. We can't see our ridge anymore, just distant hills that belong to other towns.

I swivel around to get a shot of Rory. She's found one of Olivia's fashion magazines on the floor of the backseat, the pages rumpled, the skin of the cover celebrity mottled with red slushie stains. From Rory's look of concentration as she reads, you'd think she was studying Tolstoy.

Felix has closed his eyes. I'm pretty sure he's just pretending to sleep.

Nate bobs his head to the music and seems more relaxed about the highway driving, a light–years–away look in his eyes. If I were Leslie, I'd ask him what he's thinking about. But I'm just me. I suddenly understand this about myself: I like to watch. I like to let the thing I see through the lens tell me whatever it wants to say.

FIFTEEN

SOLOMON TOWNSEND MEMORIAL REST AREA. 2 MILES.

Yeah, someday I should look up who these people actually are.

"Let's stop here," says Nate. "I'd like to call Keira."

Once we've exited the thruway and pulled into a parking space, Nate turns to me, then holds out his hand for the phone, which I had been holding. I give it to him. It's strange to have this silent language between us.

"Here goes," he murmurs. We're all quiet as he dials Leslie's number. We can hear the ringing on the other end. Ringing and ringing. "Should I leave a message?"

I shake my head. Now we hear Leslie and her voice mail greeting. It doesn't seem right to be leaving messages for Keira on Leslie's phone, even if Keira could retrieve them.

Nate hangs up. "She saw it was me who called. I guess if she doesn't want to talk, I can send her a text. I'll just ask if she's okay and tell her to call me if she can." Nate takes a few moments to type out a message on his phone.

"So, what now?" I ask when he's done. "We just head down to that address and bang on the door?"

Nate shrugs. "We have to start somewhere. I'm pretty sure that's what Keira is doing. Or has already done." He glazes over for a second, maybe picturing how that situation played out.

"Well, before we do anything, I've gotta make a pit stop," I say, and he snaps out of it.

Felix has to go too, and we walk into the building together, then separate when we get to the restrooms. When I come out, I find Felix in the snack shop, clutching to his chest a bag of trail mix and a bottle of radioactive orange sports drink.

"Please, Mom?" he says, pushing out his lower lip in a mock-pout. "It just ain't a road trip without munchies."

I'm a sucker for Felix calling me Mom, and also for anything that makes me feel like what we're doing is fun.

When we get back to the car, snacks in hand, Rory has taken my seat in the front and is busy typing something into Nate's phone.

"She offered to navigate," says Nate, noticing my confused and not unterritorial expression. "She said she's good at that."

"She is," I say, accepting the new arrangement. I slide into the backseat, then dangle the trail mix bag at him. "Care for a cashew?"

He takes one, then sees the price sticker. "Seven ninety-nine? Are you crazy? That's, like, a quarter a nut! We have to be careful with our cash if it's going to last."

"I've got some left. How much do you have?"

"Well, I've got my debit card and about . . ." He checks his pocket for his wallet, but doesn't find it. Checks the other one. Something bad crosses his face. "Oh."

"Oh, what?"

"I may have forgotten to grab my wallet."

"You *may* have."

"I was so focused on the phone and the music . . ." He bangs on the steering wheel, then collapses until his forehead is resting on it. "I'm an idiot."

Giving him a hard time about this won't help anyone, plus the self-chastising thing is cute. I say nothing until Nate raises his head, takes a deep breath, and starts the car. "I guess we can borrow money from Dylan, if we need it." He pulls out of our space and toward the thruway on-ramp. "And Keira's got Leslie's wallet, if and when we find her."

I look at the fuel tank gauge. It's still almost full. Is it possible that my sister had the foresight to gas up her car before coming to get us? Olivia does have her moments of clarity. Suddenly, I love her like crazy.

Which reminds me of the Secret MasterCard.

Olivia's recurring moment of *unclarity* is that she's got two purses, and her wallet often ends up in the one she's not carrying. She'll go shopping, load up her cart with several deals of the century, then find herself with no form of payment at the checkout counter. After the third or fourth episode like this, she decided to stash one of her two credit cards under the detritus-encrusted floor mat in the backseat of her car. "If someone is brave enough to touch that thing in search of stuff to steal," she told me, "they *deserve* a spending spree on me."

Suddenly, there's the comfort of a valuable secret. I know how to forge my sister's signature. We have financial backup, should circumstances call for it. I decide not to share this information with the others just yet and don't think too much about why.

It seems like the less we think about anything right now, the better.

Nate rolls down his window halfway as the car climbs back into high gear. The air hits me fresh and delicious, whistling promises I can't quite hear. All I know is this, which feels like enough:

We are on the road again.

* * *

We've crossed into New Jersey now, no longer on the thruway but a route that takes us down a choked-up corridor of chain stores and shopping centers.

Felix hasn't spoken once since we left the rest area, and this is so unlike him, I'm starting to worry. I reach out and put my hand on his leg, and he jumps.

"Shit, Justine." he says.

"You're sorry you came."

He doesn't answer. I guess it's not a question.

After a few moments, he turns away and says, "I was really hoping this movie was my chance for . . . something."

I want to say, *You didn't have to come*, but I know it's not true.

Instead I say, "It still will be. It still is. You know Lance and Leslie. They'll make whatever they can of what they end up with." Then I look down at the camera in my hand and add, "Don't forget about this."

Felix turns back to glance at the camera, then at me, with an intrigued look. Evaluating something. "It's okay," he says after a moment. "We owe Keira this. But I should call my mom and get that over with."

"Hey, Nate?" I call to the front seat. "Felix needs your phone."

Nate hands it back and Felix takes it. He dials slower than I've ever seen anyone dial.

"Mami," he says with no expression. "Yeah, it's Nate's . . .

good, I'm glad they called. It's all going to be fine . . . better than fine . . . I know . . . I know . . . I should be back soon . . . " Then he is silent and I can hear Ana spewing in Spanish. Felix runs his fingers through his hair, and listens. "Okay," he says, then hangs up without saying good–bye.

Felix stares at the phone for a few seconds, like he wants to make sure it doesn't start shouting at him again, then hands it back to Nate.

As Nate takes it, he says, "My Spanish must be better than I thought it was, because I got some of that and wow, I'm sorry, man."

"Why? What did she say?" asks Rory.

"You don't want to know. Felix may just want to get an apartment and stay in the city until he's about thirty, and then maybe by then she'll forgive him."

Felix snorts a laugh, and I see Nate smile in the rearview mirror, looking at Felix with something I've never seen on Nate before. I almost don't recognize it, because it seems so impossible. But I do recognize it, because I feel it every time I try to talk to Rory.

Longing.

Can't process that. Especially not on Route 17 going through New Jersey, not when we're driving behind a Toyota Odyssey with the bumper sticker *MINIVANS ARE THE NEW SEXY!*

I know this route well enough, from the occasional day

trip with my family. We'll be in Manhattan in about forty-five minutes. And I feel a little sad, then surprised that I feel a little sad. There's something about people being in a car, held fast by the speed and lack of distractions that usually keep us from interacting with one another. I'm reminded of how, when I was younger, my parents used to have long, involved discussions when we went on road trips. They'd talk about big family issues and major decisions. My dad would tell stories about his patients, and my mom would fill him in on the latest parent gossip. It was like they hadn't talked, really talked, in weeks. And they didn't care that Olivia and I were right there in the backseat, pretending to play video games or drawing but, in fact, listening to every single word they said.

Ideally, Felix would be sitting in the front seat with Nate, and Rory would be back here with me, but I know that's a configuration they'll do everything to avoid.

Suddenly, Nate's phone rings.

Rory doesn't think to pick it up and check it for him. *I* would, if I were up there.

Nate glances at it quickly, then swerves the car onto the shoulder, cutting off the car behind us and causing much honking.

"Hey," he says breathlessly as soon as we've stopped.

Keira.

"How is . . . everything going?" Nate steadies his voice into a calm, curious tone. He listens, and I can't hear her on the other end. "Okay . . . okay . . . Yeah, well . . . we came home early and as soon as I had my phone again I wanted to check on you. So you can reach me. If you need to."

Nate listens for a few more moments, nodding as if she can see him, then says, "Good luck. I'm here if you need me," and hangs up. The intimacy of their conversation was obvious even in the few words I could hear. He stares at the phone and puts it down, looks out at the traffic speeding by us.

"Did she see her mom?" I ask.

"Not yet. Apparently she's moved to another neighborhood. That's all Keira told me."

"You didn't tell her we were coming down to find her," says Rory.

"No," replies Nate.

"Are we still?" I ask.

"Oh, yeah," he says. Now he turns to face me. Just me. "We have things we need to do."

SIXTEEN

Somewhere in the Garden State, I actually fall asleep. When I open my eyes, the motion of the car has changed dramatically. Instead of the straight and steady vibration of highway driving, there's a lot of stop-and-start now. Swerving right, then left. Then the light feels artificial and the world sounds like an empty *whooshing* thing.

It's so disorienting that I can only slur the words, "Do we know where we are?"

Nate laughs. "Lincoln Tunnel. Thanks to this one." He points to Rory.

The lights inside the tunnel are evenly spaced and

endless, like a line of chorus girls in one of those old movie musicals. I'm still not completely awake or thinking straight, but I reach for the camera and start shooting. Reflections of headlights and taillights on the walls, the intimidating rigidity of the double white line between the two narrow lanes. Nate grips the steering wheel with extra firmness and looks straight ahead, driving much slower than necessary. The rest of us are quiet until Felix asks:

"You know what would be awesome? If we came out of this tunnel and on the other side it was suddenly 1956."

I see Nate crack a smile through his concentration.

Then the tunnel opens up into daylight, and reality. Unfortunately, not 1956. But it is NYC, and that still feels like a miracle.

"Stay to the left," says Rory, examining the map application on Nate's phone.

A few blocks later, Rory has us turn again on Forty-Second Street. Now there are other things to shoot. People. Buildings. Storefronts. The guy with the Mohawk riding in a truck alongside us. I pan over to Felix, then Rory, then Nate.

Already, we have traveled so far.

This morning, I woke up in a house in the woods on a mountain. I climbed the face of a rock with my bare hands. Somehow it is still the same day but now we are here, in the city, the four of us together in a car. The journey from there to here seems like it must be a lot more amazing than it felt like. Maybe the camera can see it even if I can't.

"Turn right here, on Tenth Avenue," Rory directs Nate.

"Don't you love the city?" I ask, the camera recording.

"Like crazy," says Felix, and in his eyes I can see the reflection of all his plans for the future.

"It's got a great soundtrack," says Nate, and at first I think he's misheard me, maybe he thinks I'm talking about a movie. But then I get it. The city has a soundtrack. It's different for everyone, but it beats through every second you spend here.

I turn the camera on Rory, waiting for her to say something. She doesn't notice me shooting her, but after a few moments, she whispers, "Actually, I hate it. Too many painful noises and so much happens . . . suddenly."

I think of the time we were eight years old and our moms brought us into the city to see the Radio City Christmas Spectacular. We were walking down a midtown street toward the theater, jumping sidewalk cracks in our new holiday dresses. Mine was purple velvet with white fake-fur trim; Rory's was the same, but in green. She was in front of me when we were approached by a homeless guy holding out a plastic yogurt cup full of change. He didn't even say anything; he just stepped in front of us and shook the cup in our faces so it jingled and clanged.

Rory screamed and covered her ears. Collapsed in a

green velvet pile on the nearest stoop and wouldn't move. Her mother had to carry her the remaining blocks to the theater, and she spent half the show in the gigantic ladies' room, too fascinated by all the mirrors to leave.

"Look! It's me, to infinity!" she said when I came down to find her after the performance. Her mother sat on a sofa in the corner, reading a book. She never left the house without one for just this type of occasion. In two mirrors on opposite walls, there was Rory stretching on forever. I didn't want all those Rorys. I just wanted one, who would sit next to me during the Radio City Christmas Spectacular so we could pick out which Rockettes we liked best.

"You can stay in the car if you want," I say now. "If it's easier."

Rory turns her head halfway but her eyes are on the ceiling. "I *know* that."

Maybe I should just not say anything to her ever again.

We drive a few more blocks, then Rory tells Nate to turn left on Forty-Seventh Street.

"It must be on this block," says Nate, looking at the numbers. The neighborhood feels mishmashy. A large auto repair shop, an empty lot between two brick buildings, a contemporary high-rise.

"But we know she doesn't live here anymore," I remind Nate.

"Keira must have talked to someone who gave her a new address. We'll talk to the same person."

We find the building, a blocky thing built around a small courtyard, and Nate pulls to the curb next to a fire hydrant.

"You can't park here," says Rory.

"We can't park anywhere," says Nate, huffy, and I realize how nerve-racking the driving must be for him. "It's a Saturday afternoon in Manhattan." Then he turns to me. I'm his cocaptain, back here. "Do you want to come with me?"

Nate already has that endearing All-American Boy look on his face and he'll be just fine on his own. Probably better. I shake my head.

"Be right back," he says. "If someone asks you to move the car, just circle around."

I turn on the camera and shoot him exiting the car, then climb out in time to catch him walking down the sidewalk and turning into the courtyard.

When he's out of sight, I turn to Felix, who's rolled down his window and is leaning his head against the frame, staring at the sky. I'm still recording. "Why was your mom so angry?" I ask him. "You're with friends. You're not missing school. You said you'd be back tomorrow."

Felix eyes the camera and takes a deep breath. "It's disrespectful, what we did. That's what she said. And in my family when you disrespect someone . . . not a good thing. Plus, she's afraid we violated our agreement with Lance and Leslie and they'll come after us with lawyers.

My parents are big on the legal thing, you know. They spent so many years undocumented and worked so hard to change that."

He's risked a lot to be here. It makes me feel like I've let him down somehow.

"I'm sorry, Felix."

He bites his lip. "There's something else that's really embarrassing."

"You don't have to tell me."

"Why not? At this point, I've got nothing to hide." He pauses and looks straight into the camera, then at me. "I've never actually spent a night away from home. I don't think my parents wanted it to be quite like this."

"Not even one night? You're sixteen. How can that be?"

Felix gives me one of his *Oh, you are so white* looks. "I wasn't allowed to do sleepovers. Sleepaway camp was out of the question, moneywise. So that's how it can be."

Rory unbuckles herself and scrambles ungracefully into the backseat with Felix, draws her knees up to her chin. "I've never spent a whole night away from home either."

That's no surprise. We tried a sleepover at my house. Once. Rory woke up screaming at 2:00 a.m. and started to run home, until my dad caught her two houses down and drove her the rest of the way. I was so mad. Wounded, really. *What was wrong with my house?* She'd been there a thousand times and called my parents "D–Mom" (for Diana) and "J–Dad" (for Jeff). But our sleepovers were always at Rory's from then on. Later, after I met new friends, it felt amazingly uncomplicated to have them sleep over. Dramaless.

I hear footsteps and turn to see Nate jogging toward us. Fortunately, I've had the camera on this whole time. I wasn't thinking about it. It's becoming part of my hand and I don't even feel the weight of it.

"We're golden," he says, waving a Post-it note. "I talked to the woman Mrs. Jones was sharing the apartment with. Apparently she moved last year, but the roommate gave me the address like she gave it to Keira."

At first, I'm not going to ask how he was able to swing this, because really, it's Nate. But I feel the tug of the camera's curiosity.

"What did you say?" I ask, raising it to frame Nate against the buildings across the street.

"I explained that Keira was our friend and we wanted to be there for her when she saw her mother again for the first time."

Our friend. "I'm so glad you left out the part where she has no idea we're here, and that you're really the only person she would possibly in a million years want to see right now."

Nate shakes his head sadly. "You make it sound like she hates you."

I press stop on the camera and lower it. "Um, because she does."

"She doesn't."

"And you know, of course."

He shrugs. "We've talked about it." He looks at me, his eyes darting to my feet, then up again at my face. "She admires you, actually."

I'm about to ask more when we hear a sudden honk. It's a police car. My heart jumps.

"Please move your vehicle," says an amplified voice, half-human. "You are in a no-parking zone."

Nate waves at the cop, respectful and pleasant, then jumps into the car. I slide into the passenger seat, heart racing. Why do I feel like we almost got caught doing something? We're not committing any crime. We barely even pissed anybody off. We're just four teenagers meeting up with a friend in New York City, and normal people do that kind of thing every day.

Nate pulls the car away from the fire hydrant and the police car watches us go. When it feels safe, I turn to get a shot of it in the rear window.

"Where are we going?" Felix asks two blocks later, when it becomes painfully obvious that Nate doesn't know.

Nate hands me the Post-it and his phone; I pass them back to Rory. She studies both, then tells Nate to get back to Tenth Avenue. "We have to drive through Central Park to the Upper East Side," she says. "I'll let you know where to turn."

Nate tries to turn at the next big street, but it's going the wrong way. "Arrrrghhh," he mutters. We're all quiet for a few tense minutes, because he's stressed and it's the kind of stress that needs respect.

Once we're turned around again and back on Tenth Avenue, Nate visibly relaxes. I study his face, then turn on the camera again.

"Does Keira know her way around the city?" I ask Nate.

He raises his eyebrows. "With all the theater and ballet and museums her father drags her to? Yeah, I think she's getting where she needs to go."

"I knew you guys were friends, but I didn't realize you knew so much about her."

I want Nate to tell me that they're a couple, that they're doing it on a regular basis, some kind of concrete information that would explain the mysterious signals I'm picking up.

Then Rory says from the backseat, "You love her," in this way that's so simple, it's too complex for anyone but her to say.

Nate frowns. "I guess I do."

"You *love her* love her," adds Rory.

"If you mean we're *in love*, then no. We're not in love. I mean, at one time, I had a crush on her. Who hasn't? But we . . . shared something once."

"Bodily fluids?" asks Rory, and I snort involuntarily. Felix laughs too. Rory grins because she made an attempt at a joke, and it was successful.

Nate looks at both of us and smiles. "Not bodily fluids. Just an experience. Sorry to disappoint you."

Out of nowhere, a taxi cuts us off and Nate slams on the brakes, hard enough that I have to brace my hand against the glove compartment to keep from lurching forward. My other hand instinctively smothers the camera.

"You okay?" I hear Felix ask, and I turn to see he's talking to Rory, who has curled into the fetal position with her arms wrapped around her head.

"Like I said," squeaks Rory, "too much of the sudden stuff."

Felix reaches out tentatively and touches the tip of her elbow, like this is the one secret spot that might steady her. "What helps?"

"Fresh air. Holding something familiar."

Felix leans across Rory and rolls down her window halfway. Then he looks around the backseat, finds Misty on the floor. He hands the horse to Rory and Rory takes it, surprised, as if she forgot it was here. She clutches it to her neck and says, "Thanks." It doesn't sound very sincere. To Felix it probably sounds mechanical. But I know that for Rory to even say it, to remember that she's supposed to say it and then actually do the thing she remembers she's supposed to do, is pretty huge.

What would I have done if I'd been sitting back there with her? Would I have thought to ask, like Felix did?

What helps? It makes so much sense, I probably would have overlooked it.

At the next red light, Rory says softly, "You're going to turn right here. That should take us through the park."

Nate nods and when the car is stopped, fiddles with his iPod. "We don't need road-tripping music anymore," he says. "We need techno." He turns around to Felix. "Felix, that's your thing. What do you suggest?"

Felix meets Nate's eye for a few seconds. Then says, "Hand it over," in a way that almost sounds affectionate. I unplug the iPod and pass it to him. Felix scrolls through it, making some judgey faces, then hands it back to me after he's selected something. I plug it back in and as we turn, a series of electronic chords fills the car, eardrum-splitting but beautiful. Haunting. Suddenly, it seems like everything around us is moving to the beat of this music. People on the sidewalk, a bus in the next lane, as if the world is now set to our tempo.

"Nice," says Nate. Felix turns to the window, but he looks content.

We're quiet for a little while, listening, as we drive to the east side through Central Park and then hit Fifth Avenue. Traffic is slow, but Nate seems more relaxed.

"Where are we turning?" he asks Rory.

"Not until First Avenue. The odd number avenues run north on the east side, so you'll have to turn left. Then go up to Sixty-Ninth Street and turn left."

It takes another ten minutes to get to First Avenue. But then we're turning uptown, and the lights are with us so we coast as the numbers on the street signs tick higher. Sixty-Seventh, Sixty-Eighth, Sixty-Ninth, and here we are turning onto this pretty little block lined with brownstones.

"There," says Rory, pointing to a redbrick one with a double wooden door. And just in front of it, so amazing that I don't quite believe my eyes at first, is a pickup truck pulling out of a parking space.

"Put on your blinker!" I shout, and Nate startles but does as he's told. We've made our claim.

"Whoa. That is damn good parking radar, Justine," says Felix, patting me on the shoulder from the backseat.

"It's usually impossible to park in the city," says Nate as he maneuvers into the space. "We don't even have money for a garage, thanks to my boneheadedness. What a score."

"The parking gods must be watching over us," I say. I get out of the car and check the sign. The space is legal until the next street cleaning day, on Tuesday.

Nate is suddenly beside me. "You wouldn't happen to have a comb, would you?"

I turn to examine him. It's gotten so easy to do this, now. To just look at him with purpose.

"A comb," I simply repeat. His hair does look a little crazy.

"In my rush to pack, I left mine. And I'd like to look presentable."

"Are you nervous?"

"I guess I am. I . . ." He glances down and notices the camera in my hand. I'm holding it by the handle and it's hanging by my side.

"You're not thinking of coming, are you? With that?"

I look at it, the lens like a mouth shaped into a questioning O. "I don't know."

"Let me go alone," says Nate. "If Keira's here, I'll tell her we're all here, then we'll see what happens."

I stare at him for a moment, then go to the trunk of the car, find my backpack, pull out my hairbrush. It's black with multicolored glitter all over it.

"Here," I say, holding it out to him. The sunlight catches some of the glitter and it sparkles.

"This is very girly," says Nate as he takes the brush and examines it.

"It won't cause you to magically grow a ponytail, if that's what you're worried about."

He smiles, but at the brush. "Just surprised you have something like this." Then he starts running it through his hair.

"You don't think I would own anything so girly?" I ask, keeping my voice jokey.

Nate stops brushing and runs his finger over the glitter. "I guess you've never seemed like someone who needs a glitter anything to make an impression." He hands it back to me. I'm too stunned to do anything but take it and get really interested in something on the sidewalk.

Nate runs up the steps to the brownstone's front door and looks at the list of names and buzzers.

"It's Weston on the Post-it, right?" he calls. "What the roommate told me she changed her name to?"

I nod, and he presses a buzzer. We wait.

Silence.

Nate bobs his head and seems to be counting. "Again?" he asks me.

I nod. He buzzes again. Nate bobs to the count of ten. Nothing.

"What now?" he asks.

"You're asking me? You're the one who's been cruise directing this whole thing."

Nate sits down on the top step. I'm standing on the bottom step. We're eye level this way. He rests his elbows on his knees and his cheeks against his palms for a moment.

"I think we should just wait for a while," he says.

"Can't we just call Keira and see what's up? Maybe the two of them are somewhere together."

Nate considers that for a moment. He stares at the top of the buildings across the street, the now-afternoon sunlight catching his face. The little tug at my brain starts again. *I should be shooting this.* But another tug, pulling in the opposite direction, says *Uh-uh.*

"Let's walk over to First Avenue," says Nate. "We can get a snack, hang out. Come back in an hour."

I'm hungry, and it feels good to stay put for a little while on an exquisite spring day in Manhattan, and I want some more of this experience of talking to Nate like we are regular human beings. I nod and walk over to the car, where Rory and Felix are watching from the backseat.

"We're going to go around the corner, get something to eat. We can check again later."

Felix glances at Nate, then opens the car door. "Starving," is all Felix says.

Rory shrinks further into her corner.

"You coming?" I ask.

She shakes her head.

"Rory, you have to face the city eventually. It's a quiet neighborhood. You're with us. It'll be okay."

She shakes her head again, then leans over and picks up the magazine, which she has surely read from cover to cover by now.

I sigh, frustrated, and close the car door extra tight as if hermetically sealing Rory from the world.

Felix peers back at her, worried. "We'll be back in a little while," he calls, but she doesn't seem to be listening, or caring, or aware there's anyone else in the world.

SEVENTEEN

We start walking to the corner of First Avenue. I've got Nate on one side and Felix on the other. The buffer between them, apparently. I think about shooting, but it feels good to take a moment to look at things with my own eyes rather than filtered through a lens.

We pass an elderly woman with three small dogs on leashes. She wears a straw hat tilted sideways and glances at the guys, then at me, with a sweet smile. For an instant, I see what she sees. Yes, I'm in New York City on a perfect afternoon, flanked by handsome boys. Aren't we the quintessential picture of youth? We've got everything ahead of us. We've got everything, period.

The feeling is so strong that, for a moment, I believe it too.

We round the corner and stop, scanning the block. At first glance, it's got a little bit of everything, like a movie set of a typical city street. "That looks good," Nate says, pointing a few doors down to a café, where there are tables set up on the sidewalk. We walk there together but as we reach a table set up for four, Nate and Felix hang back. At first, I think this is chivalry, but then quickly realize it's because they want to sit on either side of me.

A waiter comes by and puts water on the table, hands us menus.

"We could get the Smothered Nachos," says Nate, scanning our choices. "But it would pretty much blow the rest of our cash."

"Go for it," I say, thinking of the credit card under Olivia's floor mat. "And add on the chicken. We'll figure out the rest when we need to."

Nate nods but doesn't look convinced. After he orders, we sit in silence. I take a long sip of water. Nate starts chewing his ice. Felix watches him. At least they're actually looking at each other now.

"Do you think Rory's okay?" Felix asks after a minute.

"Trust me," I say. "She's safer in the car."

Felix looks at me sadly, then says, "I know you've been trying with her."

"Trying, and failing."

Instinctively, I glance at Nate. Because I get the sense he has been trying, and failing, as well. With Felix. There's an awkward silence and Felix gets up. "Bathroom. I'll be back."

As soon as he's gone, Nate says, "Let me ask you something."

"Okay."

"You want to shoot this?" he asks, indicating the camera with a tilt of his head.

"Sure." I pick it up, turn it on. Get him in frame.

"Why is it so important for you and Rory to be friends again?"

I stare at him on the LCD display; Leslie was right—it's easier to use this now that I know what I'm doing. His face, so close, when the camera should really be registering *my* reaction. It's weird that he wanted me to shoot him, but a good weird. A glad weird. "Because I was shitty to her, and she didn't deserve that." I watch his face soften into curiosity and add: "She shouldn't have to be alone."

After a moment, Nate shrugs. "It seems like she's doing okay. Finding her niche online, and all that."

"But that's online," I say. "It's not real. Or at least, not the same real."

"You wanna know what I think?" he asks, then takes a long drag on his water.

"Sure. You seem to have a lot of stuff figured out here."

"I think maybe it's not about her at all. I think it's all about you."

He says that with such confidence, I have the urge to punch him, and maybe this is why he wanted me to be shooting this conversation because I can't punch him, unless I do it with the camera. Which may not be such a terrible idea.

"You're tired of feeling guilty," he continues, and there's something about his voice now. His sad stare at the middle distance past the camera. Instantly, I know what he's saying is true, and I also know that on his side of the lens, Nate is feeling the same thing. He must. Something has changed and I feel like we're equals in this conversation.

"Yes," I finally say. "I am."

"But do you actually *want* to be friends again? I mean, do you truly want to hang out and do stuff and have it be the way it was? If it even could be in a million years?"

I haven't thought about that. I've only ever thought about getting to *I forgive you*. Holy crap. I don't yet see us together on the other side of that.

I'm aware of what my face would look like on camera, if it were flipped around. I can even see it framed, the window of the restaurant behind me. I wish I were shooting it. Maybe the least I can do is keep things going, build on them.

"What about you?" I ask Nate. "And Felix?"

Nate glances up to see if Felix is coming, but he's nowhere in sight.

"I hope every day that he changes his mind," he says matter-of-factly. "But in the meantime, I've moved on."

Changes his mind?

Now the waiter appears with our nachos and three small plates. Nate digs in and I put the camera down so I can eat too.

"Dear God," he says, chewing. "This is good."

I can't not ask. Even without the camera recording, if I don't pick up this notion it might drop and roll away forever.

"What do you mean, you hope he changes his mind?"

Felix reappears, seemingly from nowhere because I've been focused on this conversation. "Changes whose mind?" he asks, grabbing a tortilla chip covered with guacamole before his butt is even completely in the chair.

"Yours," I say.

Felix freezes, the chip halfway to his mouth, the guacamole sliding off. He looks at Nate. A terrible look, full of anger and betrayal. He flicks the chip back at the plate and slaps his hand on the table.

"You asshole!" says Felix. "You told her!"

"I didn't!" snaps Nate.

"I knew it was only a matter of time, with you guys suddenly so chummy."

"Oh, Felix, give it a rest. I made you a promise and I've kept it all this time. Why would I break it now? *Especially* now?"

Their voices are raised enough so that people are looking at us, even the jaded New Yorkers who aren't supposed to be fazed by anything. I feel like I just walked into the middle of a play and have no idea what's going on in the plot.

The camera sits on the table. I can't believe I'm not recording this, whatever *this* is.

Felix narrows his eyes at Nate, and Nate does not waver. He sits still with his gaze lasered at Felix, so intense I would be afraid to cross the beam for fear of getting vaporized.

"Felix," says Nate slowly. "We were talking about you changing your mind about being sorry you came. That was it."

Felix turns to me and I nod. Hating the lie. Hating not knowing what I'm covering for.

"Nate?" asks someone behind us, a voice quivering and unsure.

We all turn to see Keira standing on the sidewalk. Her mouth hangs open, her brow scrunched. It is so unlike her. She seems tiny compared with the tall buildings around us. I notice she's dressed in a dramatic red V-neck sweater and skinny jeans, but with hiking boots, and somehow this outfit she packed for the Aikya Lodge looks quirky-chic in the city.

Nate bursts out of his seat and steps toward her. He wants to reach out, to touch, to hug. But he holds back.

"What the hell are you doing here?" Keira asks slowly, not angry but overwhelmingly confused. She looks at Felix and me, lumping us in with her question.

"We wanted to be there," says Nate. His voice catches in his throat. She's made him nervous. "For you . . . if you should need it."

"How did you . . ."

But Keira's brain seems to be doing its job, because I can actually see the process of her figuring it out. The first address. The second. I slide the camera off the table and keep it in my lap. I'm not going to push my luck by turning it on right now, but that familiar tug is too much and I want it ready.

"Are you mad?" asks Nate. He turns on his trademark charm. "We ditched Lance and Leslie. We took off right in front of them, and it was all kinds of awesome."

Keira relaxes a little, but shakes her head with affectionate disapproval like you would at a puppy who just peed on the rug. "I know you mean well, Nate. I know you're worried about me. I don't blame you." Their eyes lock for a moment, serious. "But this is something I need to do on my own."

255

Keira glances at Felix and me. We don't get the naughty-puppy look. With us, it's more like, *It would be so nice if you weren't here right now.*

"Did you see her?" asks Nate.

"No," says Keira. "She wasn't home. I decided to walk a five-block square around her street five times and then try again later. I know that's weird. But it's calming me down."

"Do you want us to stay with you?"

She looks at Felix and me again, then away. "No. It's actually been . . . kind of nice, being alone."

Nate nods slowly at her, relieved, and I'm getting the sense that this is it. The end of our adventure here. No reason not to head home to Mountain Ridge and let whatever will be, be.

"Want some nachos?" asks Felix, a completely brilliant comment to insert into the moment. Keira smiles. She visibly relaxes. For her this means standing up straighter, pointing her chin higher. She steps toward the table and Nate pulls the fourth chair out for her.

I hold up the camera. "Do you mind?" I ask her. "I've sort of been documenting this whole outing." Keira gives Nate a questioning glance and he nods, then she nods. I would hate their little unspoken connection if it didn't make life easier for me at crucial moments. I press record as she sits down.

"So," says Nate. "Do you want to hear the details of the

shit hitting the fan after we all woke up and found you gone?"

"Yes, please," says Keira, smiling now. She raises her head and reaches out for a chip, and then suddenly, loudly, sucks in her breath like she's been punched. Like something came out of nowhere and knocked the middle out of her.

She's staring into the near distance. Felix and Nate follow her gaze and I do the same, but with the camera. It takes me a few moments to land on them, but there they are:

Crossing the street toward us is a man and a woman. The man is pushing an empty stroller and the woman is holding hands with a little girl, maybe two years old.

The woman is Keira's mother.

I recognize her instantly, although she looks very different than I remember. She's wearing a long plaid shirt over black leggings, and white Keds that match the ones on the girl. Her hair, which was always super long, is just to her shoulders now.

The four of us watch them reach the curb, then turn to walk up the block right past us. I keep the camera on them the whole time. They say anything can happen in New York, and now anything is.

I glance at Keira. She's not blinking. There is no expression on her face and I can't tell what she's feeling. Maybe at a moment like this, you feel every emotion at once and they cancel one another out, like how white light is not actually white but many colors of light blended together.

As they pass us, almost on cue, Mrs. Jones picks up the toddler and rests her on her hip. It's such a fluid, natural motion. Devastating.

"Keira," whispers Nate. "Aren't you going to call her name?"

Keira doesn't speak. She only moves. She moves away from us and toward the trio, following behind.

"Shit," says Nate, digging into his pocket and pulling out the rest of his cash. He counts out what should be enough, then throws it on the table before starting off after them. Felix and I exchange a look.

"Whatever happens," he says, "you keep that camera rolling. Yes?"

I nod, and now we're following too. I speed up so that I'm alongside Nate. He doesn't even notice me; he's got his sights locked on Keira.

We round the corner as the tail end of this extremely strange parade, and just as we do, the little girl drops a stuffed thing she's holding. It's like a small blanket with a cat's head. She cries out.

Mrs. Jones and the guy stop abruptly, and Mrs. Jones sets the girl on the ground so she can pick up the blanket. Keira stops. She's only a few feet behind them. Mrs. Jones must sense someone there because now she turns around, casually, probably expecting to get a dirty look from some other pedestrian who has to get around them.

She sees Keira, smiles in an apologetic way, then turns back. Keira does not move or speak.

Now Mrs. Jones turns around again, and really looks at Keira. Her daughter.

"Oh my God," she says.

I move silently to the side and take some steps away, so I can get a better shot of what's happening. At any moment, they will notice me and react to the camera, but until then, I can record every second possible. Besides, it's easier to watch what's happening on the LCD display instead of in the intensity of real life.

Keira looks at the little girl, then back at her mother.

"Keira, no," says Mrs. Jones. "It's not—"

And Keira bolts. Across the street, down the block, faster than I have ever seen her move.

EIGHTEEN

As Nate takes off after Keira, Mrs. Jones crumples onto the steps of the nearest brownstone.

The little girl watches her do this, then turns to the man, frightened. He scoops her up and walks her down the block a bit, abandoning the stroller in the middle of the sidewalk.

I'm not sure what I should do here. I don't seem capable of moving, or taking the camera off this woman who now has her face in her hands, sobbing into them. Fortunately, Felix steps into frame.

"Mrs. Jones?" She looks up, her eyes unfocused. "It's Felix Cortez. Do you remember me? From Mountain Ridge? From the movies?"

She stops sobbing long enough to make the connection, then nods. Now she notices me, and the camera.

"Is this part of the next film?" she asks, defeated, like she's been dreading this moment for a long time and now it's finally here.

"No," says Felix emphatically. "Not if nobody wants it to be."

Mrs. Jones looks down the street at the man and the girl. "She's not mine. That's my boyfriend and his daughter."

"We'll find Keira," Felix assures her. "We'll explain."

She dabs at her tears with the back of her wrist, once on each cheek, and then presses her palm to her chest like she wants to make sure she's still breathing. "It wasn't supposed to happen this way," says Mrs. Jones. "I wanted to really get my life together before contacting her."

Felix leans on the railing above her, a comforting *Go on* gesture. I zoom out a bit so they're both in frame.

"She's so beautiful," says Mrs. Jones, staring at the spot where she saw Keira, as if it were years ago and not minutes, and in her voice there's pain and love and desperate want.

"Yes, she is," says Felix.

"It's so strange. Every day, I think I see her on the street. The city is filled with young women who look like my daughter."

Nate reappears, panting and sweaty. He walks over to us. "I lost her around a corner." He grips an iron fence and tries to catch his breath.

"Do you have any way of reaching her?" asks Mrs. Jones.

Nate nods. He takes out his phone and dials. Mrs. Jones stands and holds out one hand to indicate she'd like to speak, and Nate gives her the phone. "You'll hear Leslie Rodgers on the voice mail. Just ignore that. Say what you need to say."

Mrs. Jones steps away from us, toward the man and the girl, and we see her speaking into the phone. She hangs up, says something to the man. He nods sadly, then they all come walking back to us. She returns the phone to Nate.

"Look at you," she says to him. "You're all grown up." She scans over to Felix and me. "All of you."

"Not quite, but we're getting there," says Nate, then flashes a shy smile.

"Can you make sure she listens to my message?" asks Mrs. Jones.

"I can try. She's using someone else's phone, and I don't know if she can access the voice mail."

After Nate gives Mrs. Jones a couple of cell phone numbers—Keira's, and then his own—she slips her hand into the man's, and the three of them turn around to head back down the street. We watch them climb the steps to her building and disappear.

Nate looks at me expectantly. "It's her boyfriend and his daughter," I reply to his unasked question. Nate nods, then turns to his phone. Types out a text message, presumably to Keira.

"What now?" I ask.

"I told her we're going to hang out somewhere for a while. I told her we're here if she needs us."

"I was hoping you had a slightly more detailed plan than that."

The truth is, I'm not really annoyed. I'm grateful. That we don't have to go home yet. That I'll have more time to get my questions answered.

"That makes two of us," says Nate. "But I can't leave until I know this is going to be all right. Let me call Dylan to see if he's around, because that's a totally safe place to chill and we could probably stay over if we have to."

Nate starts fiddling with his phone again so I turn off the camera and go over to Felix. He's now sitting on the step where Mrs. Jones was, and I lean my head against his shoulder. He's quiet for a moment, then puts his arm around me. I have no idea where exactly we'll spend the rest of the day and even the night or what our next meal will be, and I'm still very confused about that conversation between Nate and Felix, and stumped over what to do about Rory and what I want to do about Rory. Our lives in Mountain Ridge seem a hemisphere away. We're in a place where none of the rules of those lives seem to apply. And I find myself wishing I could stay here forever.

Nate hangs up and steps over to us. "It's all cool. We can go to Dylan's. But it's way the hell downtown and we should leave the car here, don't you think?"

"Oh, yeah," I say. "Once the Parking Gods have gifted you, you don't want to anger them. I'm sure we got the last free space in the city."

"But we'd have to walk. Can't afford the subway at the moment."

"We've got legs," I say, shrugging.

"Uh, aren't you forgetting something?" asks Felix. "As in, *Rory*? She can't stay in the car all night."

Nate visibly deflates. "Right."

"I'll explain that she's got to come with us," I offer.

Felix shakes his head. "No. Let me do it."

He walks to the car and knocks on the window, which leads me to believe Rory is sleeping. Then he opens the car door and slides in. All we can do now is wait.

Nate sits down on the bottom step. Facing the sidewalk, away from me. "You know, we shouldn't be sitting on someone else's steps."

"Thank you," I say suddenly.

"I just don't want us to get in trouble."

"No, I mean, for what you said earlier. About Rory and me. It was something I hadn't thought of."

The back of Nate's head nods.

"Have you thought about what would happen if Felix were to forgive *you?*

Now Nate turns to me, frowns. "Felix forgive *me?* I didn't do anything he needs to forgive me for."

"Is that how you see it?"

His face hardens to match the tone of my voice. "I don't know what he's told you, but I have a feeling it's not exactly true."

I open my mouth to protest, but it hits me. Felix hasn't actually told me anything. Was there a conversation somewhere in the last four years when Felix said, "Nate decided to change his life and become a different person, so he completely ditched his best friend"? It feels like there must have been. I've been seething about these events for four years.

I don't know what to say next so I do the thing that seems to be working when this happens. I turn on the camera and frame Nate below me. It's an interesting shot. He looks smaller, more vulnerable. Nothing but sidewalk and car tires behind him.

He stares right into the lens. "What did he tell you, Justine? I think I have a right to know."

The thing about having a camera basically stitched onto your anatomy is that you can't look away when you want to. The camera forces me to meet Nate's gaze on the display, even if it's through a whole bunch of electronic innards.

"He didn't tell me anything. He didn't have to."

Nate's features slide into a kind of sadness. "Ah. So you're going on assumptions."

I pause. "Why don't you set me straight?" I say, keeping my voice even, like Leslie would.

"That's not up to me. I meant what I said to Felix before. I've kept my word all this time and I'm not going to blow it now. It's on him to tell you the truth. And really, you're the one he should tell. If he can't tell you, he's in bigger trouble than I thought."

Nate turns away. What can I ask next to get him to keep talking? But just then, I hear Felix chirp, "Here we are!"

I find him with the camera and yes, here he is. And here Rory is too, staring a hole into the pavement.

"Yay, Rory!" says Nate, but she doesn't react so he switches gears. "We have to get down to Dylan's dorm and we have to walk. It's pretty far. Felix explained that?"

Rory nods.

"Why don't we go ask Mrs. Jones to lend us money for the subway?" suggests Felix, pointing with his thumb behind us.

"No subway," says Rory. "No way. Never."

Felix mentioning money reminds me of the credit card in Olivia's car. It makes sense to have it with us, in case of

267

an emergency. "Before we go, I need to grab my stuff," I say, and pass off the camera to Felix.

"Oh, yeah," says Nate. "Me too."

He starts walking toward the car and I step in alongside him. I don't want him to see me grab the credit card. I'm not sure why this is important, but it is.

Nate still has the keys so he uses them to pop the trunk, reaching in to grab my backpack and then his. He hands me mine and slams the trunk shut.

I'm focused on the credit card but there's something else gnawing at me. I think of the front seat. Leslie's bag. I know from the camera's display that I have plenty of shooting time left on the memory card but eventually, I'll run out of battery charge.

"Hang on," I call to Nate. I reach in, find the bag on the floor of the front passenger seat. As I'd hoped, inside is a spare battery, which I grab and stuff in my backpack.

Nate is distracted by something up the street so now I open the back door, crouch down like I'm searching. I flip up the floor mat on one side. Nada. Then I flip up the other. *Oh, come on, Olivia. Please don't tell me you borrowed your own emergency credit card and then forgot to put it back.* At first, I see nothing. Then, way in, almost under the front seat, I see a corner of colored plastic. Bingo.

Nate's still watching two drivers argue about who cut off the other. I tap him on the shoulder and he snaps out of it, uses the keys to beep the car locked. Then we move back toward Rory and Felix.

"Ready?" Nate asks Rory, hoisting his backpack onto his shoulders. It's like we're about to embark on some treacherous hike in the woods. Which we sort of are.

Rory just starts walking, hugging herself.

Felix falls back, returns the camera, and asks me, "Would it help if I offered to hold her hand?"

Rory has never been one for touching. She might have changed, what with all the therapy. But I see in my head the image of Felix and Rory walking down the street, hand in hand, and even though it would make a great shot I already feel the sting it would cause me. So I shake my head no, slowly, like *Don't even go there.*

We get to the corner and the light is with us, so Nate gestures and we follow, across the street and on our way downtown. I hang back so they're all in front of me and start shooting.

Nate leads us, and Felix tries to slow his pace so he's behind him and not next to him, but also not next to Rory but not too far ahead of Rory. He looks ridiculous, and maybe a little drunk. Rory walks in a steady and careful march, not taking her eyes off the sidewalk.

Traffic roars by, a tide of mostly yellow taxis, like loud breaking waves that keep coming and coming. A car parked at the curb honks, and Rory jumps, then freezes, breathes in with her whole body to the count of three, and starts walking again. Up ahead, Nate's at the corner and the light has just turned to a red hand so he has to wait, and we catch up to him.

"You good?" he asks Rory. Rory just nods. "Okay. One block down. About fifty-four more to go."

He says this with a supportive and earnest smile, but Rory turns pale.

The light changes again. We cross. As we walk, I experiment with panning the camera to the right and left, up and down. It feels embedded now. Like a second pair of eyes searching for things my regular eyes could never see.

These are the things the camera notices:

Nate walks looking straight ahead. Felix can't stop looking skyward in all directions. Rory has not glanced up from the ground.

Here in the city, Felix has lost his swagger; he moves like he's in a new body. Experimenting, trying it out. Unsure of every step.

Nate seems to be striding confidently the same way he does at home, in school. But it's like he's Superman and we're back on Krypton. He has no powers here. Occasionally I see a girl or a young woman pass him and let her glance linger for an extra second, but no longer. That's the most Nate Hunter, in all his country-boy stun-ningness, is worth in Manhattan.

Within the rhythms of Rory's controlled pace, there are tiny spasms. She winces every time someone shouts across her and at the particularly loud rumble of a truck, the cry of a baby strapped on to a woman's chest, and the sharp-pitched barking of a pair of German shepherds.

We've gone four blocks now. It feels like we're in a groove, that we can do this.

Out of nowhere, a screaming fire truck cuts through what's already become a familiar hum of city noise. It's loud and painful. I'd stick my fingers in my ears if I didn't have the camera to deal with. Then I realize why it's so intense; behind the fire truck is an ambulance, and their two sets of sirens don't match up.

We all turn to look at Rory, statue still, her eyes fixed on the pavement. This seems to be working for her, so none of us goes closer.

Then, from behind me, comes a pair of little boys, sprinting down the sidewalk like they're chasing the fire truck and ambulance, shouting with glee because this is clearly the coolest thing they've ever seen. Rory's in their way. In their rush past her, one of them knocks into her hip and pushes her off-balance.

The sound that Rory makes, at this moment, is full of so much frustration and anger that you know it's been building up, that some kind of floodgate has burst open. She throws herself to the nearest wall, a narrow strip of brick between a deli and a shoe store, and slides down to the ground. She wraps her arms around her head and closes her eyes.

Felix is the first to reach her and he kneels down, instinctively reaching out to touch her, but then he hesitates. In seconds, Nate is on her other side. I press stop on the camera and join the circle.

"I'm sorry that happened," Felix is saying.

Rory has not lifted her face yet. It's almost freakier down here, with all the feet and dog paws and stroller wheels rushing past us.

"Rory?" pushes Felix. "What can we do for you?"

She takes a deep breath, long and slow. Her whole body expands and retracts with it.

We wait.

Finally, she unspools her arms and raises her head. She doesn't look at us. She doesn't seem to be looking at anything. Her eyes are blank, unfocused.

"I want to go back to the car," she says.

Nate glances at me, panicked. I just shrug. Then he digs the car keys out of his pocket and says, "Justine, you should drive her home to Mountain Ridge."

Nate opens his palm so the keys sit there. Olivia has a tiny Lego man on her keychain and it stares up at me, ready to be claimed. Nate pushes his hand toward me. I understand the sense of it. Nate must stay for Keira, and I must go for Rory. Maybe the extra time alone with Rory will result in an actual Important Conversation. The beginnings of something beyond *I forgive you.*

The fact is, none of us should be leaving yet. The

camera feels warm and eager in my hand. But it's not up to me.

"I really want to be where you all are," says Rory, defeated, clearly fighting back tears. "I want to stay part of this." She's talking to nobody, looking at nothing. Or maybe just something the rest of us can't see.

I think of that day we went to Radio City. After the show, after the Endless Rorys in the ladies' room, we had to somehow get out of the building and back to the car. I watched her mom use Rory's favorite poem to bring Rory to the point where she could do that. Soon after, I started using the same poem when I needed her to calm down about something. I thought it was kind of fun, just another one of the songs and rhymes we learned in school.

"Rory," I say now. "Bluff King Hal was full of beans."

She just shakes her head.

I repeat it, more urgently, ignoring the befuddled looks on Nate's and Felix's faces. Knowing how crazy I must sound and almost liking it. "Bluff King Hal. Was full. Of *beans*."

Something quiets in Rory and settles into recognition. She closes her eyes and says, softly, "He married half a dozen queens."

"For three called Kate they cried the banns," I add, keeping my voice steady, hiding my own amazement that I actually remember this.

Rory takes a deep breath. "And one called Jane." Another breath, even slower and longer. "And a couple of Annes."

"You do the next one," I say gently. Rory opens and raises her eyes to me now and they are no longer focused on nothing. They are right here, deeply pooled with sudden gratitude. She keeps them this way as she starts to recite the next stanza.

"The first he asked to share his reign, was Kate of Aragon, straight from Spain. But when his love for her was spent, he got a divorce, and out she went."

Our locked gaze must be too much for her because she looks away to continue the rest of the poem, each pair of lines detailing the fates of Henry's wives. When she's done, and Henry is dead and survived by lucky Catherine Parr, Rory rests her head against the wall and takes one more shuddering breath.

"Better?" asks Felix.

"Yes," says Rory, almost dreamily. "Much better."

In my mind, I enjoy the quickest of victorious superhero moments, because that's all we have time for. I'm still not sure how we're going to avoid taking Rory home.

How did we handle it at Radio City? After the show, Mrs. Gold walked to the parking garage to get the car while my mom and I stayed with Rory in the ladies' room.

The parking garage.

A parking garage takes credit cards, and a credit card

is something I happen to have in my pocket for emergencies. Admittedly, this is not a life-or-death situation, but emergencies can come in all forms, and this sure as hell seems like one of them.

"We don't have to drive her home," I say to Nate, then turn to Rory. "We can take the car down to Dylan's. Would you be okay to stay in the city if we took the car?"

Rory finally meets my eyes, holding them there for a few long moments before closing them. "Yes. I guess so."

"Justine, we shouldn't move the car—" says Nate, and I hold up my hand to silence him. I stand up. He stands up. I reach into my pocket and pull out the credit card.

Nate stares at it for a long time, and I can feel the leadership of our little group suddenly leap from him to me. Maybe this is why I kept the secret.

"If I weren't so happy to see that thing," says Felix, still kneeling next to Rory, "I would try to stab you with it."

NINETEEN

B ack in the car, we put the blocks behind us at warp-drive speed, or at least it seems that way compared with the pace we kept on the sidewalk, where every step was full of too many dangerous possibilities. Nate drives and Rory rides shotgun, navigating us to Dylan's dorm. She's in control again, and happy.

We take turns borrowing Nate's phone to text our parents. Just texts. No need to deal with spoken words that may cause problems. Aside from the *click click* of the cell phone keys, we are silent.

At a red light, Felix reaches forward to the front

seat and tentatively squeezes Rory's shoulder. He has a younger brother and sister. I'm guessing he sees Rory that way, but what if it's more than that? Would that be weird? I don't even know what his type is, but maybe it's this. I can, if I squint sideways in my mind, sort of see them together. And then I can sort of see the *three of us* together. As friends.

I'm so grateful I'm pointed south at the moment, barreling down Second Avenue, rather than north and backward to Mountain Ridge.

Rory has Nate make a right turn off Second Avenue and soon, we are pulling up to a medium-high stone building on Fifteenth Street, just a block from what I know is Union Square.

"I see a parking garage up there," says Nate to me as Felix and Rory get out of the car. "And oh, look, it's only a bazillion dollars to park overnight."

I laugh. "Olivia will forgive us."

Nate drives off, and I see Felix has moved Rory to the nearest wall.

"Let's get inside," says Felix, as if it's raining hailstones. Rory reaches out to take his hand. He grabs hers, examines it for a second, like some strange and shy bird has just landed on him and he's afraid to move, then pulls Rory forward. As they walk, I linger long enough to start recording and zoom in on their linked hands.

Inside the building lobby, we wait for Nate, and I pan

the room. There's a low orange sofa against the wall and a guy fast asleep in a big chair, a book open on his face. I hold on him for a few seconds, then move on to the block of vending machines humming in the far corner.

Five minutes later, Nate appears, carrying our backpacks. He dumps them on the floor and walks right up to the girl sitting behind a reception desk, says something I can't hear. The girl smiles, nods, and picks up the phone. Nate turns to us and gives us a thumbs-up. It occurs to me that I have never given a thumbs-up in my life. I don't think my hands could even form the shape.

After a few more minutes, a voice shouts "Nate!" and we all turn to see someone standing in front of the elevators. This person could be Dylan Boone, if the Dylan Boone I remember from Mountain Ridge had been upgraded to a better groomed, better dressed model.

"Wow," I whisper to Felix. "It's like he got a gaykeover."

Felix laughs, louder than usual, with a nervous edge. He scoops up his bag and Rory's, then moves away.

Dylan hugs Nate and then they do that guyish thumb-handshake—another gesture I've never made. Dylan turns to the rest of us and holds out both hands, palms upward, and says, "Welcome to the jungle."

When he sees the camera, he pauses, his head tilted sideways.

"Is it okay?" I ask.

Dylan exchanges a look with Nate, then laughs. "Sure.

I'll make sure not to do anything illegal."

We take the elevator up to the seventh floor, which I realize is actually the eighth floor because there's a button L for the ground floor and a button 1 for the second floor. I can't believe how misleading this is, and find myself wondering who I can write to about it.

Dylan leads us down a long hallway that smells of coffee, bleach, and ramen noodles. The floor is tile and our footsteps echo way too loudly, which makes it seem even more obvious that we don't belong here. To add to the topsy-turvy-ness of the situation, Felix and Rory are still holding hands, and Nate, carrying my backpack and his, keeps looking behind him to see where I am.

Finally, Dylan opens a door and we're in a room that seems to be all things at once. There's a small kitchen and table on one end, a TV and a futon couch in the middle, and a twin bed in the corner. But based on what I've seen of dorm rooms in Mountain Ridge, this one rates at least three stars. The futon is on a dark wood frame and actually has throw pillows; magazines are spread out on the coffee table in front of it. There's a small alcove off this room with two doors facing each other.

Two guys emerge from one of the doors, which I now see is a small bedroom. "Is it *you?*" asks one of them, auburn-haired, well-gelled, as he stares excitedly at us.

"It's *them*," says Dylan, then turns to us. "Sorry. My roommates studied the *Five At* series in their class on documentaries, and this is apparently the most serendipitous moment of their lives."

"Hi," says the other roommate, blond, holding out his hand to Nate. "I'm Adam. This is Max." As he says "Max," he loops his arm around the dark-haired boy's shoulder and they lean into each other. "Forgive us if we're a little starstruck."

I remember what it was like to get recognized, right after *Six* and *Eleven* came out. If I was having a bad day, I hated it; on great days, I loved it so much that I almost asked the people for *their* autographs too. Right now, I'm not sure if this day counts as bad or good.

Max nods. "We knew Dylan grew up with you guys but . . ." He spots the camera in my hand, which I put on pause the second we came into the suite. "Oh my God! Are you shooting the new film?"

"No," I snap, instinctively moving the camera behind my back. "I'm just . . . this is just personal."

"That's a mighty big rig for just personal," says Adam.

"It's complicated," says Nate, in a way that lets them know they need to drop it. That protectiveness. I've only ever seen it come out for Keira or Rory. But this time, for me.

Max and Adam look disappointed, so I add, "Is it okay if I shoot some stuff in here with you?"

"Uh, we'd be *thrilled*. But let us declutter first," says Dylan. "The place is embarrassing like this."

As Max and Adam pick up, Nate gathers our bags into a pile in the kitchen and starts talking to Dylan about swimming. Rory asks to use the bathroom. Felix walks the perimeter of the room, checking the place out. I find myself turning the camera back on and following along with him.

If we didn't already know Dylan was gay and hadn't just met one of his roommates and his roommate's *boyfriend*, the décor would seal the deal. There are art prints of male nudes. There's a poster of a well-known underwear ad, some athlete I can't remember the name of, in his tighty whities. I'm looking at a handmade ceramic platter hanging above the crappy, beat-up microwave, and it's such a contrast that I can't help but think the placement is intentional.

"Adam's mom made that," says Dylan, stepping up next to me. "Isn't it beautiful?"

Somewhere in my exploration I lost track of Felix, but I see he's now standing near the bathroom door, becoming one with the wall.

"Justine," says Nate, coming over to me. "Food."

"Yes. Food." I am loving our shorthand language.

"Do you feel comfortable using your sister's credit card for a *hunger* emergency?"

TWENTY

The sky's already changed colors when Nate and I step back onto the street. All the lights have that early-evening blurriness along their edges, and it feels like the rhythm of the city has shifted too, at once sped up and slowed down.

We're headed to get takeout at some restaurant that's reportedly the second coming of Chicken Kebabs. Felix volunteered to stay in the dorm with Rory. When we left, they were watching some reality show about a matchmaking service for millionaires, and Rory was saying, "If he's so rich, you'd think he'd have that growth on his eyebrow removed."

"That's not a growth, Rory," I heard Felix say as we shut the door. "It's a piercing."

It's been a while now since Nate and I were alone, and it's like those few moments of honest conversation at the café uptown have been rewound, and we have to start from the beginning again. It's awkward and I don't know what to say to him. I turn on the camera and shoot, but the *Wow, look at the city* shots are getting a little old.

Finally, I ask a dumb question I already know the answer to. "Nothing from Keira?"

Nate shakes his head. "Not yet. I'll call in a little while."

We walk for a few long seconds in silence. We're parallel to Union Square now, and Nate keeps looking at the crowds of people gathered there. A dance crew is performing in the center of a circle of spectators. He's so focused on the scene that he doesn't see a woman with a stroller coming toward him, and he stumbles right into one of the wheels.

"Oh! Sorry!" says Nate. The woman gives him the hairy eyeball and keeps walking.

"Is it really that fascinating?" I ask, indicating the park.

"I sort of have this habit." Nate steps up to the wall that separates us from the park. "Whenever I see a big group of people, I'm always looking. You know. For *him*. I can't stop myself."

I'm very confused for a second, and then I get it. *Him.* Nate's father. All I know is what I saw in *Five at Six.* When

284

she was still in high school, Nate's mother had a boyfriend from another town. She got pregnant. He left the scene and moved away from the area. At age six, Nate had never met him. I'm guessing this is still the case.

"Do you even know what he looks like?" I ask, and this comes out harsher than I mean it to. I'm asking for more of the story, but it sounds like I'm criticizing him.

"No," he says bitterly. "At least, not what he might look like now. My mother showed me some pictures once. *Once.*" He watches for another few moments, then shakes his head as if it's an Etch A Sketch and he wants to erase what he drew.

"I'm sorry," I say. It never occurred to me that Nate would be craving the sight of his father. He has those grandparents who clearly love him so much.

I run my fingers over the camera and Nate must sense it, because he glances at it, then me, and slowly shakes his head no. His pleading eyes mean business. I drop the camera to my side.

"When Keira's mom left . . . that really got to me," he continues, maybe feeling safe now. "But I couldn't process it because of all the things that happened to me in that movie." He says it like they only happened on film and not in real life.

Suddenly it all makes sense. Their connection.

"Did you talk to her, after?" I ask.

He shakes his head. "No. She disappeared with her

dad too fast. But when she came back to town, we ended up at a party together. This one girl was drinking and got really sick. Keira and I helped her and I don't know, I guess we bonded over that. When you're fourteen, helping someone find a place to puke in a backyard is a pretty intense experience." He pauses and makes a silly, cringey face, trying to break the tension. It works. I laugh.

Then he continues. "But she asked me about what it was like, living without a dad, knowing you had a parent who wanted nothing to do with you. Didn't try to see you or talk to you or anything."

We're quiet, looking at the crowd, and now I, too, find myself scanning for someone who might look like Nate, but in his thirties. I actually see two men who sort of fit the bill. *This city is full of people who look like my daughter*, Mrs. Jones had said. I can't imagine the feeling that such a huge, lost part of you could reappear at any time. I know there's more to be told here. What would Leslie ask without asking?

"So now I think I understand," I say slowly. "Why you wanted to be there for Keira. Are you wondering how it would be, if you ever go looking for your dad?"

"There's that," says Nate, "and also, well, she always seems to be one step away from losing it completely. It's not obvious to everyone. But if you see her up close all the time, like I do, it's pretty clear." He sighs. "When I found swimming, I found a way to deal. I don't think Keira's found any other way except to bottle it up."

Then he starts walking again, putting a sudden stop to this assault of information. But I don't yell at him to come back and finish. I don't call him a jerk for holding the reins so tightly and completely in his control.

I just run to catch up to him.

The kebab place is on the corner and our order is waiting. I pay with Olivia's credit card, in my head saying, *I'm sorry I'm sorry I'll pay you back I promise* as I forge my sister's name. I know I'll have to do it again later when we get the car out of the garage.

We're silent on the walk home. We stay on the other side of the street, opposite the park.

Back in the dorm, Adam and Max have joined Rory and Felix in front of the TV. While Rory and Felix are sitting on the futon with eyes glued to the set, Adam is sitting on a leather beanbag chair and Max is lying on the floor in front of him, leaning against Adam's legs. Adam's got his left arm draped across Max's chest, and Max grabs it with both hands like he wants to press it closer to his heart. I suddenly miss Ian. Or maybe not the Ian part. Just the having-someone-care part.

Dylan spreads an Indian-print tapestry on the floor and we unpack the meal, enough food for all of us and perhaps two more suites. We just wanted to seem like good guests.

I eat a little, quickly, because I'm ravenous but also want to get the camera going as soon as possible. I put it on the coffee table and frame the shot so we're all in there, pretty much. It's close enough so there's decent audio. Look at me, saying words like *audio*.

Dinner is fun. Dylan and his friends talk about college, about their courses and their professors and some of the student films in the works. They ask us about *Five at Sixteen*, and Nate tells the story of the retreat weekend and everything it set in motion.

"How much did they shoot before this weekend?" asks Adam.

"Several weeks' worth," says Nate, so casually it's almost obvious he's leaving something out. "I think they spent a decent amount of time with each of us so far."

"Will they shoot more once you get back?" asks Dylan.

Nate looks at me, as if I know the answer, and I just shrug. It's something I haven't thought about.

The whole time we're eating, Felix and Rory have not said a word.

We're almost done with dinner when the fourth roommate, Kyle, arrives. He has no reaction whatsoever to the presence of strangers in his suite.

"Hey," says Dylan. "You got my text about our visitors?"

"Yeah," says Kyle distractedly, like *who cares*. "I just ran into Vijay and he said they're having a party tonight."

"Cool," says Dylan. He turns to Nate and me, beaming.

"Vijay and his suitemates throw the best parties. You guys picked the right night to hang here."

It's been an hour, and Dylan and his friends are still getting ready to go out. Granted, there's just one bathroom and all four of them need to shower. But by contrast, I was ready in five minutes. That simply involved changing into a sweater, the only nonslob item I packed for the weekend, and running the *girly brush* through my hair. Even if I had my eyeliner with me, I'm not sure I'd put it on. At least I've got the pink streaks. I'm beginning to see them as built-in fashion accessories.

Parties are just not my thing. I tried drinking once. It messed up my stomach for two days. When you're totally sober and everyone around you is totally not, you feel like an alien who's landed on a planet of shouting idiots. I wonder if that's how it is for Rory wherever she goes: like she's always the only nonwasted person in the room.

Nate has opted to wait his turn for a shower, so he finally takes one, and Felix and Rory are watching TV again. They've made no indications that they're getting ready to go to a *college* party in the middle of Greenwich Village in the middle of New York City. Very possibly the coolest thing they will get a chance to do all year. Then again, maybe I'm biased because I can already see the shooting possibilities.

"You guys are coming, right?" I say, keeping my voice as light as possible.

"I would like to come, yes," replies Rory. "I'm curious to see what it'll be like. As long as I can leave whenever I want."

"I'm not sure," says Felix.

"How can you say that?" I ask, smiling. "When else are you going to have an opportunity like this?"

A phone rings from somewhere deep inside Nate's backpack, which is sitting on the floor of the common room.

Nate comes out of the bathroom, wearing jeans and a long-sleeved shirt with Iron Man on it. His hair sticks out on all sides and frankly, he looks adorable. I just want to reach out and smooth it down, or at least give him my hairbrush again. He whizzes past me and the smell of *clean boy* almost knocks me over as he digs into his back-pack, finds his phone, and answers it.

"Hello?" he says hopefully. A pause, then: "Oh. Yes. She's here." He flicks his eyes toward Rory. "She's totally fine. Do you want to talk to her? . . . Okay. I'll tell her. . . . Yes, as soon as we can. We'll be in touch."

Nate hangs up his phone and turns to Rory. "Your mom wants to remind you to take your meds," he says.

"Already did," says Rory. "Thanks, Mom."

Rory smiles at her microjoke, and we all laugh ner-vously. Nate does a good job of hiding his disappointment.

Surely he thought we'd hear from Keira by now.

I can't stop the urge to reach out toward him. My hand takes off and lands, gingerly, just the fingertip, on his wrist.

"She'll call," I tell him.

"I think I should try her now," he says.

"She knows we're here, right? Then let her be. Let's give it until ten o'clock before we try her. That's a reasonable time to be checking up on someone."

I'm not sure how these words, which make actual sense, came out of my mouth. But suddenly, the rest of the evening rolls out before me. I can see exactly how it should go, and there's no reason why it can't go like that.

Ten minutes later, our hosts are ready and we're all headed out the door. Rory pulls herself off the couch, but Felix does not. I go over to him and kneel down, rest my chin on his thigh.

"Come on, Felix. You'll hate yourself if you don't at least go for a little while. You'll always wonder."

"I know," he says sadly.

"Besides," I add, "I think Rory needs you there." God, I'm awful. Playing the cards I know will beat him.

Felix takes a deep breath, turns off the TV, then nods without meeting my eyes and stands up. I follow him out the door.

TWENTY-ONE

I do have to hand it to Vijay and Company, because this is one hell of a party.

The suite is identical to Dylan's, except decorated much more ornately, every square inch of wall covered with posters, strings of colorful plastic beads draped everywhere. The ceiling is covered with shimmery CDs and old vinyl records, and a layer of little white Christmas lights that shine up into them reflects a galaxy of electric stars.

I'm standing with Felix and Rory against one wall, shooting the room. Dylan's been introducing us as freshmen. "She's just getting some B-roll for a student film," he said, pointing to me. I get the feeling they're used to this kind of thing and don't care that they're getting caught on camera as underage drinkers.

There's actually a DJ spinning in the corner, and I'm told this is one of Vijay's suitemates, hence the assumed awesomeness of the event. His gifts, apparently, are related to being able to produce great sounds at minimal volume so as not to break dorm rules.

The room is small, so it feels more crowded than it really is, and already a dozen people are dancing. Adam and Max are grooving together and not even touching, but their attraction, their chemistry, is so loud I can almost hear it buzz along the bass line of the music. Felix watches them, his face all curiosity and examination. He's barely looked at these two so far, but now, it's as if he's the only person at a private screening of the Adam and Max movie.

Something about it seems off and decidedly un-Felix. When I think he won't notice me, I get a shot of his expression, then pan to the guys.

But he notices me.

"Why did you just do that?" snaps Felix.

"Why are you staring at them?"

"I'm not . . ." He stops, knowing he can't deny it. Embarrassed, and a little vulnerable, maybe. He adds, "Justine, don't shoot me anymore. Not here. Okay?"

"Okay." I put the camera on pause, then look over at Rory. Even *I* feel overstimulated in this place, and there are bodies coming dangerously close to her every 1.4 seconds, but her curiosity seems to be overriding all that.

"What do you think?" I ask her.

"I don't think I've ever seen people having so much fun," she says, glancing quickly at me and then down to the floor. "Real fun. Not fake fun."

I smile, thinking of the gatherings I used to attend with Ian. Everybody trying to look like they were having a great time, constantly glancing around to see who was noticing them looking like they were having a great time. But there's something *pure* about this party. The people here seem to have crossed over some bullshit barrier.

I haven't seen Nate since we first got here. He disappeared into one of the bedrooms with Dylan and Kyle, and I'm trying not to get mad about it. What's happening in there? It's sort of obvious. They're smoking a joint, or doing shots, or something worse. It's not like I want to be included. Two days ago, I wouldn't have expected anything less from Nate. But tonight, it feels like a betrayal of who he is now, to me.

Nate reappears, looking worried. He comes over to stand with us, taking a place against the wall next to me as if we're all in a police lineup. After a minute, he leans in close to my ear and says something that sounds like, "You wanna dance?"

There's no way he could be saying that, so I move my ear closer and ask, "What?"

He breathes in and out, and I can feel his breath on my skin. "I said, do you wanna dance?"

"With you?" This just escapes me. A reflex, like a blink, or my knee after being hit with the doctor's mallet.

Nate looks hurt. "Never mind. I'm just not one for standing here."

He doesn't seem drunk or stoned. "What were you doing in that room?" I ask, before I chicken out.

Nate glances in the direction of the room, and I can't read his expression. Finally he leans down again. His breath, again. "Rabbit."

"Rabbit?"

"One of the guys who lives here has a rabbit. It won't eat. Dylan remembered that I used to raise them, so he asked me to take a look."

Nate's voice even saying the word *rabbit* seems unnatural, like he has trouble wrapping himself around the sound. It's the first time I've seen him connect himself directly to the person he used to be.

I must look really shocked, because he adds, "You thought I was drinking or smoking or snorting something. Right?" When I don't answer, he shakes his head and mutters a word I can't hear, then launches himself off the wall. Walks over to Rory. I see him hold out his hand, and she shakes her head. Then he holds out his other hand and says something else to her, and she smiles shyly. Rory grabs on to both his hands and he pulls her, walking backward, to the very edge of the dance cluster. They start to move.

Why didn't I say yes to dancing with him? Here, of all places, it would have been okay. More than okay. But I can't seem to break us out of our old boxes, despite everything we've been through in the last twenty-four hours.

I don't have too much time to dwell on this, though, because in the middle of the floor, Adam and Max have suddenly frozen. Adam whispers something in Max's ear, Max nods. Max steps around a few people to get to the wall. Where Felix is.

"Hey, man," says Max, holding out his hand with an earnest smile. "Come dance with us."

Felix looks so terrified, Max may as well be holding a wooden stake against his chest. He doesn't even speak.

"You've been watching us all night," adds Max. "It seems like you really want to." He nods ever so slightly, as if giving Felix permission for something.

Felix glares at Nate. Quick, but *whoa*. Intense and hateful. Nate's so focused on Rory, moving side to side with her the way ten-year-olds do at a painful school social, he doesn't notice. Then Felix looks back at Max, still offering his open palm.

Something happens to me here. It's like my brain has been wrapped in a fog that's now lifting, moving across the night to reveal a crystal clear, oh-so-obvious moon.

Felix pushes Max away, both hands against his chest,

sending him stumbling into a group of people, then bolts from the room.

Nate and Rory freeze, but I take off after him, gripping the camera. In the hallway, above the noise of the party, I can hear footsteps in the stairwell. *Ping ping ping.*

"Leave me alone!" I hear Felix call before a door opens and booms shut, and there's something in his voice that tells me he's not sure exactly who's chasing him. I don't yell that it's me, in case that means he'll just run faster.

Now I'm at the door and I throw myself through it. It puts me out in another hallway, but I see the building lobby up ahead, and Felix at the front door, rushing outside. By the time I'm outside too, I just get a glimpse of him at the corner, crossing the street into the park. He's not running anymore. He slows to a walk, deliberate, angry. Each hard footstomp on the pavement is like a silent shout.

I keep up my speed, though, and I'm able to get across the street during the same traffic light. I don't have to go too far into the park to find Felix. He must have grabbed the first empty bench he saw, but it's a nice one, right under a streetlamp. He sits hugging his knees to his chest and when he sees me approach, he doesn't react. He just watches me. I slide into the bench next to him and struggle to catch my breath.

"I thought it was you," Felix says flatly.

We're silent for a little while, breathing together, as we watch a pair of young women with identical shopping bags walk by. Elsewhere in the park, someone's playing a clarinet.

"Go ahead," he finally says. "Ask what you want to ask." The first part of his sentence comes out casually, but by the end of it, his voice is shaking, breaking down.

I don't ask what I want to ask. I ask something else. "When you asked Rory what helps, I thought that was brilliant, really. Can I steal that? Can I just ask how I can help *you*?"

"You can't help me, but thanks anyway." Felix shakes his head. "Goddamn Nate. He planned this whole thing."

I assume he means the trip to find Keira. "It was my idea, originally. Remember? But he does seem to be in charge at the moment."

"I mean, coming here to Dylan's. We could have hung out in a park or gone to Macy's or *something* while we waited."

"I think he wanted to find a place where we could borrow money and sleep, if it got too late . . ."

But Felix is not listening to me. "Nate knew Dylan is . . . out," he continues, "and that his friends were probably like that." He turns to me now, tears welling up in his eyes. "But I'm not. You know that, right? I'm *not*. I can't be."

"You mean gay."

Felix shrivels at the sound of the word, into a smaller version of himself. I don't want to ruin this. The camera's off, but this must continue. I draw a mental line back to what he said about Nate, then connect that conversation to the rest of what just happened.

"Felix, why would Nate think you're gay?"

Now Felix is really crying. He puts his hands over his eyes and sobs. They are little-boy-lost sobs, the-world-is-ending sobs. I rest my hand on his knee.

"Felix?" I prod.

Felix sucks in a deep breath, and the sobs disappear into it.

"Because maybe I am." He raises his eyes only halfway to me, and I still can't see his face.

I want to ask something practical here, like, *Why? Are you attracted to men?* But I decide to take a different tack.

"And how would Nate know that?" I keep my voice easy. Totally nonjudgmental.

For this one, Felix has to turn his head so he's looking away from me, toward the music, wherever it is.

"Something happened. When we were kids."

I wait for him to go on. I'm tired of filling in the blank spaces with questions.

"We were eleven. It wasn't long after they shot *Five at Eleven*, but before the movie came out."

"Can you tell me what it was?"

"No. I don't want you having that image in your head. God knows it's burned into mine." He pauses, then slowly pivots toward me, still not meeting my glance. "Let's just

300

say we were messing around, wrestling, you know, and I had this overwhelming need to see what would happen if—" He stops dead, jammed against the thing in his mind that blocks him from going further. But I don't need him to go past it right now. It's all making so much sense. Felix's eagerness for us to start dating. All the cryptic things Nate said.

Seeing Felix every day, right in front of me, but not seeing him at all.

"Wow," I say. "I really had no clue. You're going through all this and you kept it completely hidden? Impressive. Terribly unhealthy, but impressive."

Felix shrugs. "Well. That's something, I guess."

"I can't believe you didn't think you could tell me. It would have been fine."

"But if I didn't tell anyone, then it didn't have to be true. I can't be gay, Justine. I just can't."

"Why not?"

Now, at last, Felix looks me in the eye. "Do you know what my dad would do? He would kick me out of the house. And my mom . . . she'd kill herself, if she didn't die of a broken heart first."

"I think you're being a little overdramatic."

"You don't know what it's like, with my family. We may as well be living in the eighteenth century when it comes to certain things." Felix's face takes on a sadness that's so raw, so unself-conscious, it pierces me. "Then there's everyone else. The whole freaking world. You think I want to open myself up to that kind of persecution from total strangers?"

"You could look at it a different way. If Lance and Leslie were aware of this, you'd be the focus of the film no matter how angry they were. It would be a great story. Inspirational, even."

Felix shakes his head, hard. "If I'm going to come out, it's not going to be for public consumption. Even *I'm* not that much of a media whore."

I think back to that first question. That simple question, the one so basic, nobody thinks to ask it anymore. *How can I help him?* What will take him just one single step past this place? What will get him off this bench, to start?

"Felix," I say, trying to break this huge thing down into the smallest possible pieces. "Nobody's asking you to come out. Not even to your parents. Why don't you focus on coming out, you know, to yourself first."

Felix bows his head and stares at my hand on his knee, like he's just noticing it. He puts his hand on top of mine.

"I don't know if I can."

"So what are you going to do, live in the closet for the rest of your life?"

"I hadn't thought that far ahead. I guess I was still hoping I would . . . change."

This hope must be superstrong because I can actually

302

feel it, sitting on this park bench, vibrating off him. If hope can be depressing, that's what this is.

"Nate," I add, still working on the puzzle in my head. "That's the real reason why Nate stopped being friends with you."

Felix bites his lip. "Actually, no. *I* stopped being friends with *him*. I wouldn't see him anymore or hang out with him. I sent him, like, a breakup letter on X-Men stationery."

Now I reach over and put my fingers under Felix's chin, push it up so I can finally see his face straight on. "He didn't dump you?"

"No," he says sadly, with a sigh. "I mean, he was definitely weirded out. But he had his own problems, as you know. He needed his friend. But I couldn't . . ." Felix yanks his face out of my grasp and turns away again. "I'm the one who bailed on him when he was still getting tormented on a regular basis. It sucks having to live with that, in addition to this other thing it sucks having to live with."

I think back to the apple cider donut and the whole gesture changes. It didn't come from hurt and loneliness but rather, guilt, and maybe a little self-preservation.

"All this time, I hated him for ditching you," I say. "And you let me."

"I guess I was too busy hating *myself* to correct you."

The music in the distance stops. It's like a cue for something else to be said here, a cutaway or at the very least, a change in scene. A shift in the mood.

I come up with this: "So now that we know we're attracted to the same gender, you have to tell me. Butch or Sundance?"

Felix actually laughs now. "I am so not telling you that."

"Come on. I'm with the Sundance Kid. All the way."

"Okay," says Felix, biting his lip. "Me too."

Another pause. This feels like the right direction.

"I think you should go back to the party and dance with those guys."

"That is very much not going to happen."

I look down at the camera, which is nestled in my lap. Felix follows my gaze.

"No," he says emphatically. "No way."

"Understood. But it's here if you change your mind."

Felix nods and we sit in silence for a little while. Then he takes a deep breath and says, "We should go back. I'm worried about Rory."

"Yeah," I say, "me too."

He stands up and offers his hand, which is the kind of macho thing Felix never does, but I don't make a snarky comment about it. I just take it, and let him pull me back to where we came from.

TWENTY-TWO

ory is dancing. Not just dork-stepping with Nate as we left her, but actually *moving her body in a rhythmic fashion*. With a guy. Who's not Nate. He's tall and smiling down at her and she stares at his chest for five seconds, then at his face for five seconds, then back at his chest.

Nate's watching nearby, like a bodyguard. I'm not sure how he managed to create this situation in the short time Felix and I were gone.

"Was this a naturally occurring phenomenon?" I ask him. Felix has disappeared to the bathroom to splash water on his face.

"He asked her. She said yes. These things do happen, Justine. Even to Rory." We watch for a few moments, then Nate asks, "Can you stay and keep an eye on her? I want to go back and see the rabbit."

"Sure," I say, and as Nate moves toward the room he was in earlier, he crosses paths with Felix. Felix nods quickly at Nate. Not really a greeting. Barely an acknowledgment. But still.

When Felix finds me, he looks at Rory and the guy and says, "Whoa." The guy has moved about an inch closer to her. It feels like any second she could scream and run away. Or, alternatively, she could throw her mouth onto his and they could mack out in front of all these people. I'm not sure anything could surprise me anymore.

I move so she can't see me easily, turn on the camera, and shoot her and the guy for a good minute. Nate still hasn't reappeared, so I lean in to whisper at Felix, "Can you watch her? I'll be right back."

"Does she know she's got the Secret Service here?"

"I think it's the only reason why she's able to do this."

When I get to the door, I knock twice, then pause, before walking in.

He's sitting on the floor with a black-and-white lop-eared rabbit in his lap. He looks a little nervous, but seeing me, he relaxes, and his hand starts moving again along the rabbit's back. It has its nose burrowed into his elbow and seems to be shuddering with joy.

I take a seat on the floor facing him, also cross-legged, like we're back in kindergarten and this is the multi-colored carpet at the front of the classroom.

"Felix okay?" asks Nate.

"I think he's going to start kind of eventually being okay, yeah."

Nate raises his eyes to me, questioning, and I nod. He seems to relax even more. Now we're silent. I'm not sure what I had planned, coming in here. I just wanted to see him, having this fresh information. I just wanted to see if he looked different.

And he does. He is Bunny Boy again. Obviously, the rabbit helps. But there's something dug-up about his manner now, a shiny trinket found in the mud after years of being buried. There's so much I want to ask him. I start with this:

"Do you mind if I shoot?" He doesn't look up but shakes his head. I turn on the camera and zoom in on the rabbit, then zoom out slowly to frame a shot of them both.

"His name is Ratso," says Nate, as if knowing what question I'm about to start with. "They bought him from some guy on the sidewalk one night when they were drunk."

"Ratso Rizzo," I say, nodding. "That's a disturbingly appropriate *Midnight Cowboy* reference."

Nate laughs, but only a little. "They have no idea how to take care of a rabbit. They're not even supposed to have it in the dorm. He's pretty skinny, but nothing a good diet won't fix."

Now I know exactly what to ask Nate. I need to ask him about Nimbus, and the boys who made his life a living hell that year, and why he never asked Lance and Leslie to come forward with all the footage they must have had.

But just then, Nate's phone rings in his pocket. He contorts himself in order to get it without disturbing Ratso, and actually this is pretty funny. He looks at the phone and his face lights up.

"Hello?" he asks, in that way where you pretend not to know who it is despite the caller ID.

He listens. He stops blinking and slows his breath. This is how I can tell he's alarmed. Also, I can hear Keira's voice on the other end. It doesn't really sound like her. She sounds too *something*, like she's running on the wrong speed.

"Just stay there. We're a couple of blocks away. Give us a few minutes."

Nate hangs up, stares at the bunny. "That was Keira," he says.

"I figured."

"She's at a bookstore down the street. She's changed her mind about seeing her mom and now she's scared to be in the city at night by herself. We need to get her."

But he doesn't get up, and neither do I. Why don't we get up?

We won't get to be alone again. Maybe ever. Can that be it? Or is this about a rabbit in his lap?

"I'm going to bring this rabbit with me," he says, then looks at me with such seriousness, I almost bust out laughing. "The guy asked me if I wanted him. I do."

"Okay. How will we carry him?"

Nate finally stands up and gingerly places the rabbit on the bed. The rabbit makes a strange whimpering noise I didn't know rabbits could make. Nate looks around the room and sees a backpack on the floor, grabs it. Empties it of its contents, gray sweat socks and a balled-up T-shirt. With extreme purpose, he grabs a towel from a hook on the back of the closet door, folds it carefully, puts it inside the backpack. Then he picks up the rabbit as if it's a newborn baby, with both hands, so gently it nearly breaks my heart.

"Okay, Ratso, you're coming with us. I promise it'll be okay." He places the rabbit in the backpack, zips it up so that a few inches stay open at the top. "He should be fine like that, until we get to Keira's mom's place."

"Is that the plan? Take Keira to her mom's?"

Nate shrugs. "We have to try. It makes sense to finish this." Now he smiles that smile, and once again it's easy to feel like he laid this all out ahead of time, like everything that's happened and hasn't happened so far was for a specific purpose.

Back out in the common room, Rory and her Mystery

309

Guy are still dancing and I swear, they're even closer now. It's going to suck to break this up. Felix is still watching her, and fortunately, Adam and Max are nowhere to be seen. I find him and lean in.

"We're on the move. Operation: Get Keira."

"I don't think Rory wants to leave."

"*You* break it to her," I say. Felix gives me a dirty look, but he knows he's the one.

Me, I just need to get it all on camera.

Felix makes his way through the swarm of bodies and taps Rory on the shoulder. When she freezes, he leans in and whispers in her ear. After a moment, she nods, and Felix walks away. She doesn't follow him immediately. She turns to Mystery Guy, stares right into his eyes. She makes an *I've got to go* gesture, and he looks deflated. Then she does something I'm so glad I'm getting visual proof of:

She leans in and hugs him. Halfway. Loosely, like she's draping a pretend blanket over his shoulders.

When she turns to face us, she's smiling. But it's a totally private smile. Totally not meant for us, or for the camera. I get a good shot of it, then stop recording. Rory walks toward us and gives me a brief but electric glance. It's the kind of look you give a BFF when your world has just shifted on its axis, and it thrills me.

"So we're going to get Keira?" she asks me. *Me.*

"Yup," I say. She nods and then leads the way out of the room.

It's ten thirty on a Saturday night in Greenwich Village, which means the sidewalks are crowded. I see Rory's confidence falter a bit once we hit the pavement. Groups of students, moving en masse, make walking down the street feel like we're in a gigantic pinball machine. Rory holds Felix's hand, looks straight down at the pavement about five feet ahead of her.

"How far away is it?" I ask Nate.

"Two and a half blocks. Think she'll make it?"

"Are you prepared to carry her with a jacket over her head, if it comes to that?"

"Yes," he says, without hesitating.

With Rory walking much faster than she did the first time we tried this, and Nate gingerly carrying the rabbit-filled backpack by its top handle so it totally looks like he's carrying a purse, and Felix constantly swiveling his head back and forth to catch every interesting thing around us, I've got plenty to shoot. Each one of them is somehow different as a result of this party, and it shows. I wonder if this happens to everyone, and that's why Vijay has such a rep.

The bookstore is on a corner and we see it coming from a half block away, lit up and glowing, a big picture window facing the street.

In an overstuffed chair just inside that window sits Keira, her hands folded in her lap, looking down at the floor. She's so still that she could easily pass as part of the window display.

One by one, we pull to a halt when we see her, but none of us says anything or taps on the glass. I guess we're just watching to see what she's doing and what she might do next. After a few moments, Keira raises her eyes to see us.

She looks scared. Tired. Something familiar in those eyes is gone and in its place, a vulnerability. It's almost like I can really see her now. Some kind of transparent wrapping has been removed. Her gaze sweeps over all of us, one by one.

Now Keira sighs, a sigh that visibly travels the length of her body, down then up. She stands, grabs her bag off the floor. Moves to the door and then out onto the sidewalk to be with us.

I had the camera off, but now I turn it on again.

"Hi," she says to Nate. I think she's expecting him to hug her but he really can't, not with the second backpack in his hand, so now she hugs him. "Thank you for coming."

"Where have you been?" asks Nate. "Are you okay?"

Keira nods. "I went to the Metropolitan Museum for a while, until they closed. I ate. I walked."

"But you got your mom's message?"

Keira nods again, a far-off look on her face now. "Yes. I kept planning to call her. Or to just go back. But I couldn't do it. For some reason it's harder, now that I've actually seen her."

Nate thinks about this, and I imagine he's projecting this idea onto his own situation, evaluating what he would do if it were his father.

"So you guys have a car here?" Keira continues. "Can I ride back home with you? I left Lance and Leslie's car at the Trailways station in Mountain Ridge."

"Ride home *now*?" asks Nate.

"Yeah," says Keira.

"Without seeing your mom?"

Keira looks like a little kid caught doing something dumb, scolded for taking an extra cookie from the jar.

"I told you," she says, her voice growing soft, her eyes darting to the rest of us. "It's too hard."

This time, it's Felix who steps forward. "You came all this way. You actually found her. And now that she's waiting for you to come, you're not going to do it?"

Keira opens her mouth to reply, but nothing comes out.

"No," says Felix. "We're taking you to see her."

"I can't," says Keira, backing up.

"This is the time," says Nate. "This is it. We're here and we'll stay with you."

Keira looks at us one by one, and when her eyes land on me, they slide down toward the camera hanging at my side. There's something about the way she's looking at it that makes me speak without thinking.

"Finish your story, Keira," I say. "Finish it tonight, and get on with your life."

She's frozen silent for a few moments, then finally, she says simply, "Okay."

TWENTY-THREE

Rory is navigating us uptown to Mrs. Jones's block, but this time she uses only her memory and not a map. Felix and I sit in the backseat with Keira wedged between us, and Nate drives more confidently now that there's less traffic.

After we ride in silence for a few blocks, Keira asks, "How late did she say she'd be up?"

"Late. Come on, K. You're her daughter. She'd stay up all night for you."

It's pretty weird, crammed in next to Keira like this. She's trying hard not to look at me, and in her efforts, she keeps glancing down at the camera. She notices me noticing.

"So have you been shooting everything that happens?" she asks. There's no judgment in her voice.

"Pretty much."

"And what about the big *reunion*? Lance and Leslie would never forgive you if you didn't get that."

"It's really up to you and your mom," I say, and mean it.

Keira pauses. "Can I think about it?"

"Of course." I want to be kind here. I want to have an interaction with her that will help, not hurt, the experience she's about to have. "This moment is totally, completely yours. They took the other one from you, but this time you know better. Right?"

Now Keira looks straight at me, with an expression like she's just been punctured. *Pop.* She stares for several very long seconds, and I work to keep my eyes connected to hers.

"Right," she finally says.

"We're going to stay on this until Sixty-Seventh Street," says Rory. Nate nods and picks up speed. We see nothing but green lights stretching for blocks in front of us, as if an unknown something is shouting, *Go, go, go!* When we finally see a red light, Nate slows, but it changes to green before we get to the intersection and he speeds up again. I put my hand out the open window, fingers spread wide, feeling the air slide through them. Felix sees me do this and puts his hand out his window, and now we pretend our arms are wings on either side of the car and we flap them, in unison.

Then something amazing happens. Keira laughs. Rory takes her cue and laughs as well, then Nate notices what we're doing and cracks a smile.

Finally, a light turns yellow, then red, as we approach, and Nate gently pulls the car to a full stop. But my heart keeps traveling in a joyful trajectory, soaring through the windshield and up into the air, higher than the buildings. Weightless for several infinite seconds, before it rebounds and when it does, everything in the car feels changed again.

"So, Rory," says Keira into the sudden stillness. "Tell me about this epic party."

Mrs. Jones's street is lit all pretty from streetlamps now. Welcoming. This is going to sound weird but at this point, it almost feels like home.

After putting the car in a nearby garage, we stand at the foot of the steps leading to Keira's mom's brown stone. I really want to get a shot of it like this, the dark wood of the front door glowing a little from the reflected streetlamp, but don't want to ruin the moment. Keira's moment, like I said in the car. Although in a way, it belongs to all of us.

"Hey, Keira," says Nate.

"Yeah?" She doesn't take her eyes off the door.

"I'm really glad you're here."

I don't know if he means here *with us* or here *about to visit the mother you haven't seen in five years*, but it makes her smile. Then she walks quickly, almost businesslike, up to the door and rings the bell.

"Nate?" says Mrs. Jones's voice on the intercom.

"It's us," Nate says loudly as he runs up to the door, and yes, it's a bit strange that she didn't say "Keira," but we're ignoring that.

"Second floor," she says, and buzzes us in. Once inside, I can tell Nate wants to lead the way, like he has been all day, but I'm glad he lets Keira go first.

Mrs. Jones is waiting on the second-floor landing. I can see her but Keira hasn't noticed yet because she's climbing the stairs looking at her feet. This is a risk I have to take. I hang back, press record, and frame the scene. I have to zoom in a bit and the light in the stairwell sucks, but it will work. I'll show the footage to Keira later and if she asks me to destroy it, I will.

Keira looks up. Sees her mother standing there. Stops cold.

There's a bit of traffic backup as Nate must now stop abruptly, then Felix, then Rory.

"Hi, sweetheart," says Mrs. Jones, her voice unsteady.

Keira climbs the last few steps and nobody's sure what's going to happen next. She freezes again when she reaches the top, and looks like she might actually be shaking.

Then she throws herself into her mother's arms. There's a noise now, echoing through the stairwell. It's the sound of Keira crying. And now Mrs. Jones is crying, and their crying together is the strangest, sweetest duet I've ever heard.

According to the digital clock on the kitchen stove, it's officially Sunday now.

The sofa bed in Mrs. Jones's living room is lumpy and I can feel a coil on my hip as I lie on my side, but holy shit it's good to be still.

Felix and Nate are already asleep on the floor on blankets a few feet apart. I've never seen anyone crash that quickly. It was literally *head* plus *pillow* equals *out cold*. Don't guys ever lie awake worrying about recently lived-through, world-changing experiences?

Rory's in the bathroom and I think maybe I'm waiting for her to come out. Ratso the rabbit is sleeping in a cardboard box in the corner and still looks absolutely bewildered.

"You must all stay," Mrs. Jones said earlier. "I can't let you drive all the way to Mountain Ridge this late." None of us protested. As strange as it is to be crashing at this woman's apartment, it seemed a far better choice than going home and facing our parents in the middle of the night. It was hard enough to text them with the news that

319

we wouldn't be back until morning.

Keira's in the bedroom with her mother. I haven't heard a word from either of them since they went in there. I imagine them just lying in bed, holding each other. Maybe talking is too big, or too small, for where they are right now. I'm not sure how or if or why I would forgive my mother for walking out on me. I know it's more complicated than that. The force that brought Keira here is something I will hopefully never have to understand.

The bathroom door opens, throwing a beam of light across the floor and right onto Nate's sleeping face, which I will admit looks overwhelmingly *touchable*. Then Rory shuts off the light and the beam vanishes. I see her silhouette moving across the room, then sinking into the sofa bed next to me. The coil on my hip moves and that hurts, but I take it.

I listen to Rory's breathing for a minute, and suddenly I'm not in an unfamiliar apartment in the middle of Manhattan but Rory's bedroom, and we are eight or nine or ten. We have just completed a one-thousand-piece puzzle and eaten popcorn with M&M's and worked on our comic book and looked at all the pictures in her latest biography of Queen Elizabeth I. Rory's called the shots on all of this, which is annoying as usual, but I focus on the fun parts as usual. She's wearing one of those floor-length flannel nightgowns with lace across the chest, and

I'm in my black pajamas with white skulls on them that I found in the boys' department at Target.

Rory shifts. Something about this movement lets me know she's not asleep yet, or anywhere near it.

"What was his name?" I whisper toward her.

In the darkness, just breathing. Then: "Brennan."

"Nice."

"Or maybe Brendan."

"Also nice."

"It could have been Brandon. I'm really not sure."

"He was cute," I say.

"I know," says Rory. She's quiet for a few moments, then adds, "Was I supposed to do something else? Like, get his number or something?"

"If you really want to stay in touch with him, I'm sure Dylan can connect you."

Suddenly it strikes me that Brennan/Brendan/Brandon might have been familiar with the documentaries and known who we were, and who Rory was, and his motivations might not have been entirely innocent. But I'm not going to mention that. That's not about Rory.

"Justine, you really helped me today."

Her voice is all business and I know from experience that she's just processing the facts. But I want her to get these facts straight.

"You helped yourself, really."

She's silent for a few moments. Someone on the floor

is starting to snore. I can't help but giggle, and now Rory giggles too. I hope it's because she legitimately thinks it's funny.

This is my chance. I'm getting a total break here, with it being dark. I don't even have to see her face.

"Rory, there's something I've been wanting to say to you for a long time."

A pause, then she asks, "Is it bad?"

"I don't think so."

"Okay. You can say it."

"I've just . . . I've wanted to tell you that I'm sorry. For abandoning you as a friend." I pause, but she doesn't answer. I take that as a sign to continue. "I was . . . an idiot. I'm not anymore. At least not in the same way. And I think I've missed you every day since then."

It's quiet for a moment. I stare at the shadow of the light fixture above us, a round paper lantern that in the darkness reminds me of the earth, floating in space. Just being.

Then Rory says, "Good night, Justine," and rolls over, away from me.

Alrighty then. I know her response could mean anything. But it must be enough, for now, because a wave of something washes over me, and I'm not sure if it's relief or plain old exhaustion, but within moments I'm no longer awake.

* * *

The rumble of some behemoth vehicle on the street takes me out of a dream so messed up I forget it instantly. *Where am I?* Slowly, reality comes into focus. The clock glows a very red 4:32 a.m.

I roll off the sofa bed, gripping the cool metal frame with my hand for leverage, find my way to the bathroom, and turn on the light. It feels like a sudden refuge from the darkness, from the unfamiliar apartment, from the snoring—not sure if it's Felix or Nate, will have to check for the record—and from The Weirdness.

But it's also kind of exhilarating, this fresh, unpredictable, vaguely dangerous state. I think I might love it. I got nowhere near enough sleep but it's a done deal: I'm up.

When I'm finished in the bathroom, I open the door and leave the light on for a few extra seconds so I can figure out who the snorer is. Then I flick it off and find my way to a corduroy armchair in the living room, where I remember leaving Leslie's camera bag. I pick it up, sit down, and put the bag on my lap. For a few moments, I stare out the window at a light from the building across the alley. Someone's left their living room lamp on and I can see the top of a sofa, some framed art, a tall armoire. Another person's whole world, right there. Close but untouchable.

I open the bag and remove the camera, then fish out the headphones and poke around a bit until I successfully get the right jack to plug them into. I turn on the camera display and navigate to the playback menu, where I can watch every clip I've shot since yesterday.

There's the road leading out of Aikya Lodge, the trees and sheets of rock, the side of the mountain where it drops away to show us the entire valley below, the patchwork of farms and river and the cluster of buildings in the center of Mountain Ridge that means the college.

I see Olivia driving, and Nate and Felix and Rory in the backseat. Where we started.

The chain of video clips takes me through town and onto the thruway, toward the city, in and out of our day. The street and the dorm and the party.

Keira and her mother hugging. The way their sobs blended, each wrapped inside the other. Then the image jumps to black, and even though I know I didn't shoot more after that moment, I keep waiting for the tiny screen to show me something else.

The Cramp, which I haven't felt since we left home, hits me hard as if to make up for lost time. It raises the hair on my arms and the back of my neck. Something else starts to happen too, but I won't let it. I mentally stomp on it and grind it into the ground with the toe of my shoe.

I'm not going to cry.

But I do have to get the hell out of here.

It's light now and the clock says 6:07 a.m., and there must be someplace open for food. I fumble for my shoes and sweatshirt, then scribble a note ("Went for bagels"). I leave that on the bathroom mirror where the first person with a full bladder will see it, and take the liberty of grabbing Mrs. Jones's keys from the handmade pottery bowl by the front door.

I've headed toward First Avenue simply because we were there before, and it's practically an old stomping ground compared with the rest of the city. The air's still night-fresh but the light's already getting strong, and there's a feeling, something you can't put your finger on, that the day is going to be beautiful.

As soon as I turn the corner and point my feet downtown again, I remember a playground we passed yesterday. It was packed with parents and kids, vibrating with noise and energy. Now, though, it's deserted.

Once inside the gates, I notice that in between the swings and this massive maze of a climbing structure sit two small elephant statues. I get a closer look and realize they must be fountains, because their trunks look quasi-functional. I can imagine children in bathing suits on a summer day, running across the pavement as they get sprayed with water, squealing like they hate it but in fact are really loving it. I sit on one, then feel stupid, so I get up and go over to the end of a spiral slide, which really is not any less stupid but at least now I'm not squatting on a concrete animal.

This is where I let it happen. The switch gets flipped,

the cord gets cut, and I face-plant into my own hands. They're instantly wet and the tears are seeping through the cracks between my fingers. My eyes burn so much; why do they burn so much? Maybe they're simply not used to this.

I'm totally losing it in front of people walking down the street and the city sanitation crew that's arrived to empty the park garbage cans. Nobody even looks up, though. Like a girl crying on a playground by herself in the early morning is just another part of the city's landscape.

"Please don't," says a voice. I part my hands and see a familiar pair of sneakers on the pavement in front of me.

"Why not?" I ask.

"Because I was just getting used to seeing you smile," says Nate. He leans against the play structure above me, sleepy-looking and adorably bed-headed.

"Ah," I say, brushing the back of my hand across my eyes and nose. "That never lasts long. You've completed Lesson One about me." Now I force myself to look at him. "How did you know where I was?"

"I woke up just as you were leaving, so I followed you."

"That's creepy."

"That's *concern*. Anything can happen to you alone in the city, even during daylight."

Nate was worried about me. This might start the crying again.

"Lesson Two," I say, digging back into my arsenal of

smart-ass self-defense. "Nothing ever happens to me."

Nate motions for me to scoot over on the end of the slide, and I do, and because it opens wide at the end, there's just enough room for both of us.

After he settles in, his elbow digging into my side and me not leaning away, letting myself absorb the raw pressure of it, he says, "You can't make a statement like that and not elaborate."

I sniffle back the last remnants of the tears. "I woke up early and started watching all the footage I shot since we left the lodge. And I have to say . . . it's pretty amazing. In those clips I can really see everyone. Keira and her mom. Felix, facing the big truth about himself. Rory, pushing through things she's never done before and moving that much further, finally, along her own storyline." I hold my thumb and forefinger apart, to illustrate what a small but precious amount I'm talking about. "And you . . ."

I freeze. I'm not even sure how to finish that.

"Do you really see *me* too?" asks Nate. His voice catches on a nervous edge.

"I know I see a different you. Not the one I saw before." And now, because he is *right here* and smells like sweat and sugar—*Is it apples? Can it be that he actually sweats apples?*—I add, "I hated that guy."

"Uh, yeah," says Nate. "I got that. Was that because of what you assumed I did to Felix?"

I wince. He had to use that word, *assume*, which only

makes me think of that "when you assume, you make an ass out of you and me" saying, although he certainly has a right to.

"Partly," I reply. "I guess I felt you sold out somehow. Remade yourself, just to look good on film. But who am I to say that? Maybe that's just who you became."

Nate collapses backward so he's lying on the slide, his feet still planted on the ground. He puffs out a long breath. "Actually, you were right the first time."

Now he hooks one arm over his face, smothering it with his elbow.

"Go on," I say.

"After those jerks stole my rabbit and totally humiliated me, *on camera*, I knew I had to change things. I like to think I did it for myself and not for the films, not because Lance and Leslie would be coming back in a few years and I wanted to show everyone I'd won the game. But that can't really be true."

"I wish I could have changed like you did," I say, and as soon as it comes out, I realize why I resented Nate for his morphing abilities. I was jealous.

"Into someone who wasn't actually you? I'm glad you didn't." He takes his arm off his head now, but his eyes are still closed, and even though there's a decent amount of pain on his face, I can't help but want it to stay that way because it's quite gorgeous, really. From an artistic standpoint.

"Besides," he continues. "I'm not sure how much I changed at all. There was the version of me I created to show the world, and the version of me that felt like me . . . and I can't tell where they overlap." He takes a deep breath, in and out, and shudders on the *out*. Is he going to cry too? I can't begin to plan how to deal with that.

After a few more breaths like this, Nate continues, calmer now.

"You know where it all started? Lance and Leslie shot some stuff between Aidan and Tony and me. When my grandfather wanted them to share any footage that could prove what was happening, I begged them not to." He looks up the slide, like he's worried someone's going to come crashing down on top of him. "I was such a chicken, it makes me sick to think about it."

I try for something positive to say here. Something Nate needs to hear.

"Getting those guys in trouble would have made your life more difficult down the line," I offer. "They would have come for payback. What you did was smart."

"Maybe. I just know that I wanted that whole episode gone, along with everything people saw and felt about me. I actually asked Lance to destroy the tape that had the footage—they were still shooting on videotape back then, remember?"

"And did he?"

Nate shrugs. "He sent it to me."

"And you destroyed it?"

"More or less."

"I'm not sure what that means."

Nate looks at me, his eyes twinkling. "We got off the subject. Do you really think you might know who I am?"

"Aside from being an epic snorebeast, I think I might."

Nate smiles. It's the smile I've seen a hundred times, the smile I used to want to slap away. Now it's something I'd just like to hold for a while, cupped in my palms.

"I think I might know who you are too, Justine."

The hair on my arms suddenly stands up straight. I need to say something to cover.

"How could you? You should see this footage. I'm not in a single second of it."

"You should have asked one of us to shoot for a while."

"Even if you had," I say, "what would you have shot? Me walking down the street. Me watching everyone else. Me watching, not doing."

"You did something for Rory at the right moment. And you went after Felix at his right moment. I don't know if I would have done that."

That word, *moment*, hits me on the jaw. I can even feel the sting of it as I say, "I guess I'm sad that I haven't had a moment."

Now Nate sits up, his body shifting against mine, and I expect him to put his arm around me but he doesn't. Instead, he knocks his left sneaker twice against my right one. Like, *Hello? Anyone in there?*

"I think you have a moment," says Nate, "in every second of footage you shot. You weren't just watching. You were telling the story. You were telling *our* story. And I think that's *your* story."

We look at each other now and I see he's rather proud of this theory. Maybe before, I would have seen it as arrogance. Now I understand, instinctively, that it's just pure delight at making some sense of the world. Joy in the possibility of helping me.

This could be the kind of moment I've been seeking. One that belongs to me, or even better, to us. For the first time in my life, I think, there is no distance between me and another person. We are connected in ways too scary to understand. How can I stay here? How can I make happen what I will admit, now, I want to happen? Neither of us glances away or even moves.

Suddenly, the shouts of a child break the silence, and Nate turns to see a little boy bolting across the playground toward the swings. A weary-looking dad lags behind him, coffee cup in hand. We watch them for a few seconds, a chance to recover from this thing we just shared.

"Come on," says Nate finally, scrambling up and nudging my shin with his foot. "I hope you were serious about the bagels."

TWENTY-FOUR

I bet you forgot you have this," says Felix, clutching the iPod and reaching to turn up the volume on the car stereo. He's riding shotgun next to Nate, who's behind the wheel.

Now here comes classic David Bowie through the speakers. Those first powerful electronic chords, instantly tapping your inner pipeline, not wasting time with any slow buildup. Nate laughs and just says, "Shit, yeah." Felix beams at him and turns to look out the window, nodding to the music. I'm about to ask whether this song is called "We Can Be Heroes" or just "Heroes," because I've never looked it up, but I don't want to interrupt this silent conversation between them.

I peek through the camera's viewfinder—I'm back to using this rather than the LCD display, there's something much more immediate about it—and frame a shot of the East River on our right, sunlight bouncing off the water, a bridge in the middle distance. The song provides the perfect soundtrack, the car traveling at the exact speed of its rhythm, and I keep recording even though the second battery's starting to run low. Rory sits next to me, and Keira's on the other side of Rory. We'll be home in ninety minutes.

After Nate and I left the playground, after we came back to the apartment with bagels, after we all ate and washed up and called our parents to let them know we were still alive and well and on the way home, we sat on the steps of the building while Keira said good-bye to Mrs. Jones.

"You don't want to stay for a little while?" Nate asked her. Keira shook her head, lacing her fingers a little awkwardly through her mom's hand. "There's time now," she said. Mrs. Jones did not take her eyes off Keira once in a three-minute period, and I know this because I was filming it.

All morning, Rory kept glancing at me when she thought I couldn't see her. I'm not sure what to do about that.

Keira has fallen asleep and Nate and Felix are quiet in the front seat. I've set the camera down so I can just stare out the window, too tired to think about anything except the scenery. When the song changes to something much slower, Rory taps me on the leg.

"Hey," I say.

"Can you turn on the camera?" she asks.

I take off the lens cap and slip my hand back in the strap, press record, and look at her expectantly.

"Last night you said you were sorry about blowing me off. About our friendship."

"Yes," I say. I'm not sure where she's going with this, but I keep the shot framed on her, her face so close and unfiltered.

"How do you know I wouldn't have gotten sick of you at some point?" She asks this scientifically, with no accusation. I can tell Felix and Nate are listening intently but neither of them turns around.

"Maybe you would have," I say. "Maybe *you* would have dumped *me*."

"That wouldn't have happened. You were my only friend. I was a difficult person to be with and still, you stayed around."

I realize she's just trying to understand the situation. Looking at all sides in order to see it as a whole.

"We're just talking hypothetically here," I urge. "Just pretend, like this is a story in a book or something."

Rory considers that. "If I had been the one to dump you, would you have wanted me to apologize?" she asks.

"If I missed you as a friend, yes."

"And you would have forgiven me, if I'd done that?"

"Yes . . . but, Rory, this is really about you. If you think we're done and we should go back to ignoring each other, then I'm okay with doing that."

"But you'd rather not."

"No," I say. "I'd rather not."

Now Rory bites her lip. "Me neither."

She leans in and hugs me, sideways and quickly, and on camera it looks weird because her face just gets closer closer closer, then disappears, then reappears. But actually, it's perfect.

I turn the camera off.

"Did you get it all?" she asks.

"Yeah."

"Good. Because that's why I didn't say it last night. I wanted to do it when you could shoot it. Because I know that's better. Right?"

"Yes."

Rory folds her hands into her lap and bows her head.

"You know that email I sent you?" she suddenly asks, looking at the gross car floor mat. "When I heard you weren't going to do the film?"

"That was *you?*"

She raises her head to look at me again, even more surprised than I am. "Yeah. I thought you'd figure that out right away."

"No, I assumed it was Felix."

"Oh. Well. It was me."

"You said we were part of a whole."

"We are. And I can't stand missing puzzle pieces. Remember?"

Now we look at each other and smile at the same time. One thing has closed and another has opened, and I'm not sure which is which, but it doesn't matter.

"I remember, Rory. I so totally remember."

It's almost ten o'clock by the time we see signs for the Mountain Ridge exit. I can't believe it's still Sunday morning. The rest of the day may as well be the rest of my life, the hours unfurling with possibilities and uncertainty.

The first stop is Keira's. Nobody discussed this. It just seemed the obvious choice. When we pull up to the house, Mr. Jones steps out the front door wearing running pants, a sweatshirt, and sneakers, as if he's not waiting for us at all but just on his way to work out. He takes a few steps forward, then stops at the last stone of the front walk.

"Good luck," says Nate to Keira.

"I won't need it," Keira says with determination.

She opens the car door and turns to glance directly at me, giving the slightest of smiles, before she climbs out. I don't know what will happen the next time I see her. Will she say hi to me? Hug me? Ignore me completely? Any of these things seems possible. I guess I'll just have to stay tuned.

Keira walks slowly to her dad. Nate doesn't back up right away. It's only when Mr. Jones reaches out for her, not hugging but putting a firm and protective hand on her shoulder, maybe making sure she's really there, and Keira nods, that Nate feels okay to leave.

"Who's next?"

"May as well get this over with," says Felix. "Although if anyone else is interested in a last-minute trip to, say, Canada, for about a month, I might be up for that."

I pat the top of Felix's head as Nate drives deeper into town. We both know that, unfortunately, Felix is only half-kidding. The iPod has dialed up some melancholy one-hit-wonder from a few years back, so unoriginal it's catchy.

"I'm not sure why this is on here," says Nate.

"Uh, because you're a tween girl at heart?" asks Felix, and they both laugh. I don't think I've heard them laughing at the same time in years. It's like pure glee, uncorked. At least, to me.

But Felix gets quiet quickly as we pull onto his street, and he sighs.

"One thing at a time," says Nate, full of extra meanings.

The car stops in front of the house and after Felix jumps out, I do too. Nobody's come out of the house to greet us, which feels like an ominous sign.

"I love you," I say to him, and his eyes fill with tears. He circles me into a Felix bear hug.

"You rattle my world," he whispers.

We let each other go and after he turns, I don't see his face again. Just his slightly hunched figure under the backpack, carrying a keyboard case with both hands, moving reluctantly toward the front door. I think of how much farther Felix has to go, beyond that door and his living room and his parents and the disorienting maze of his own head. I wonder if it's further than the rest of us have to go, or if it's really just a question of direction.

At Rory's house, I exit the car along with her. Nate does too. Rory's parents rush outside and aren't bound by paving stones, the way Mr. Jones seemed to be, but close the distance between themselves and their daughter as quickly as possible. There's an instant three-way hug.

Mrs. Gold draws away and smoothes Rory's hair, then spots me over her shoulder. She's not sure what to say or even how to react. Rory follows her gaze, then steps toward me. She slips her hand in mine and it feels just the same as it used to.

"Justine made everything okay," she says. I'm glad for all the ways this is true.

"You should have seen her in the city," I add. "So brave. Really strong."

Rory's mom's smile turns inward so she's biting her

lips, like she's trying to contain something. "I knew she could be," she says. Anything else Rory wants to share with her parents is totally up to her.

Nate shakes hands with Rory's mom, then dad, before they all turn and go into the house. Nate opens the driver's door and pauses. Oh. *Duh.* He's waiting for me to change seats so we don't have a cab-driver-esque situation for the final leg of the trip.

I climb into the front passenger seat, and he gets behind the wheel, and we are driving in silence again. It should take only a few minutes to get to Hunter Farms. I don't want us to. I wish we could drive all day, although to where I have no idea.

Do I want this because I don't want to go home yet? Or do I want it because I want to be with him for a little while longer?

Ugh, it's so much easier to just stare out the window.

"No more shooting?" asks Nate after a little while.

"It doesn't feel necessary right now."

That sounded kind of cryptic but Nate doesn't question. We drive on.

"The Cannibal Apple sign," I say as we pass it.

"That?" He thinks about it, then laughs. "Never saw it that way. You know, I'm the one who came up with the idea for that sign."

"I've felt sorry for that poor helpless fruit for, like, years."

"I was imagining a world where everything was apples. The creatures, the food, the buildings. It didn't seem cannibalistic to me. Just . . . uncomplicated. I used to pretend I lived in that world, actually. I'd go out into the orchard and lie under a tree and *see* all of it. Felix too."

He pauses, clearly lost in the memory. Takes a deep breath in, then out.

"God, I feel like I just got a piece of myself back. With him. Do you feel that way about Rory?"

A rush of heat into my eyes, the middle of my forehead. I refuse to cry in front of Nate Hunter twice in one day. But I am able to say, "Yes. Yes, I do."

Now here we are at the driveway to the house, and Nate makes the turn more slowly than seems necessary. When he brings the car to a stop, he takes an extra few moments to put it in park, to pull up the parking brake higher than I've ever seen it go. We sit, watching the back of the house. Nobody comes out.

"Mom works Sundays," he says, "and my grandparents are still at church."

"Did you want them to be waiting by the door for you?"

He shrugs. "I'm glad they trust me, I guess. Besides, now I can get Ratso all situated without having to do the whole permission thing first."

I pick up the backpack from where's it's been nestled on the floor of the front passenger seat and hand it to him.

He slowly unzips it and peers inside.

"It's okay, little dude," says Nate, then reaches his hand in to pet the rabbit. He turns to me. "Wanna come with us to the barn?"

I answer by jumping out of the car.

The barn is a few hundred yards behind the house. Inside, there are three stalls with goats, who appear way too excited to see us.

"They think it's time to go into the pens by the store," he says. The goats watch him with their disturbing horizontal pupils and such a familiarity, I get the feeling he comes here more often than anyone knows. Nate leads me to a stall at the back of the barn. It's empty and scrubbed clean.

"Can you help me with some hay?" he asks, opening the stall door. We grab some from a bale on the ground and pile it into the stall. He puts the rabbit inside and closes the door. "You'll have to hang here for a bit," he says to Ratso. "I'll be back with some food and water." The rabbit just looks at the wall.

We stand there in the middle of the barn, which smells like mildew and damp fur, and there's this awful *What next?* hanging in the air between us.

"Do you have a minute?" Nate finally asks.

Yes, I have a minute. I have many. I have millions, for you right now.

"I really need to get going. . . ." And why I say stuff like

342

that at moments like this, I'll never understand.

"There's just something I want to show you," says Nate.

He indicates with his head for me to follow him, and I do. Into a far corner of the barn, where wooden shelves contain animal feed and unlabeled metal cans. Nate grabs a ladder that looks like he made it as a kid with toy tools, and positions it against the wall of shelves.

"Hold this," he says, and I do. He climbs the ladder and with each step, I'm convinced it's going to break and he'll fall backward onto me. Which wouldn't be a terrible thing, but probably best to avoid anyway. When he reaches the top shelf, he moves some containers aside and produces a rusted coffee can. It rattles as he climbs back down. I step aside as he makes the jump to the floor.

"You asked me about the footage Lance gave me," he says. He peels off the plastic lid and reaches in, pulls out a digital videotape. "This is it."

The way he holds the tape, clutches it really, tells me the emotions and experiences recorded on it haven't worn off in the years it sat on a dusty barn shelf.

"So, not destroyed," I say.

"I couldn't. Even stuff like this, you can't let go of."

The fact that he's kept it, the fact that he's showing it to me—I can't imagine anything more intimate. Except this:

"Here," says Nate, holding it out on his open palm. "Take it."

"What . . . why?"

"When you give the other footage to Lance and Leslie, give them this too. They'll know what it means. It's part of the story and I'm ready for it to be told."

I see how, at a certain point, keeping the tape could hurt a lot more than letting it go out into the world. I take it from him and slip it into the front pocket of my jeans.

Silence. I stare at our feet and remember his sneaker tapping against mine on the playground. Any more animals to tuck away in their new homes? Any more coffee cans full of secrets?

"I guess I should head over to Lance and Leslie's. Give them their stuff back."

"Do you want me to come with you?"

I do, but I don't. "I think I need to go on my own," I say, with genuine regret. He nods. He gets it.

There should be more here. I don't know who it's supposed to come from.

Finally, I just mutter, "See you," and turn and walk out of the barn, resisting the overwhelming urge to look back.

Outside, the light is extra bright, screaming at me like *Find a way to stay longer, bonehead!* After my eyes adjust, after I move through that cloud of regret, I turn the corner to the side of the barn and start walking back to the car.

What will happen when we see each other at school? Will it be like nothing's changed, when, in fact, everything has? I can't imagine it another way. I can't imagine how we could possibly keep things the way they are at this very moment. Or were. Because the moment is already over.

"Justine!" calls Nate.

I turn to see him rounding the corner of the barn toward me. Doing that walk-jog thing where you want to run but don't want to run. He stops when he reaches me and takes a deep breath.

"I forgot to say thanks. . . ." He holds out his arms. Without even thinking about it, I'm opening mine to him and then we are holding each other. I feel the familiar reflex to pull away but ignore it, because he's not pulling away either. His shoulder, his neck, his ear. He's so warm, and it could be that I've been cold my whole life.

The hug lasts a few seconds and then Nate breaks apart first.

"Thanks for what?" I ask.

"I don't know," he says, and we laugh. "I guess there's just so much that wouldn't have happened this weekend, if it weren't for you."

I'm about to give him a *You're welcome* but it feels like another lame-ass substitute for all the things I really want to say. Suddenly, I'm so sick of not saying them, and all the rest too. Sick of watching and not doing. Of wanting and not taking.

"No," I say.

"No?"

"This," I say, and lean forward. I'm not sure what's going to happen and I haven't thought through the consequences. But now Nate's leaning forward too.

And here, his lips.

His lips, which taste new yet familiar, scary but safe. It's like taking off and landing at the same time. I give myself over to this blood-thudding rush of contradictions.

My hands are in Nate's hair and his hands are on the back of my neck. I'm unsteady on my feet and maybe he senses this, because suddenly he's pressing me against the side of the barn and kissing me harder. I kiss back harder.

After a few moments I open my eyes and see the ridge in the distance. The tower, straighter and taller than ever, watchful and protective. Always staring back.

When Nate finally steps away from me, I feel shaken loose.

"Whoa," he says.

"Is that good?"

"That's good."

We move back toward each other and meet halfway, and kiss again several times quickly, as if to get in as much as we can before this *good* wears off.

"Can you stay awhile?" he asks, his voice a little wobbly.

I don't know how to deal with what just happened, so my old impulses take over. "I should go do what I have to do. Lance and Leslie, then home."

Nate nods, looks stricken.

I fight those impulses back down. *Be gone.* "But then . . . later?"

"Will you meet me later?" Nate's face is earnest now. Hopeful.

"Where?"

"The boat launch down by the river. Three o'clock?"

I brush my fingers across his. "I'll be there."

And now I do let myself flee, running to the car, but this time, not away from something. For once, I'm running *toward*.

Look at me. I'm in such a state.

Olivia's car may as well be flying, one of those jet cars you see in bad futuristic movies. I don't even care that Lance and Leslie might be home and I'd have to face them.

The sweet spring sun and air on my face through the open window, this road I have traveled a thousand times in my life. The trees, fully swollen with leaves at last. I breathe it all in and glance at my reflection in the rearview mirror. Then again, and again. Each time, I recognize that girl.

Lance and Leslie are renting half of a duplex just outside of town. I've never been there before, but I know where it is. When I drive up, I notice the front door open and just the screen door closed. I'll have to be quick.

I hop out of the car with the camera bag, prepared to drop it on the porch, knock, then dash off. Even if they see me, they can't stop me. But when I get to the porch and put the camera bag on the doormat, I find it hard to pull my hand away. I picture the camera sitting in there, feeling abandoned. Missing me.

Or me missing it.

No, no. It's not mine. It's one thing to borrow but at this point it would be stealing. I will return what doesn't belong to me.

I take a step away, but look back at the camera bag again.

Then I figure it out, what's calling to me. It's not the camera. It's the footage inside it.

You were telling our story. And I think that's your story.

Suddenly, the thought of handing over the film, our film, *my* film, to Lance and Leslie seems wrong in every possible way.

I hear movement inside the house. Someone running down the stairs.

I unzip the bag and scoop up the camera, and the old videotape Nate gave me. I'm holding them tenderly in my arms when Leslie appears in the screen door, only half-visible.

"Justine," she says. "Oh, Justine."

"Leslie," I say.

Then she opens the door and I see her face, flushed with concern and regret. She starts to reach for me, out of instinct, I guess. Or out of love. I can accept that. But she stops herself.

We know each other so well. I can accept that too.

There is so much else I can say at this point: apologies and explanations and confessions. But when I open my mouth, this is what comes out first:

"Listen, I have an idea."

TWENTY-FIVE

I f the audience only knew how well I can hear them. Every time a seat creaks with someone shifting their weight. Every whisper, laugh, and sniffle. I listen to all of it, even over the sound of the film, and even from where I stand backstage, which is so close yet also so far removed from the hundreds of people watching *Five at Sixteen* on the other side of this theater curtain.

I hear them loudest when they make no noise—when what they're seeing on-screen has them riveted to silence.

"Just a few more minutes, right?" asks Felix, who's

standing nearby. He swigs from his water bottle and glances nervously at me.

I listen for the voices on the audio track, then nod.

Rory's here too, traveling the length of the dark, narrow space by putting one foot precisely in front of the other along the lines in the hardwood floor. Keira sits on a folding chair, reading the film festival guide. We are one of the highlights, apparently. This screening was sold out.

Keira raises her eyes to me and points to the guide. "I love this picture of you," she says warmly.

"Thanks," I say, touching my hair. I recently changed out the pink streaks for turquoise, and I daresay I'm rocking that color.

We've already been told what's supposed to happen. The film will end, and they'll take a minute to set up chairs for the Q&A session before a moderator—some famous magazine movie critic—introduces us one by one. We'll listen for our names and fill in the chairs starting from the far end of the stage. It all sounds so simple, except for the fact that we're terrified.

Here it comes. The last lines of dialogue I now know so well. Then, the moments of a blank screen—I count them out, *one, two, three*—followed by the song that runs over the closing credits. It's a great song. Perfect, really. I'm still so proud of that. But I only hear the first few notes, because it's suddenly overpowered by wall-shaking, whooping applause.

Felix, Rory, Keira, and I look back and forth to one another with various combinations of surprise, relief, and curiosity. Felix peeks his head through the curtain that separates us from them, then turns around with a smile. "They're standing."

"You bet your ass they are," says Nate, who is suddenly beside me. Lance and Leslie asked that we not be in the audience, so we were escorted backstage through a special entrance only ten minutes ago. That was fine by most of us, but Nate sneaked out to watch the last scene.

My pulse is pounding and my stomach, of course, is churning, and I have to keep looking down at my feet to make sure they're still there, because I don't feel connected to the ground.

A petite young woman with blue horn-rimmed eyeglasses and a clipboard ducks through the curtain. She could be twenty-five, or thirty-five, or fifteen. She's one of those.

"We're ready! Do you hear that applause? You've got a great audience out there."

Nate slips his hand in mine and squeezes. Just like that, I'm plugged back in to where I need to be. I squeeze back.

The moderator introduces Keira first, who takes a deep breath and shakes out her wrists before stepping onstage. Then Felix, who flashes us the smile that will somehow get even bigger as soon as he sees that audience—the confident grin that pulls you into his world. Next is Rory,

353

presenting us with a carefully drawn *Gah, can you believe this?* look before marching out there.

As soon as she disappears, I turn to Nate. "You're on."

He grabs my face with both hands and stares at it for several long seconds. I have seen so many versions of him in the past year. Nate at six and eleven and sixteen, over and over in a computer's video editing program. Nate in real life, present tense. From a distance, and in extreme close-up. I know them all by heart.

The moderator calls his name. Nate doesn't move, except for stroking my cheek with his thumb. For a moment, I'm worried he hasn't heard. He just gazes at me and I gaze back, and between us swings the weight of everything we've discovered about ourselves since that weekend in the city.

Then he kisses me, quickly but deeply, before turning to run through the curtain.

I'm still feeling Nate on my lips and his palms on my skin when someone else touches me on the shoulder. I turn around to see Leslie, and Lance behind her.

"Ready, kiddo?" she asks, her eyes welled up in a good way.

"No," I say. "Never."

"There's a lot of love out there," Lance says proudly, "and you deserve all of it."

I hear the voice of the moderator now.

"And finally, please welcome the three codirectors

of *Five at Sixteen*: Lance Rodgers, Leslie Rodgers, and Justine Connolly!"

Leslie nudges me forward through the curtain.

A blur of hands clapping, their flutter like wings in a flock. Warm faces with bright eyes. Unfamiliar, but affectionate.

I step fully onto the stage now, and let them all see me.

ACKNOWLEDGMENTS

Whoa. Now that I sit back here, past the book's final pages, I can feel the rush of gratitude. This space won't fit individual mentions of everyone who bolstered me creatively and emotionally on my journey with this novel, but I'll start with a sweeping shout-out to my family, friends, author compadres, and heck, even my cats, who all sure know how to make a writer girl feel loved.

Thank you as always to my agent, the whip-smart, bunny-loving Jamie Weiss Chilton. I'm blessed with an amazing editor, Rosemary Brosnan, who empowered me to accomplish everything I set out to do with this manuscript . . . and then some.

Heartfelt thanks to Andrew Harwell, Andrea Martin, Olivia deLeon, and Barbara Lalicki, along with the rest of the wonderful team at HarperCollins—a publishing house I'm thrilled to call home. Designer Laura DiSiena and art director Cara Petrus created this dazzling cover, and thus I think they pretty much rule.

I'm forever indebted to Bari Pearlman for letting me tap in to her expertise as a documentary filmmaker, and to Nora Snyder for sharing her gorgeously personal insights on teens with autism. Thank you also to the folks on Facebook who weighed in on such important story points as dorm decoration, drunken pet-naming, and barn animals.

Ten-gallon plastic tubs of Thankful to my readers—every one of you who has written to me or shown up at an event or recommended my work, or simply connected to it personally, silently, and held it close. To all the booksellers, librarians, and book bloggers who have so enthusiastically supported what I do: I can't fully express my appreciation without a lot of colored markers and heart stickers, and maybe not even then.

Finally, I send infinite thanks and love, love, love to Bill, Sadie, and Clea. You make so many things possible.